I0547601

Flabius Flaximus and the Superstars of Antarctica

Michael Parker

Table of Contents

For Dad

Table of Noncontents

(The following chapter titles failed to make the cut)

Table of Continents

Preface

In the backwater village known as New York City, where the trekkers of vast fortunes and the fortune hunters of obscure Trek merchandise meet on snowy evenings, the story of a young girl and her all-pink panda bear found its genesis. The girl is based on *Samson Agonistes'* Dalila, as highlighted in the May 1984 issue of *Highlights*. The Panda bear is an amalgamation of Danny Kaye, Ludovico Ariosto, Francois Mitterrand, Def Leppard, Donner the Reindeer, Mitch Albom and the Island of Molokai. The villain in all of this is the writer. Don't ask for my help, though, I don't know the man.

Thus, this is thusly the continuing story of the conniving Cockney fortune hunter from Corto Maltese who left on a Tuesday without any hamburgers or tofu substitutes, whom we have all come to know and love as that guy whom we don't know or love, and never will, so stop asking me about it already, Tifa Lockhart, I don't care how hot and spicy you are. I will also try, of course, at least mostly, to the best of my ability, with the deepest of commitment, no matter who, what, where, how, but never when, to avoid using commas, although highly unlikely, unless of course required by the Associated Press or common vernacular, in which case, even if I don't want to, I will likely, in part, or perhaps less than whole, but not without feeling ill at ease about the matter, attempt to structure the story in such away, when it seems least contrived, to use one or two commas, although I will likely, no doubt assuredly, not feel the slightest bit distressed, diatomic, deprecatory, dietary, dyspeptic, duplicable, discombobulated, declamatory, diabolical or deleterious about the entire ordeal. Which leaves us at an impasse.

Act I:
The Saga of the Spoon

In an unrelated incident, the leftover portion of chapters 1 through 4 will never be released because there are no leftover portions to release. Slowly Dave begins to realize his true mission, Flabius tries to find peace in a world of pacifists, *I punch some people*, and the Fairy doesn't buy any pizza.

1 Terms of Endowment: Dave's Shiny Old Car

What had all begun with a small practical joke was now turning into a violent mess of blood and some other stuff that goes flying when a body gets chopped up. Little Davey thought he knew his hamster, but found out all too late what evils lurk in the hearts of small rodents. Middle-aged Dave discovered the truth behind the presidential scandal, and had come so close to revealing it, before the NSA, CIA, NARAL, FBI and NASA teamed up to freeze his brain via Hershey's dark chocolate ice cream. Old Dave could tell the world the secrets of immortality, as he had taken the eternal life potion himself, but died before the formula could be revealed. People began to suspect that Old Dave might have been lying when he said that he was going to live forever, but the world would never know if Old Dave was telling the truth, now.

And so it started on the night that Dave was found dead. The moon was dark. Dave looked out over the landscape. Dave couldn't see the landscape because the moon was dark. Dave thought it odd that the moon was dark. Then he realized it was just that the moon was hurtling toward the Earth at an incredible speed, no longer lit by the sun's reflection. The moon hit the Earth. Dave died. He was found dead.

The end.

Epilogue

It was midnight in Munich, as opposed to lunchtime in Rarotonga or dinner in Albany. That line is hilarious if you are looking at a world clock, because then you'll see that

Rarotonga is 12 hours ahead of Munich and Albany is six hours behind, unless, of course, you're talking about Albany, Ga., not Albany, N.Y., although I think Albany, Ga. and Albany, N.Y. are in the same time zone, so same difference, either will work, although I may have ruined the joke for you by this point. It was a terrifying place, where things go bump in the night, like if somebody threw soft mushy bananas at you, and one of the bananas hit you in the face, it would probably make some kind of thud-type noise and therefore be terrifying. Munich might not be scary at midnight if people weren't throwing soft mushy bananas, though, so go ahead and imagine that people were throwing mushy bananas.

For Dave, Munich was a big juicy pile of Animal Crackers. Except no camels, Dave hated camels. And juice. Dave also despised dry cleaners, gourmet bakeries, Post-It notes, the color periwinkle, fancy cheeses (mostly because they left him bloated and gassy – like the Marcellus Shale formation), potato chips, chipwiches, the remake of *Goodbye Mr. Chips*, and anything starting with the letter W. But that was just his way, the way of a super spy.

On this night, Dave was not found dead. Nope, he had work to do. Old men lurked in the shadows of a red light district alley. Some were not so much lurking as bumping into things because they couldn't see very well. Dave's nemesis exited a brothel across the main street. He watched as the young woman in the blue dress adjusted her stockings. She was a beauty, and she put on quite a show. Dirty blond hair, a silk scarf, and all the right curves; a super spy's type of woman. She made her way north along the avenue, staying just outside any light source, be it from a porch or the fireworks erupting over the Chinese New Year parade.

A car pulled to the side of the road just behind the femme fatale. A man exited, moving rather hurriedly toward Dave's quarry. Dave darted through traffic at elephant-like speed. The

3

villain was moving more quickly, a hand raised, as if to strike. Ten yards, five yards, three feet, inches, then Dave's fist met him like a soggy tomato. The man turned to face his attacker, shuddering in fear.

"Stinkov. I should have known, You will die, today, mortal enemy," said Dave. He wasn't about to let another villain intervene with his plans to capture the girl, and bring down her secret organization bent on world destruction... kind of like Cobra.

"What? My name is Gus Weatherby. I've never seen you before in my life!" Stinkov was a master manipulator. Only Dave's keen spy sense kept him from being fooled.

"Oh, sorry. I could have sworn you were one of my mortal enemies or something. Hey look, you dropped your wallet." Sure enough, the evil Agent Stinkov had dropped his stuff. Dave took the time to read his ID. "Agent Waldo Sta... Sti... Splackoff, Spiffnarf... What's this last word here?"

The agent of doom looked down at the card. "Stinkov."

"Got it, thanks. Well, here you are," said Dave, returning Stinkov's personal effects. "See ya Gus, have a fun time in Berlin." Dave's deviously meticulous scheme had worked to perfection. But then he forgot about his plan, so it ended up working slightly less effectively than originally anticipated.

"Berlin? Aren't we in Munich?" asked Stinkov.

By this time, Dave had turned his attention to the lady walking away. He quickly chased after her. Agent Stinkov laughed a hideous cackle, kind of a combination of Margaret Hamilton and Rudolph Valentino.

The villain, having eluded his greatest foe, confidently stepped off the curb and was run over by the New Year's dragon. Blood and some other stuff went flying, including, but not limited to, a bunch of coconut cream pies, the left two-thirds of the Great Pyramid of Giza, R5-D4, a Fabergé egg, the uneaten portion of Archie Bunker's last grilled Reuben

4

sandwich (because obviously if it were the eaten portion, that would have been disgusting), Q*bert, six or seven maids-a-milking, and Gus Weatherby. Stinkov wasn't going to recover.

Dave's victory was secured, but he had lost her again. He stood at the corner of Concord and Lexington, with his nose in the air, hoping to catch her scent. A police dog patrolling the city noticed his horrible methodology, and went over to offer some constructive criticism. Before the big German shepherd had a chance to speak, however, his human partner butted in. "What do you think you are doing, American? We have laws in this country. You can't just go around sniffing the air anytime you please..."

Dave was deep in thought, so he decided not to kill the officer. Instead he tried to throw the lawman off his trail. "I am here to prevent the destruction of the Berlin Wall, if you must know. These orders come straight from PROTOCOL."

"You're in Munich. Besides, the Berlin Wall was torn down years ago."

"Well, I guess this mission's over. I'm headed up to my grandmother's house for milk and cookies. See you later." The cop waved goodbye as Dave sped away on foot. His streak was still intact. He would live to fight another day.

Dave's story was all too common among secret agents: a high school genius who was kicked out after failing kindergarten, eight-sport All-American at UCLA, wrote the megahertz manifesto at 24, ran guns to the Belizeans in 92' when they were screaming for Philly cheesesteaks. He made his first kill shortly thereafter, leading PROTOCOL to initiate contact. Of course, Dave had only accidentally shot that rock in the foot, and he was wielding only 14 of Baskin-Robbins' 31 flavors, as opposed to, say, a Howitzer or a bazooka, but the wound did turn out to be fatal, and the heads of PROTOCOL had never been wrong about an agent.

After his recruitment, Dave spent every waking moment

5

either traversing the globe stopping international crime syndicates or visiting his grandmother. Having lost the trail of his curvaceous nemesis, there was nothing to do but head back to the U.S. and await further instruction...

Los Angeles, a fortnight later (a.k.a. two weeks)

Dave, dressed in all black, made his way through the murky swamp to his grandmother's house. What Dave had failed to realize was that Grandma didn't live in the swamps anymore. In fact, she had never lived in the swamp. Dave began to wonder if he ever really had a Grandmother. He was angry that they lied to him. But he couldn't harp on old news. No, Dave had to meet someone else on this night, someone who was not his grandmother. And so, in this depressed, disgruntled state, Dave headed out of the swamps.

Dave was on his way to that city by the bay, the mistake by the lake, El Paso, Arkansas. The dust from the road swept up into Dave's eyes. A gigantic tumbleweed hit Dave repeatedly in the bottom, until he retaliated with a right jab and a left winky that sent the displaced bush into oblivion. Dave was then back on track. He soon saw some bright neon lights in the distance. The cold water Dave had been swimming in had led him to his goal. Suddenly, Dave realized he wasn't supposed to be in the water at all. No, in fact, Dave was supposed to be on dry land, where it is dry, unlike water, which is not dry at all. He waved his fists and shouted in anger.

"I'll get you for this, bad guys," said Dave. "If it's the first thing I do, you will pay!"

The genius super spy rechecked his super spy manual. His secret decoder destination was a place known as the 'Windy City.' Yes, Dave knew of this place all to well. Also, Dave was a human compass, as he had been magnetized as a young lad during a misadventure with Go-Gurt and Gobots. He built a signpost before beginning his expedition. Next, Dave grabbed

6

a ball of twine, took a hop, skip and flop and was off.

The journey was treacherous. Dave knew that he must be going in the right direction because of all the large motorized enemies he had to face. Dave shook his fists with abandon to show these bad guys that he was on to them. But as he looked around himself, Dave had to face the fact that not only was he lost, he had no idea where the heck he was. Some signage hinted that Dave had entered the City of Angels.

"Drat!" Dave was the master of arcane exclamations, as well as geographic reference points. Dave circled back and began again, just like Michael Finnegan.

Eventually, after a laborious trek through vicious jungles and snowy mountain cliffs where every turn could be filled with danger and despair, through the sands of a seemingly endless and disastrous desert where a drop of water was worth more then a man's life, Dave found his way to the city he had been searching for. Soon he even got to Los Angeles, which was just a little further away.

"Ah yes, the city that never sleeps. Now, to find out my mission." Then Dave took a nap.

Dave was a loner, a drifter, a man of the streets. Hollywood was his forest and he was the Cowardly Lion, except that Dave was not really a coward, so he was more like a combination of Toto and the Scarecrow. L.A. was at that time a crazy place, filled with people who were not entirely stable.

"Not entirely stable?" asked Dave.

"I'm glad you're here to tell us these things," said Keith Moon, drummer for *The Who*. "John, old boy, take the Professor in back and plug him into the hyperdrive."

John Entwistle, or possibly someone who looked like John Entwistle dressed in a Chewbacca outfit, reached out for Dave. It was difficult to ascertain if it was the real John Entwistle, as hundreds of individuals, wearing any number of costumes, would often mingle with actual celebrities up and down

7

Hollywood Boulevard.

Only Dave, and a few other highly trained super spies knew the difference. Dave slowly began to retrieve his *The Who Sell Out* album and his pink Sharpie from the lining of his secret agent black turtleneck sweater.

"Hey, I'm trademarking black turtlenecks," said an evil agent standing nearby, dressed as Sterling Archer.

Dave grabbed a tall, skinny guy dressed as Christopher Reeve and threw him at the fake Sterling Archer. The plan was a success, as the cartoon charlatan was knocked back into a Genesis circa-1977 tribute band. The fake Steve Hackett leveled the guy with his real Gibson Les Paul.

"Couldn't you have at least thrown the Christopher Reeve wearing the Superman outfit, rather than the Christopher Reeve dressed up from *Somewhere in Time*?" asked Sterling, before passing out.

"Excellent team work, fake Steve Hackett," said Dave.

Unbeknownst to Dave, it was in fact the real Steve Hackett. But just then Lou Costello, completely out of breath, came running up to Keith Moon. He grabbed him by the shoulders, and gasped, "Heh, heh, heh... wh... wha... who's on first?"

"Yes."

"Wha... wha... well, go ahead and tell me."

"Who."

"The... the... the guy on first."

"Who."

"The guy pla... gack... playing fir... fir... first base."

"Who."

"The guy... the guy playing first..."

"Who is on first."

"What are you asking me for? I'm asking you," said Costello, before also passing out.

"Ah, I see, the old, *The Who* and 'Who's on First' trick," said Dave. "You should know, Keith Moon, that deception may have worked with the Flint, Michigan staff of the Holiday Inn, but it won't work on me. Also, can you sign my *The Who Sells Out*, album?"

"I assumed as much, old boy," said Moon.

"Ah, the old 'assumed as much' retort, in reference to both the 'Who's on First' trick and the request for an autograph of the world's greatest rock drummer," said Dave, as he retrieved his album and his pink Sharpie, completing the final dialogue exchange of passwords with his field boss.

"Correct again, old boy," said Moon, secretly encoding the record with a mission synopsis. Many had known the British rock legend for his tenure with *The Who*. Unbeknownst to the general public, however, was the fact that Moon had been recruited during the fateful 1967 U.S. tour to join the ultra-secret branch of a multi-governmental counterintelligence organization known as PROTOCOL. The head of the society, known only as 'The King,' enlisted Moon to serve as West Coast operations director. A short time later he brought his colleague, bassist John Entwistle, into the fold. Entwistle had a penchant for disguises.

Dave quickly saluted his boss by tapping two fingers to his brow. Moon acknowledged the salute with one of his own, codename 'Thunderbird.' He then directed Entwistle/Chewbacca to pick up the elderly Costello, and the three vanished into the background.

Dave quickly perused his mission brief: he was to investigate a villainous guild of individuals known as 'actors.' They had been engaged in a most despicable form of torture, where they would show moving pictures of themselves to their victims, and then charge these poor fools $140 for popcorn and soda. PROTOCOL believed there were some even more despicable bad guys who had the real power. It would be up to Dave to investigate and stop them, if he had the capacity.

Dave traversed Los Angeles on this night in an Elgin

9

Baylor-esque mood. He brushed off his mud-stained outfit and peered around. 'These wicked bad guys are going down,' Dave thought to himself. I'm assuming when he said 'wicked' he was referring to a synonym of appalling, dreadful, contemptible, or distasteful, as opposed to the Gregory Maguire book or the Broadway play, or 'wicked' as in 'wicked rad,' like something the Teenage Mutant Ninja Turtles (of whom Michelangelo was clearly the awesomest) would say.

Leaving the friendly confines of Hollywood Boulevard, Dave was nearly trampled by a pack of pontificating bloviators. After successfully dodging the fiendish madmen, Dave was able to continue his quest for the Holy Grail... um, the lost temple of... island of Atlantis... ah, Dave had stuff to do. He flipped through his spy manual, past his notes for some of his recent assignments, such as finding those responsible for sabotaging the 1919 World Series or determining who was to blame for inserting some kind of fruity, grapelike substance in his jelly donuts. He paused briefly on the file detailing his recent encounter with the beauty from Berlin.

"That's Munich," said a nearby German shepherd.

"Right," said Dave, still searching for a lead on his quest to disrupt the actors' guild.

Then Dave decided to get some takeout from TACO SUPER BURRITO. Oddly, the store did not sell any burritos, or jelly donuts. Nonetheless, the super spy was sufficiently satiated after devouring a plateful of fruit-filled cookies.

And then, from out of the sky, came an updated dossier from PROTOCOL. The file hit Dave right in the face, in the form of yesterday's newspaper. Dave quickly skipped pass the world report, which detailed an imminent nuclear attack and something about the moon hurtling toward Earth, and took the opportunity to skim through the local news.

"Finally, there's a sale on those booty-enhancing sneakers from Sketchers," said Dave, drawing more than one or two odd looks from the other patrons of TACO SUPER BURRITO. Dave noted their peculiar behavior before finally reaching the classified ads, in which he found the addendum to his standing orders: to stop the ring leader of a crazy cult of cannibals known as 'Producers.' They were the despicable bad guys responsible for every evil scheme, past, present or future, since the dawn of the Neoproterozoic Era. And it was going to be Dave's job to eliminate the ringleader of these 'Producers!'

PROTOCOL often gave Dave his mission in this manner: The advertisement would say something along the lines of "Come to Shorty's Gin Joint, on the Corner of 13th & Honker." Dave would then decode the message via the cardboard toy he received on a specially marked box of Cap'n Crunch shortly after his acceptance into the PROTOCOL brotherhood. Of course, there were no traveling pants, nor Traveling Wilburys inside the cardboard container, only sweetened corn and oat cereal. The key to it all, of course, was Dave's spy manual, which he had originally found wedged between his grandmother's house and Wedge Antilles' X-Wing. Now imagine Patrick Stewart saying 'advertisement.' He puts the emphasis on 'VERT,' whereas we Yankee blokes put the stress on 'AD.' What's the deal with that?

Dave scanned the soggy pages of his journal. 'Shorty's,' according to Dave's super spy manual, meant 'stop the ring leader of a crazy cult of cannibals known as Producers.' As for the rest of the message, 'Come to' and 'corner' translated into the location where this cult leader was to be found. In this case, the location was a gin joint somewhere around Honker and 13th. The rest of the message, 'Gin Joint, on the' and 'of 13th & Honker,' was designed to throw off any covert or clandestine organizations, foreign or otherwise.

Location in hand, Dave quickly threw the newspaper away, as the mission briefs always self-destructed after the information was received, like in *Get Smart, Mission: Impossible*

11

and *Steel Magnolias*. He was ready.

And so, with the fate of the world resting on the shoulders of PROTOCOL's greatest agent, Dave embarked on his most important mission; cool, confident, almost arrogant, with an extra pair of boxers just in case.

He fought past the traffic cops, bullied his way through a school crossing, and performed a super-jump across a gigantic six inch waterfall that was understood through out Hollywood to have caused more deaths than any single natural disaster known to man. For most women, however, it was just a little sewer drain. 'You know, I wonder if my arch-enemy could assist me in tracking down these Producers,' thought Dave.

As if on queue, Dave saw his beautiful nemesis enter a club just a few yards from his present location. It was called *Shorty's*, near the intersection of 13th and Honker, opposite the law offices of Donald P. Bellisario.

"I seem to remember reading something about this place rather recently," said Dave, wondering if there was any connection to the evil lair of cannibalistic producers he was tasked with thwarting.

The bad guy agents were quite clever. Theorizing that they could time travel within their own lifetime, they shoved author Samuel Beckett into the Quantum Leap accelerator, where he promptly vanished. But Dave was smarter than they were. This time he shook his left foot in the air with abandon.

"You can't fool me, bad guys. The next leap *will* be the leap home," said Dave, eager to converse with his nemesis. Only she could help him locate the producers' secret hideout on the Corner of Honker and 13th. "That lair has to be around here somewhere." Dave followed his enemy into the club, ready for all forms of malfeasance.

Her friends knew her as Don Juan de Marco Polo, and she was a real looker. Dave recognized her from Munich: same blue dress, lovely curves, and the bouffant hair. He was having

12

trouble keeping his concentration to the task at hand, which is probably how Don Juan de Marco Polo gave Dave the slip. Dave was no cross-dresser though; he was strictly a blouse and bloomers kind of guy.

After realizing he had lost his suspect, Dave discovered to his great surprise that Don Juan de Marco Polo had also left.

Dave slowly made his way from the back of the room to the exit, where he was met face to face with the backside of the bouncer. The man was a monster: at least 4 or maybe even 5 feet tall. Judging from the enormously broad shoulders, Dave figured the man to weigh at least 80 or possibly 90 pounds.

In order to discover the man's name, Dave had used a super spy method that only he had perfected. It was called "look at the device known as codename 'Tag' on the individual's shirt." Dave had taken a quick, 15-minute glance at just such a device pinned to the bouncer's shirt that had the letters S-H-O-R-T-Y written on it in bright pink neon letters. Dave then incorporated his deductive reasoning skills to decipher just what name those letters really stood for. The letters that were written in the order S-H-O-R-T-Y often times spelled out 'Carnival,' according to Dave's spy manual. However, Dave could go beyond his manual to realize that S-H-O-R-T-Y actually stood for 'Space Haggis Over Rutabaga and Tatties = Yummy.' Dave knew that evil, vial, cunning villains use trick words all too many times, since clearly haggis should only be enjoyed with neeps and tatties (a.k.a. turnips and mashed potatoes) not rutabagas. In addition, space haggis had a tendency to leave in the middle of most poker games, especially if it held all of the chips, chip dip and turnips, and it had repeatedly shorted the pot. When Dave heard the bartender call the man 'Shorty,' his theory was not only proven, but it also caused Dave to leap into action.

Peering down at the gigantic man, Dave could tell he was in for one heck of a fight. While Shorty still had his back to him,

13

Dave took the advantage by reaching for the first bottle he could find. It was only a 60-gallon water jug, but it would have to do the trick. As Dave crashed the jug over the head of Shorty, he could see the man turn and say, "What was that for?" as he stumbled into unconsciousness.

"As if you didn't know, pot-shorting space haggis?" Dave shouted at the top of his lungs.

He quickly made his way out of the bar, dodging several turnips and rutabagas that spilled out of Shorty's pockets, and resumed his pursuit of Don Juan de Marco Polo, who by this point was all the way across the street entering some sort of public transportation machine. Behind him, *Shorty's* exploded into tater tots.

Dave quickly accelerated after his enemy. He had reached her escape vehicle mere moments after she entered the device, known as codename 'bus' in Dave's secret agent lingo. Dave attempted to board, but was thwarted when he realized he would have to ascend possibly up to two stairs in order to continue his pursuit. Being deathly afraid of heights, Dave decided he would just have to pick up the trail later on, rather than risk serious injury or possible death.

In a dejected state, Dave slowly made his way down Hollywood Boulevard. Secret agents and street performers alike reached out to give Dave a high-five, acknowledging some great success in dispatching the cannibal producers who had threatened to destabilize all of California. Apparently they had all been crushed under the weight of imported potatoes. But Dave was in no mood for ovations. The mysterious lady had eluded him, once again.

"Some spy I turned out to be," said Dave. There was a chill in the air, and it was at this juncture that Dave realized that he was completely naked. Dave finally understood why everyone had been running away from him screaming, "Look, here comes some guy that is completely naked!"

While Dave was no math major, he could put two and fourteen together just as fast as the next super secret agent guy.

Dave searched around to find a place that would be suitable to his needs. Then he saw it in big bright lights: "Fredrick's of Hollywood." It was the perfect choice. After all, Dave had known a guy named Fred once and he was a swell individual. In addition, Dave knew he was in Hollywood, and as the saying goes, "When in Rome, la vaca está en el baño."

Now, formally attired in a pink blouse and Victorian-era bloomers, Dave was ready to get back on the case. It was at this time that another of Don Juan de Marco Polo's henchmen attempted to assassinate Dave. He had been following him around with a big Ben Franklin waving in the air, and Dave knew when he said, "Oh, come on, sweet cakes!" that the man was attempting to poison Dave with some sort of laced pastry.

"First jelly donuts, and now this," said Dave. He wasn't going to be captured alive, however, as this man was about to learn. More exactly, he wasn't going to let the man poison him with any sweet cakes, because otherwise he would be dead, and the story would be over. So skip that last part. Sweet cakes have too many carbohydrates, anyway. "Sweet cakes have too many carbohydrates," said Dave.

When this failed to dissuade the man, Dave put his five-inch pumps to good use and apprehended him with an ultimate super-super kick, like Shawn Michaels. Hoping to infiltrate Don Juan de Marco Polo's underground hideout, Dave decided to use her henchman's clothes to see if he could sneak in. He switched duds with the man, picked up the Ben Franklin and headed off, now in a dinner jacket and black tie.

Dave searched his pockets, looking for clues as to the whereabouts of Don Juan de Marco Polo. The battle with her underling had reinvigorated Dave. He was ready to get back on the case. Dave quickly found a torn straw wrapper inside the villain's vest. It was his only clue, but it was all Dave needed.

15

He carefully placed the straw wrapper in his mouth in order to do the famous 'read the label' test. As the paper slowly dissolved, Dave tried reading the name found on the wrapper. Then, Dave realized he couldn't see the wrapper. As he expelled the paper, using the super spy spitting method, codename 'loogie,' Dave found the clue he was looking for. The paper landed on a sign for another club. Now if Dave could only find the club itself, He would be back on track.

After a brief three-hour jog, Dave caught up with his prey, entering an establishment at least three or possibly four inches from the sign where he had started his search. Then Dave saw Don Juan de Marco Polo enter the club, as well. Dave attempted to follow her, but was thwarted by another bouncer. This time, however, Dave was prepared. He applied a mega karate chop to the other man's hand that used so much force that the bouncer did not even notice. Unfortunately, Dave forgot that this was the hand in which he was carrying his Ben Franklin, and it ended up with the bouncer. Gladly accepting this payment, the bouncer let Dave enter.

Dave realized almost immediately that he must be in the bad-guy-super-hideout, as everyone in the place was wearing large moose antlers in the shape of outdated Abercrombie and Fitch attire. Everyone, that is, except Mr. Franklin, who had on his usual 18th century garb, and of course, Don Juan de Marco Polo. Dave surmised, however, that as he was the one who had brought Mr. Franklin, there was only about a 40 percent chance that the "Fart Proudly" author was an enemy spy. (Franklin actually wrote an essay called "Fart Proudly" while serving as the U.S. Ambassador to France. I swear to God. Or Shiva. Or the Flying Spaghetti Monster. Or the deity of your choosing.) That was not the case for the people wearing the moose antlers. They were indeed evil super spies, and Dave could prove it. Dave was a master of the association theory. He knew that moose antlers signified that these people had been

16

to Hawaii, where all of the great ski movies were made. "First the producers, and now the actors. Time to complete this mission," said Dave.

Just then, someone dropped a hat. Quickly realizing his life was in danger, Dave flung himself through the nearest window. Unfortunately for Dave, what he had thought to be a nearby window was actually a small piece of ravioli. Dave, now lying on the ground, quickly surmised it was time to find his prey, before he attracted any attention. He could see his cover was still okay as he arose from the floor. Only a few hundred people had seen his super spy dive.

"I'll dispatch these torture-inflicting actors after I converse with my arch-nemesis." Dave thought this aloud to himself in a low volume shout, similar to the decibel level of a minor volcanic eruption, such as Mount St. Helens or Yellowstone. All of the antlers were focused on Dave.

But there, in the middle of all the antlers was Don Juan de Marco Polo. Now was Dave's chance to confront her in a secluded setting. As he made his way from the door toward his suspect, he traveled past table after table, knocking antlers all over the place. But in order to be cool as ice about the whole mission, Dave decided at the last moment against pulling out his rapid-fire bazooka and randomly shooting people. Instead, he would deftly go over and introduce himself.

"So Don Juan de Marco Polo, we meet again. As I am quite sure you all ready know, I am Dave."

"Don John de what the heck did you just call me?"

"Let's not play games Missy, the jig is up."

"Who's Missy?"

"I don't know, and what's all this about asking me to dance? I hate the Irish Jig."

"Dance?"

"Who, you and me? Why I would love to! Say, what did you say your name was?"

17

"I'm pretty sure I didn't, but it's Cecilia."

Just then, Ben Franklin whizzed by their table on a jungle vine. The two spies both glanced at him before returning to their own conversation.

"Nice to meet you! My name is... ah... umm..."

"Dave."

"No, I'm Dave, lady. Boy, you sure do seem confused..."

"Well, you sure are a funny one. Come on, let's go."

And then Dave and Cecilia proceeded to dance up a storm as only two of the top secret agents can do. Now was Dave's big chance to take Cecilia out of action, finally completing his Munich assignment. Dave slowly worked his way toward the back exit of the dance club, but lost track of where he was and ended up in the orchestra pit.

It was at this point, by some freak act of nature that the Timpani drummer, world renowned as the greatest in his field for never losing a Timpani stick, fell victim to his first colossal failure. I'm pretty sure it was that guy from *Spaceballs*.

The drummer was just about to go into the great Timpani solo that ends the song (likely either the Chariots of Fire theme or "Call Me" by Blondie) when the stick in the drummer's right hand flew out and made a beeline straight for Cecilia. Dave, with his lightning fast reflexes, decided to sacrifice himself rather than have his beautiful partner harmed. Apparently Dave forgot that this was his archenemy. The soft, foamy tip struck Dave at the base of the elbow, knocking him out instantaneously.

Cecilia, feeling sorry for the poor devil who had just risked his life to save her's, dragged Dave back to her dorm, fireman's carry style, and threw him down on her roommate's bed.

2 What's that Under the Bed?
The Entrance of Flabius

The legendary journeys began long, long ago, in the age of the dinosaurs, when man ruled the earth. Flabius Flaximus was the commander-in-chief of all he surveyed. The eagle-eyed Flabius could see at least two feet in every single direction (maybe even three feet), and within that awesome circumference Flabius was the ultimate alpha mega omega super Emperor of everything.

But all was not well in the empire of the great Flabius Flaximus. A powerful force of evil was slowly weaving its way into the prosperous community of the Rambo Brighteaens, as the residents of the Kingdom of Flabius were known. This evil weaver was the most evil of evil weavers in the history of evil weavers. She could weave such evil that even bad guys were often saying, "Man, I might be a bad guy, but that weaver is really evil," or, "You know, I bet caramel corn is better than a futon."

One particularly nefarious morning, Lucy the evil weaver was scampering around from one side of the kingdom to the other. It was obvious that she was up to something. Lucy looked left. Lucy shot a glance to her right. Then, from out of an unquestionably neutral piece of shrubbery, a small three-toed sloth named Larry 'The General' Stanfrackle emerged carrying an apple-scented porcupine pie.

"Now you die, General Folivora," said Lucy the evil weaver, as she lunged for the sloth.

Missing completely, Lucy rolled directly into the path of an oncoming squadron of duck-billed platypuses. The force of evil was over. The empire of Flabius Flaximus was safe.

But another evil was lurking in the shadows, an evil that had not reared its ugly head in eons. Does evil actually have a head? I suppose evil beings have heads, unless the celery stalks at midnight. Then again, there is such a thing as a head of celery. So an evil that had not reared its celery in eons was once more afoot, like Bunnicula...

Years Earlier

Years earlier, when Flabius's father Fattus Flaximus was in power, a depraved sorcerer attempted to take over the kingdom. The name of this despicable wizard was Weemus Bobeemus. He knew the secrets of the four corners of the world, (as the people of that time still thought the planet was round.) Weemus Bobeemus could control earth, wind, fire and water, which made him more powerful than Earth Wind & Fire, although the wizard did enjoy "Boogie Wonderland."

Weemus also had unmatched physical strength, and he was in possession of unbelievably no extra super powers that shocked, frightened, and amazed us; while at the same time made us wonder why we were so shocked, frightened and amazed.

Weemus entered the kingdom of Fattus Flaximus with only two thoughts on his mind: the total and complete control of everything and an all-expenses-paid week at Walt Disney World.

Fattus had no problem with this, as he didn't have any idea what he was even doing as Emperor of this noble land, but when Weemus stole the Sacred Spoon of Chocococolate La, the great Emperor had to put a stop to the madness. He sent his best men to find Weemus, but they were unsuccessful. In fact, they were completely wiped out.

And so the great leader and his young son went in search of

20

the evil Weemus Bobeemus themselves.

Across the great ocean they came to the land of Giants: of really big castles and mountain citadels, where Weemus had a little cottage in the enchanted forest, which was not really enchanted.

Armed only with their great faith and a couple of small Mig-29 super jets fully loaded with nukes, Fattus and the young Flabius set out for Weemus's heavily guarded cottage.

When they approached, they were met face-to-face with the most fearsome goldfish the world had ever known. There it was: perched in its enormous 12-ounce jar, high atop a three-foot pole, standing guard at the great cottage.

Inside the cottage, Weemus could be seen using the sacred spoon for the most unthinkable crimes.

Fattus, the great man that he was, knew fear for the first time in his long and revered life.

But the young and foolhardy Flabius was not about to let any stinking super tough goldfish stand in his way. Surveying the landscape, Flabius decided to incorporate the ancient super-roll method of his ancestors, where one scurries along the ground on all fours before flinging themselves across the enemy in an attempt to surprise their opponents into surrender. Sometimes, of course, the procedure was mistaken for feckless ferrets rummaging for leftover meatloaf, but when executed correctly, the super fresh roll technique was extraordinarily powerful.

As Flabius approached the vile and cunning goldfish, Fattus and the others held their breath, hoping against hope that the young prince would not be spotted. And then it happened: Flabius made his mega-dive attempt at the goldfish, but miscalculated, and fell a good two or three hundred feet short of the mark.

The enormous quake, however, that resulted from the "Great Leap" as it is now known, caused the ground to open

21

up and swallow the goldfish, the cottage, and Weemus Bobeemus. As if on queue, the Sacred Spoon of Chocococolate La flew up in the air and landed right in the face of the great king Fattus Flaximus.

The forces of Fattus decided that it was now the time to depart, and so with victory in their collective hands, they set off for their homeland.

Back to the present (which is also the past, since this is a tale from long ago)

The good Emperor Fattus the Good was never the same after the battle, and died shortly thereafter, some 70 years later. Flabius, now reaching his maturity, took over the throne. The Rambo Brighteaens lived in peace and prosperity for the next 30 years or so. Then came the 100th anniversary of the great Flabius Flaximus's victory over the evil sorcerer Weemus Bobeemus, and rumors of the wizard's return began to rise.

Flabius, now 25 years old, had a whole kingdom to worry about, stretching further than ever before, so the first thing he ordered was that his entire army be sent back to guard the ancient spoon. Flabius would not allow anything to happen to the great ancestral utensil this time.

Feeling secure in the knowledge that his spoon was safe, Flabius embarked on the next of his great quests. He was off to the east, where legends had surfaced of an awesome device known to wreak havoc on entire countries. It was known as the "Great Fork That Has Been Known to Wreak Havoc on Entire Countries." As legends of the fork spread, Flabius became more and more convinced that this was indeed part of the missing set of which the Sacred Spoon of Chocococolate La was also a piece.

Flabius, traveling with his trusted captain of the Rambo Brightus Guard, Biffus Palookus, began the journey east to the land of Gimpus Foo Foo, and hopefully to the great Fork, as

22

well. They rode out of the city walls through a hero's welcome. This was all quite unusual for someone who was leaving, but who's counting?

Regardless, the two adventurers left the safety and comfort of home for the first time in nearly one hundred years. It was up to them to retrieve the fork before it fell into evil hands. With the fork in his possession, Weemus Bobeemus almost certainly would be able to match the strength of the great Flabius Flaximus and his spoon. Besides, Flabius had never seen a fork before, and so they were off.

"Tis' a good day for travelling, sire."

"Stay alert, my trusted friend, the forces of evil may be all around us. Look there! What's that?" Flabius peered down at some strange string-like creature attacking his shoes.

"That's your shoe lace, your highness."

"Of course, I was only testing you, trusted test-taker. Excuse me one moment as I adjust my chastity bel... as I brush my teeth." With that last exclamation, the great Emperor went off to relieve himself, and upon his return the caravan was underway again, except that there were only two people, so it wasn't really a caravan at all.

"Come let us get started," said Flabius.

The two travelers and their sturdy stallions would have to make their way through the great mountains that separate the kingdom of the Rambo Brighteaens from the mysterious, distant land of Gimpus Foo Foo.

The journey was not more than 23 seconds along when the two gallant fighters came across their first true test. It was the second greatest challenge that Flabius had ever faced up to that point in his life (the first being the battle with Weemus Bobeemus.) Biffus was an emotional wreck. Flabius found it difficult to concentrate with the screaming and crying of Biffus piercing his ultra-tough eardrums.

The problem was vast: the gates of the city were closed.

23

Slowly Flabius approached, constantly looking over his shoulder, checking every bush for evil beings. He was almost to the gates now. The rusted portals seemed to reach to the heavens. They had to be at least as big as the ones from the 1976 Dino De Laurentiis remake of *King Kong*. Biffus was sure that they would be impossible to move. But Biffus Palookus was not there the day that Flabius defeated Weemus Bobeemus. He was not fully aware of the exceptional prowess of the great Flabius Flaximus.

The Emperor peered up at the formidable obstruction. This was indeed going to be difficult. He turned around, shrugging his shoulders as he looked back at his cohort. As he attempted to steady himself by placing his hand on the massive gates, they moved. Flabius turned back around, ready for a duel. He shook his neck from left to right, and began doing some exceedingly difficult stretching exercises, such as putting his hands in the air and then slightly lunging in multiple directions.

Finally, he was ready for the challenge. Flabius reached out with his left hand and gently leaned forward, ever so delicately. The force of the 'lean-forward' maneuver shattered the mighty gates into oblivion.

It was finally over. Biffus breathed a sigh of gaseous relief. The two adventures could now concentrate on the task ahead.

"Sire, before, when you spoke of evils..."

"Yes my trusted servant, ask your question."

"Do you think the evil wizard, Weemus Bobeemus, may be coming for us? Why, just the other day, I overheard a story down at the beauty parlor. The hairdresser, some lady named Johnny..."

"You know, my trusted captain, that gossip is not a particularly becoming quality. It makes you sound like some sort of broccoli." Flabius was stern in his warning.

"Broccoli?"

"Yes. You know, when a woman gets old you call her a

24

broccoli."

"No, I believe you would call her an old lady, sire, and I was only telling you the story because I thought it might affect our imperial security."

"Of course, my trusted valet! Please, continue with your great story of chaos and doom."

"Chaos and Doom? Where?" Biffus searched the surrounding area for the wanted criminals, Doom and Chaos. Doom, though slightly less infamous than Weemus Bobeemus, had nonetheless assembled an extensive rap sheet, including charges of robbery, cyber terrorism, assault with a deadly floppy-eared bunny, and loitering. Chaos, on the other hand, had a prior for motor vehicle theft, but more importantly was a known associate of Lucy the evil weaver, so people generally kept their distance.

On this morning, neither could be found in the immediate vicinity, so Biffus returned to his conversation with the Emperor. "As I was saying, this hairdresser named Johnny, in the lowest voice I have ever heard a woman speaking in, was telling of her great exploits to all the ladies. She spoke of love affairs, great and powerful battles of Connect Four, beer, and she even knew the latest Footus Ballus stats."

"Pardon me, my trusted little tadpole, but where are you going with all of this?"

"That's not even the most important part, sire." Biffus was getting quite excited as he was coming to the punch line and nearly fell off his horse. Flabius, confused, leaned over along with his sidekick to hear the remainder of the story. "This evil hairdresser spoke of a great battle she had participated in years ago, with a young prince I am sure you are familiar with."

"Oh? Who? I love guessing games!" The Emperor loved guessing games. "Now, don't tell me. Is it Prince Emumus? No, forget that. It's Prince Hugeous Bootus, isn't it? No, no wait, I know, it's Prince Big Butt Brutus! Gotta be him! Did I

25

guess? Come on, tell me!"

"Sire, I'm fairly certain there is no such person as Big Butt Brutus," said Biffus, sounding kind of like Wil Wheaton in the Ziggurat Brothers' production of Tennessee Williams' *The Lady of Larkspur Lotion.*

"Yes, but there could be," retorted Flabius, carefully surveying the landscape for Mallomars.

"It's you, sire," said Biffus. "She spoke of a great battle with you, in which she lost her most precious possession."

'Oh, man, I thought I had it with Prince Big Butt Brutus. Shoot. So what's so important about this hairdresser, anyway? I don't recall doing battle with any hairdressers."

Flabius and Biffus both returned to the upright position. Flabius, distraught at not guessing correctly, carried a gloomy expression.

Biffus, however, took no notice. "Sire, there are a lot of things you don't recall."

"Yes, this is true. But what does this have to do with Weemus Bobeemus, the evil sorcerer? And, for that matter, what were you doing at a salon?"

"You see, I've got it figured like this: salons always have chicks getting all done up, so I figure, what better place to meet a lady?"

"What's all this about meeting little baby chickens?"

"I think the words are interchangeable."

"Who would ever trade a baby chicken for a salon?"

"No, sire, I think baby chickens and ladies are interchangeable."

"Listen, my trusted not-a-veterinarian, remind me to have a word with you when we get back from this adventure. Salons? Baby chickens? Hugeous Bootus? You have some issues we need to work on."

Biffus was about to respond when the great Flabius Flaximus began looking about. A peculiar expression crossed

26

his face. Biffus began to speak, but Flabius signaled him to keep silent. The two warriors surveyed the land. Something was afoot.

Biffus could no longer stand the silence, so he spoke. "Your Highness, what is it?"

"Shhh. The Earth is calling. Be silent."

"Sire?"

"I said silence, my trusted be-quiet-please-man." Flabius looked from side to side. He began to shake his head. "Applesauce! Looks like the Earth is done speaking. You must have startled it, my trusted talk-too-loud-man."

"Let's get back to the issue, your grace."

"Fine. Then what about Weemus Bobeemus? What does this salon story and 'Johnny,' as you call her, have to do with him?"

"Oh. Yeah. I think that this woman may in fact be Weemus Bobeemus."

"Yes, but Weemus Bobeemus was a man." Flabius seemed very doubtful of his friend's logic concerning the matter.

"I know that, sire, but don't you see? The low voice, the big bulging muscles, using the men's room instead of the ladies room; I think that 'Johnny', as she called herself, is really the evil wizard in disguise."

"How do you know? Did you see this 'Johnny' lady naked? Maybe she just has really bad vision or something," concluded Flabius. "And, I might add, Weemus Bobeemus was all ready in his eighties when we first battled. Add up the years, my great companion, the guy would have to be like a thousand million bazillion years old by now." Flabius gestured wildly, hoping to accentuate his exclamation.

"Yes sire, but even if it was 100 years ago, you were there, and now you are only 25." Not to be outdone, Biffus also gestured, but in a more domesticated fashion.

"I see your point," said the Emperor. "Regardless, I don't

27

think we have to worry about Weemus Bobeemus returning."

"I have to worry sire, it's in the job description," said Biffus, pointing to a line in his contract indicating 'worrying' as his fifth daily responsibility, after protecting the Emperor, managing the Rambo Brightus Guard budget, foraging for elderberries, and overseeing the cleaning of the royal stalls.

"Never fear my trusted friend. Weemus Bobeemus would not dare return to our sacred homeland after the pasting we gave him on the day of the 'Great Leap.' Now I want you to erase those demon thoughts from your mind."

"Yes, of course sire."

Flabius was quite serious on the matter. He no longer wanted to hear of Weemus Bobeemus. Flabius knew what sort of a threat Weemus posed. It was just that his companion's story about the salon had brought back other memories, painful ones. Flabius had heard Biffus talk about the beautiful women of the salon and could only think of his own beloved, the girl that got away. Her name was Buffy. She was beautiful, blue-eyed, and loved to steeplechase. She also had a thing for steak. It seemed only days ago when they first met...

The Tale of when Flabius met Buffy

The setting was one of those eccentric royal family parties. Most of the old folks were out getting stinky. Fattus Flaximus, Father of Flabius, was not even the top dog, yet. The kingdom was still under the rule of the mighty Flinibus Flaximus.

Flinibus, father of Fattus, grandfather of Flabius, had friends from the furthest lands. He was the 13th Flaximus to take the throne, but only the second who had to defend his capital.

The first, of course, was the Fearsome Flarnius Flaximus the Formidable, whose name was so terrible, grandiose, mighty, magnificent, ostentatious, duplicative and terrible that he was installed as king without contestation. Flarnius did,

28

however, do battle with a roving horde of iambic pentameters who stormed the city gates one Tuesday afternoon. It was a rather polemic, pastoral affair.

Flinibus, on the other hand, had to defend Rambo Brightus from the Foo Fooian Armada, the most abominable host of scum and villainy to appear in print or film since 1977.

The Foo Foos were the vilest of all the people known to exist. They plundered, pillaged, ravaged and devoured entire continents. Worst of all, they used to torture their prisoners by constantly flicking the poor captives' ears. The Foo Foos devastated every town, city, kingdom and outhouse they came upon. Under threat of annihilation, the victims left in their wake had no choice but to surrender.

The Foo Foos were unbeatable, until they encountered the kingdom of Flinibus Flaximus. The beautiful land was too rich and bountiful for the Foo Foos to ignore. And so they invaded, and promptly got their blucks klicked (That's the expression Rambo Brighteaens used to refer to people who had their rear-ends handed to them).

Flinibus, the most intelligent ruler in Rambo Brightus history, pointed out to the leader of the Foo Foos that an armada of naval vessels attacking vast swaths of the countryside might find it difficult to navigate on dry land. Never had the Foo Foos faced such ingenuity. The reign of Foo Fooian tyranny was at an end.

As a result, the former rulers of all the conquered lands came to pay homage to their liberator.

Conquering was not the way of the Flaximus family, however. So, upon their arrival, the old kings were given their lands back, which had been taken from them by the Foo Foos. The other rulers, however, insisted that Flinibus take the title of Emperor. It was entirely unclear if this was meant as a sign of respect, or if the minor royals were afraid of other, more powerful enemies, and wanted the Flaximus family to deal with

29

any and all threats to their safety. Nonetheless, Flinibus became the new top dog, and everyone else pretty much spent their days acting like Delta House.

It was one of these kings, a man by the name of Boogus MacDoogus, who had a young daughter named Buffy.

The party was on the tenth anniversary of Flinibus's victory over the Foo Foos. All of the neighboring kings came to the great city of Rambo Brightus. A young nine-year-old Flabius met a six-year-old Buffy at this party. She proceeded to kick Flabius in the shins for no reason whatsoever. Because all of the adults were drunk, Flabius could not tell on her. Instead, he had to toughen it out. He wouldn't give the unpleasant child the courtesy of tears, however.

From that moment on, Buffy had fallen in love with the big, limping kid who hadn't told on her.

Years later, they met again. It was...

"Sire?" Biffus startled the king out of his memory.

"Yes, my trusted companion?"

"How come you never say my name? I mean, I know you're Emperor and all, but you are always saying 'my trusted servant,' or 'my trusted comrade,' or 'stop eating all the Mallomars.' You know of course, that my name is Biffus."

"Of course, my trusted, ah, guy riding the horse next to me, but it just wouldn't be proper, being in a story set in ancient times, for the protagonist to use a servant's first name."

"I'm not sure I follow you sir."

"Just forget it, my trusted guy-not-named Larry 'The General' Stanfrackle."

"Yes, sir."

The two weary soldiers slowly made there way to a secluded, flat piece of earth, no larger than Siberia. It was the perfect place for Flabius and Biffus to make camp and rest for the evening. They had been traveling for nearly fifteen minutes, and neither could muster up the great strength needed to continue.

The large, monstrous, imposing, Great Flat Mountains lay dead ahead. A good night's sleep would be needed before the adventurers could attempt to scale those impossibly high cliffs.

Besides, Flabius was unable to get the thoughts of the beautiful Buffy from his mind. It had been so long ago that she disappeared, at least seven or eight minutes before Flabius and Biffus had left in search of the fork. It was right around the time that Biffus had his run-in with 'Johnny.'

But now was not the time to harp on old loves, and unresolved issues. The two adventurers needed to work on the task at hand, which was to find the 'Great Fork that Has Been Known to Wreak Havoc on Entire Countries.' And so they tied up their lovely mares, and proceeded to make camp.

"Sire, didn't we ride in on stallions?"

"I am sure it must be some sort of typographical error, my trusted guard."

"I just think that things seem pretty peculiar all of the sudden," said Biffus. "Just seconds ago we were making camp at the foot of the Great Flat Mountains, and now it looks like we're in some sort of evil lair."

Flabius, who by this point was already in his sleeping bag, looked around to see what all of the commotion was about. To his amazement, Biffus was indeed correct. Somehow they had been transported into an evil barn, with chickens, cows, sheep, and even little evil ducks roaming around.

In the center of the stable a great flame shot up into the air, and formed into the figure of the evil Weemus Bobeemus. "Well, Flabius Flaximus, we meet again. Only we aren't really meeting since this is only an image of me and I am actually somewhere else, so WE DON'T MEET AGAIN!"

Flabius fell back asleep in his sleeping bag. Biffus tapped him on the shoulder, to no avail. He looked over at the ghostly

31

image of Weemus Bobeemus and shrugged.

It would be up to the villainous wizard to rouse the Emperor from his most excellent slumber. "Wake up sleepy head. Time for my ominous warning!"

Flabius started snoring.

"Wake up, wake up! I've got some Mallomars!" Weemus shook a box of marshmallow cookies. He used his deceptive arts to cause the barn to smell like s'mores. It was enough to cause the Emperor to stir.

"What?" Flabius picked his head up, scratched his cheek and then began looking for the source of the yummy scent.

"I said, so WE DON'T MEET AGAIN!"

"Yes, Weemus, it is good not to see you too." Flabius sprung out of his sleeping bag. But as he got up, he proceeded to trip into the fire-image of Weemus. This made Weemus quite unhappy.

"Do you mind, Flaximus? It cost a lot of money to pull off this special effect, and you're completely ruining it." Yes, Weemus seemed quite flustered by his ancient enemy.

"Um, did you say something about cookies?"

"Oh, sorry Flabius, I do have cookies, but I have them with me, and since you're only seeing an image of me, I can't really share them with you," said Weemus Bobeemus.

"Well, do you have any milk, at least?" asked Flabius.

"There are cows right over there," said Weemus.

"Yes, but those are evil cows. How do I know their milk is homogenized?"

"Yeah, it probably wouldn't be. Although I'm not sure that has anything to do with the fact that the cows are evil," said the malevolent wizard.

Flabius stared down his mortal enemy with the most piercing of piercing glances. It wasn't a glance though, but a stare-down, so it was actually even worse than a piercing glance. Weemus tried to return the complement.

32

Flabius, always trained to expect nothing out of the ordinary at all times, had been expecting a stunt such as the one Weemus had pulled, ever since the rumors of Weemus's return had spread through his kingdom.

"Oh, that's a bunch of malarkey, sire, and you know it," said Biffus. "Joe Biden even knows it. I'm the one that told you Weemus might come back. I'm the one that said he was dressed up like that..."

"Shut up, my trusted shut-up-or-I'll-be-peeved!"

"Your grace, that makes no sense."

"Give me a break my trusted overly ambitious grammarian, I'm trying to stare down this evil image of Weemus Bobeemus," said Flabius.

The Emperor was furious about the Mallomar slight. "All right, Bobeemus, no cookies or milk? It's time to face your destruction." Flabius began chasing the evil spectral image of the wizard.

The frightened Weemus began dodging and moving to the best of his abilities, but the image was only of his head, so dodging was quite difficult.

Flabius was having similar difficulties. He couldn't get his hands on Weemus. This was not because Flabius didn't have hands, as the spectral image of Weemus suffered, but because Weemus wasn't really there. He was only an image.

The results of these problems meant that Flabius would dive at the image of Weemus, who would attempt to dodge, and both would fall on the ground, except that Weemus didn't fall, so Flabius would fall for the two of them. Finally, exhaustion set in, and the two battling champions called a temporary truce.

Gasping for air, but not willing to show signs of weakness, Flabius spoke. "What do you want, Bobeemus?"

Also gasping, not because he was tired but because he thought it was proper etiquette, Weemus answered. "Let it be

33

known, Flabius, that my transporting you, here, to this barn of dread, was a minor display of my powers. I have a mission for you, and if you don't complete it, I will be forced to use some more of my powers, like my major powers where I can do even more powerful stuff than this."

"How did you find us, Weemus?" asked Flabius Flaximus. "Why do you dare tempt my great abilities once again?"

"I placed a tracking device on your henchman when he came to my salon. After I knew you left the city, I made my way into the great hall of Chocococolate La (which was surprisingly easy, I might add) where I was met face to face with the entire Rambo Brighteaen army, crammed into a little room with the Sacred Spoon. Stealing the spoon was easy, as the army was packed in so tight they couldn't get their arms up over their heads to stop me from crawling on top of them."

"See sire, I told you, we should have left at least some of the men outside." Biffus felt it necessary to get his two cents in, which were actually two coins with the imprint of Fattus Flaximus on them. So in fact, Biffus felt it necessary two get his two Fattii (Plural form of Fattus) in.

"Do not speak, my trusted I'm-so-perfect-all-the-time-captain-of-the-guard friend," said the Emperor.

Flabius then turned his attention back to the evil wizard. "And by the way, Weemus, what's all this about a tracking device? This is supposed to be some long-ago time, where people rode horses and spoke high Valerian, like maybe the Bronze Age, or Copper Age, or some other metal-themed age." Flabius was quite distraught with his archenemy's lack of respect for the sword and sorcery-themed narrative.

"Bad cabbage?" The evil Weemus Bobeemus's spectral image shrugged at Flabius, which was bizarre in and of itself, considering the vision of Weemus did not have shoulders. Flabius was not in the mood for forgiveness, however. He made his anger known.

"Listen Weemus, if you think I am going to let you get away with stealing my spoon, you have got another thing coming. It doesn't matter to me that you used a device from the 24th and-a-half century to deceive my friend, here. I'll still beat you, with out cheating. You see, it doesn't matter, Weemus. Soon I will have the second element from the set of doom, 'The Great Fork That Has Been Known to Wreak Havoc on Entire Countries,' and with the fork in my possession you will never be able to defeat me." The anger in the voice of Flabius nearly chased ghost Weemus out of the room. Weemus would not go without revealing his plan, however.

"I could defeat you right now if I wanted, Flabius."

"I would never submit to your evil ways, Bobeemus."

"I know that, which is why I have something else to show you."

"All right! What is it? Did you get me a puppy? Is it an Irish Setter? A Soft-coated Wheaten Terrier? Is it a Great Dane?" Flabius always enjoyed seeing new things. He also thought that now that he was top dog (like his father and grandfather before him) he was supposed to receive a dog.

"No, this is a bad something else." Weemus didn't want Flabius to get his hopes up or anything. He was a nefarious, yet thoughtful warlock.

"Man, I really wanted a puppy," said Flabius, once again thoroughly dejected. Still, he had a kingdom to save, and that meant he had to put his game face back on. "So, are you saying bad as in good, or bad as in 'eat your vegetables or you can't play with your Voltron lion force toy set that actually transforms like in the TV show,' bad?"

"I think the second one, but I'm honestly not exactly sure," Bobeemus consulted with an off-screen presence, apparently an iPad with WiFi capability. "Yes, the second one."

Just then, a new image began forming in the place of Weemus Bobeemus. A wave struck Flabius Flaximus like never

35

before. It was still low tide and he was a good 15,000 feet above sea level, so the whole thing was pretty weird.

After he dried himself off, Flabius responded to the image. "Buffy? My awe inspiring, Angora sweater-wearing Buffy? What have you done with her, you mischievous necromancer who isn't really here?" Flabius was wild with anger, and possibly flatulence from his dinner of beans-and-greens made with Swiss chard and a little bit of garlicky-buttery sauce.

"Relax, Flaximus, I have not harmed the girl, yet," said Weemus Bobeemus, as his ghostly visage returned to the flame. "But if you do not perform the tasks I have told you, Buffy could meet with the most unfortunate of circumstances."

"What sort of circumstances are we talking about here, Weemus?" Flabius sought clarification as he snacked on some Triscuits and a diet cola, in hope of settling his unsettled bowels.

"The unfortunate kind."

"That clears up everything," said Biffus, wanting to make sure people knew he was still there. And by people, I mean Weemus Bobeemus and Flabius Flaximus, because there wasn't anyone else around, although I suppose it's possible that Biffus also wanted to let the evil mini-ducks know he was there in case they got scared because it was past their bedtime and this really long, drawn out conversation between WB and FF was dragging on interminably.

"So then go and perform the tasks I have set out for you to perform!" It was now Weemus giving the orders, and he was going to enjoy every moment.

"Hey, I do this for real. I never act my way through anything!" Flabius was confused by the orders of Weemus to go out and give a performance.

"No, that's not what I meant. You have to complete some tasks for me. Like, perform, as in do," said Weemus,

36

attempting to clarify his earlier remarks.

"I'm not following you, Weemus," said the mighty Emperor. "Are you are likening my performance to doo doo? As in poopy? Are we really now at the level of scatological humor? Is that the best an evil wizard has to offer? I must file an objection. After all, you are holding my future bride hostage, and I don't want our children learning any bathroom humor."

"You've totally lost me, Flabius."

"I see that, now," exclaimed the Emperor, as he flipped through the latest issue of *Sportus Illustratedus* while utilizing the barn's services. After reading an excellent article on several new high definition television innovations coming to the broadcast coverage of the professional Footus Ballus League, Flabius returned his attention to the evil wizard. "Well, you haven't told us of any tasks."

Weemus had momentarily dozed off while waiting for the Emperor to finish his business. "Oh, yeah. Let me see here. I have to find my notes. I wrote it all down so I wouldn't forget." Weemus began rummaging through his pockets, looking for the instructions. He put his glasses on to aid in his search.

Biffus laughed at the foolish old man, and offered a suggestion to solve his memory issues. "You should get one of those zip organizers so you don't lose everything."

"Aren't those only for women?" asked Flabius.

"No, I saw Joey use one on this episode of *Friends*. He kept sandwiches in it."

Weemus interjected. "Wasn't that a purse?"

"I thought it was called a manny," said Flabius.

"No, a manny is a male nanny," interjected Biffus. "That was in the episode with Freddie Prinze Jr. By the way am I the only guy who saw *Wing Commander* in the theatre? I sat through it so I could see the *Phantom Menace* trailer. Boy, what a

37

disappointment that was. Although, *Wing Commander III* with Mark Hamill was one of the greatest games in the history of the 3DO."

"You had a 3DO? Sweet." exclaimed Flabius.

Weemus was in agreement. "My point exactly. Ah yes, here it is. You, Flabius Flaximus, will seek out for me 'The Great Fork That Has Been Known to Wreak Havoc on Entire Countries.' You will also retrieve for me the 'Plastic Butter Knife of Wonder,' and the 'Paper Super Napkin of Destruction.' If you fail to deliver the items I have listed, your poor Buffy will meet with the..."

"Most unfortunate of circumstances, but let's not get into that again, Weemus Bobeemus," said Flabius.

"Do you make sport of me, Flabius Flaximus? I have all of the marbles here, my petulant boy!"

"Marbles? What's all this about marbles? First you said I had to get that other stuff, and now you come in talking about marbles, which you apparently already have. I think you are a little confused, Weemus," said Flabius.

"I give up. This is just not worth $10 an hour."

"What are you discussing now, Weemus? You're worth? I'll tell you what you are worth, you evil person. It's a very low amount. That's right, it's not a very high worth at all!" Those strong words of Flabius struck like a dagger into the evil, twisted heart of Weemus Bobeemus.

"Just go get those items, Flabius, or Buffy will meet with the most unfortunate... either get me the silverware, or I'll see to it that Buffy sleeps with the fishes."

Flabius grew deeply concerned. He knew how much Buffy despised seafood. "And if I retrieve the items, what then?"

"Then Buffy will be returned to you, while I, the great and powerful Weemus Bobeemus, will become Grand Master Ruler of the Universe and Beyond. And this time, I'll get my trip to Disney World!"

Biffus Palookus, trying to stay out of the argument between the two adversaries, had heard enough from Weemus. "Boy, he sure is full of himself, sire. I would have said something like 'I'm gonna be the guy who runs everything,' or 'look out, here comes the greatest guy around,' or, 'I'm almost as good as Bruce Lee,' or..."

"I heard that, Biffus Palookus," said the evil wizard. "And don't think you won't be punished, either."

"Now, just hold on one minute, Weemus, your fight is with me. Leave Biffus and Buffy out of this." Flabius, willing to sacrifice himself for the lives of his friends and his country, attempted to bargain with Weemus, albeit unsuccessfully.

"You have 73.673 hours to deliver the fork to me. After that it's bye-bye to Buffy. You'd better get started, Flabius. I've even helped you by getting you across the treacherously high Great Flat Mountains."

"Bye-Bye? Is that the best you could come up with, Weemus? Why don't you just go bye-bye yourself?" Biffus, once again, was trying to voice his support for his king.

"Relax my trusted better-be-silent-or-will-no-longer-be-trusted friend, I'll handle this." Flabius knew of the good intentions of his servant. "So you want me to retrieve a fork and some other stuff. Is that correct?"

"Yes. So I can take over the universe. And other stuff."

"You know, Biffus and I were heading out on an adventure to find some sacred plastic utensil. I wonder if that's related to this fork thing you want us to find."

"What was the name of the device you sought?"

"I think it was called 'The Great Fork That Has Been Known to Wreak Havoc on Entire Countries.' Maybe the forks are brothers?"

"No, I'm pretty sure you were looking for the same thing as me," said Weemus.

"Well, what do you want them for?"

"Stuff. Why did you want it?"

"Other stuff. Mostly I wanted to impress my girl. Maybe you know her? Her name is Buffy," said Flabius.

"Yeah. I kidnapped her, remember? Now, where was I? Oh yes, the Great Fork. I shall be sending you one of my faithful servants. You will give the fork to him, and he will tell you where to begin the search for the next item on the list."

"That's really great, of you, Bobeemus. Otherwise we would have walked around aimlessly," said the appreciative Flabius.

"Well, you're welcome. Your stallions are outside the barn, and you'd better get moving. Remember, 73.673 hours, no more. No, wait; it's 73.669 hours now. Until we don't meet again, Flabius Flaximus! Ha ha ha ha..." The image faded away with that last ominous warning.

"Like you said, Weemus, Buffy is to be returned to me unharmed. And she better still be a virgin when she gets back," The enraged Flabius shouted at the void left from where the image of Weemus once was.

Then, the image came back. "What was that? I was just fading away."

"I said she still better be a virgin when I get her back. I heard that was important in these chivalry narratives."

"So you want me to ask her if she wants to switch to Virgin Mobile?" asked Weemus. "How's their 4G coverage?"

"She's going mobile? Like Pete Townshend, or Alabama?" asked Flabius.

"Hey, do you think if I play Buffy some mountain music that she'll go out with me after you die on your mission to retrieve the Great Fork? No, she probably prefers the Oak Ridge Boys," said Weemus.

"Wait, who's Elvira?" asked Flabius.

"You know sire, I think you may have a bad connection," said Biffus, before returning his attention to his mighty steed. "Giddy up, ba-oom papa, oom papa, mow mow..."

40

"Quiet, trusted this-would-be-totally-unfair-if-I-kicked-the-bucket amigo," said Flabius. "Ok, Weemus, I fully expect to return, and Buffy and I will get married and have lots of little Flaxiumuses. So no, I do not think she'll go out with you."

"Find my stuff or I will erase you from existence," said Weemus, as he faded away for good.

"What are we going to do, sire?" shouted Biffus, "We can't just give him the fork, even if he does Erasure existence."

"I know, trusted companion, but what choice do we have?" said Flabius, humming and tapping his left foot. "And if I should falter, Would Buffy open her arms out to me? I just hope she refrains from breaking my heart. I'm so in love with her. I'll be forever blue. That you give me no reason. Why are you making me work so hard?"

"Don't you tell me, you know," said Biffus.

"Don't you tell me no," said Flabius.

"Don't you tell me, you know, sire," said Biffus. "As in, you have knowledge. As in you know that Weemus will destroy the world once you collect these ancient powerful devices and hand them over to him. Think of all the people who will get hurt, besides Buffy. And do you honestly believe he is going to give her back to you when he completes the sacred set?"

"Um, yes?" asked Flabius. "Hey, how about a little respect here? I am the Emperor, after all. Look, I know you're right, trusted clear-thinking think tank man. We must devise a plan. Let's rest now and at first daylight we'll start off."

And so the two soldiers of fortune laid their heads down on the hardened, supple earth. Neither would sleep. Not necessarily because they were worried about their quest ahead, but more likely because they spent the entire night trying to defeat Bald Bull on *Mike Tyson's Punch-Out!!*

41

3 Annie of Green Gables Part 2: The Revenge of Daddy Warbucks

Natasha moved away when I was only six. I knew the love affair wouldn't last, but some how, I couldn't let it end. We had known each other, those past twenty years, as friends and more then friends, and then just friends again, and then not friends at all, and then more than friends for one night, but back to not friends at all the next day, and then back to less than friends, but more then not friends at all, and then back to more than friends. Sure, she was fifteen years older than me, but when you're born on a leap year, things are tough all over.

Then came the shocking news that turned my world upside down forever: Leap year only counts if you're born on February 29th!

Why they changed the rules, I will never know.

Now was not the time to wallow in self-pity, however. I must gain admittance to the CIA so that I a might discover the whereabouts of Natasha. I would tell her all those things I was afraid to say all those years ago. Now I was nine, and after three years, all I could think about were those gorgeous legs, the firm breasts and the great curves, and the gorgeous legs, and those firm breasts.

But I still couldn't drive, and the CIA didn't like it when you used all their secret devices for your own ends. They said it was illegal, and that none of their agents would ever do such a deed. But I told them I had seen the movies and read the books and washed the cars, and that I knew everybody was illegal. Then they said that I meant 'illogical,' and so I punched the guy who said it and told him never to talk about my mom again.

After that, I found out that if you screw up with that whole birthday thing you could always find out how old you really are by using your birth certificate. So I went back to the old neighborhood and discovered to my disappointment that all the papers burnt up in the fire.

Then I asked who started the fire and they said I did. Then I said "oh yeah," and then the cops came. But I told them I was working for the CIA and they said "yeah right," and I punched the guy and told him that was the last time I'd warn him about talking about my mother.

Then I found my birth certificate stuck in the lining of my fedora, and so I went back to the golf course.

Realizing that what I was really looking for was the post office when some guy with a putter said "your looking for the post office," I shot the guy with a rubber band gun and told him he was fat and stupid and that I thought his mother was, too. Then he got angry and punched me and told me not to talk about his secret agent headquarters again or he would get angry again.

Then I said, "say what you will about your dumb fire truck, but I think your toys stink." Then he blew up.

I was almost two feet away from the post office when that blew up, too. As I looked around I noticed that everything was blowing up when I saw all this stuff that was without blown-uppiness, all of the sudden blow up. I wasn't positive, but I wagered that I should be on my way.

So I decided to go across the street that had just blown up and get some food from the city hall that wasn't there anymore. Then I found out that your supposed to eat at restaurants and that city halls are where they make the laws to lock up people like me when some guy that hadn't blown up yet said "you eat at restaurants; city hall is where we make laws to lock up people like you." Then he blew up, too.

Since all the restaurants were all blown up or in the process of blowing up or soon to be in the process of blowing up or likely to be soon in the process of blowing up, I decided to go to the park and feed the ducks the sandwich I had in my pocket because I wasn't hungry.

Then I realized I was hungry so I only gave the crust to the ducks because they like that part the best, too. Soon I found that the only thing that hadn't blown up was me and the ducks, because I was still I and everything else was all blown-uppish, except the ducks, but they were evil so they don't count.

Then I thought I might be dead, but I quickly changed my mind when I thought that if I was dead I wouldn't be able to think, because I would be dead, which would make thought processing difficult, so I decided I wasn't dead. Also a duck tried to bite my finger, but I bit him first and no, he did not taste like chicken.

Then the guys that had been blowing everything up came and took me away on their motor scooter. Once on board, they said, "it's a space ship, not a motor scooter," but I said I wasn't hungry so they would have to cook their own chicken. Then I found out that they blew up all the chickens, so we had roast duck and potatoes, which were not so bad either.

But then the ducks got angry again because we didn't leave them any leftovers, but then they blew up and we decided to stop listening to them. Also they spoke in duck, and I'm no fan of foreign languages, unless its English. Or Portuguese. Or the Portuguese Man o' war, although nobody wanted jelly with their potatoes, except the ducks.

Flying through outer space can be weird. If you're going really fast, the space men don't like it when you relieve yourself because you can't roll down the window. I said everybody does it, so why don't we, but then I realized that they couldn't hear me because I said that to myself, so I just forgot the whole thing.

The space ship was small and pink, except that the doors were more of a violet color, so I told the spacemen this. They didn't know what colors were, because they said, "we don't know what colors are."

I said that was stupid, because even the ducks knew what colors were. Then I got angry that the aliens blew up the ducks, because at least they knew the difference between pink and violet.

But the aliens said I blew up the ducks and I said they were liars and should keep their jellyfish to themselves or else me and the ducks would beat them up.

It turned out the ducks were hiding in the can, so I told them to stop hogging all of the potatoes and we all decided to blow up the hogs.

But the hogs didn't blow up all that well, so we blew the ducks up again instead, and ate the hogs with jelly.

Then the aliens said something about making a mistake and they tried to throw me out of the space ship. I said outer space is for losers and that they were losers, too, because they were from outer space, so I threw them outside. But they were little so they blew up real fast and it wasn't as much fun as I thought it was going to be.

But it turns out the ducks thought it was funny because to them, space guys are pretty big, so I tried to see it from their point of view.

Then the duck leaders said, "I saw that," and I told him it was the hogs, not me, so the ducks threw the hogs out as well and they blew up big time.

But it turns out the hogs took the desserts with them so everybody got mad at the duck leader and threw him out with the aliens and the hogs and all the pieces of the planet that had just gotten blown up and some undercooked bacon.

But it turns out that ducks can swim in space, so he didn't

45

blow up, and me and the other ducks thought that was pretty lame. After that, the rest of the ducks blew up again.

Then I was flying through space and I got this great idea to have a party at my house. But I said that it would be stupid to have a party because everyone blew up. Then I said I didn't care, but then I found that I didn't have a house any more either, so I decided to take over the spaceship.

After a while the space ship got boring so I tried to turn on the TV. But they didn't have cable so I looked for a radio station. They only had AM, though, so there wasn't anything good on except the Sean Hannity Show, but that too was in the process of either being blown up or had blown up already or was just what I wanted, a big hunk of cheese. I bet it goes great with corned beef and pumpernickel. It's Stilton, L.J. Thank you Mr. Stilton. Thank you Captain Stubing. After a while I figured that the space men must stink because they didn't have any game systems either. Then I hit this button and the whole ship went crazy.

When the ship went crazy I knew something bad was going to happen because the computer said so. Then I told the computer that she was no fun either and she said the ducks would have been better and I told her she hurt my feelings. She got all apologetic but by that time I had thrown her out the pod bay doors, that were not pink or violet, Hal, but more of a fuchsia color, Mr. Fox. Give him a pale lager, Isaac, and let her eat cake. The computer didn't really say anything after that, she only played Oktoberfest music, but you couldn't dance to it, so Ed McMahon wouldn't let any of the judges give her anything more than a four, which was generous.

Then some other ships appeared after the ship went crazy and I found out that I was at the home of the space men. I didn't like their home, though, because they didn't have any bathrooms and I had to go real bad.

After I went, one of the space men said that I was an alien,

46

but I said he was and then he said I was because my planet blew up and I was on his planet. Then I punched him and said he wore a dress because he did.

After that I found that other space men lived on the planet too, so I must be on a different planet then mine.

Then someone said that I was talking out loud and that I couldn't be on a planet that blew up because that's impossible and then I said he was short so then he shut up, too. When I found out other people from my planet were brought to this planet, I thought that everyone was really weird, so I decided to take over.

After I took over, everyone said I was the best because I took over, but I knew that they didn't like me and that they were just saying that so they didn't get blown up, either. Then I said that they were funny, and they thought that I meant that I liked them and that I wasn't going to blow them up either. Then, I said it was just a big test to see where their loyalties lie, and then I decided to blow them up because they didn't have any pumpernickel to go with my cheeses of the world variety pack.

Suddenly, I found myself back on the pink spaceship with the violet doors, but it was a different color because now it was blue with big green sliding doors. Then I saw other people like me and they said I was the greatest because I saved the universe. But I didn't like them because they were stupid so I jumped out of the green doors and then they blew up.

Then I found out that some one was trying to kill me by planting a bomb on my spaceship, but I decided that I didn't care who was on late night TV, and then I swam to another space ship. Once I found out that you couldn't swim to a space ship because there is no water in outer space, I said "oh, yeah," and then I made like I was going to go ballistic but I didn't and started laughing.

Then the other people jumped out of the spaceship I was in

and said "we'll take our chances in outer space." But they were stupid because you can't swim in outer space and you can't breathe under water and I told them so, except they were gone, so I decided not to tell them.

After that, Natasha came out of the kitchen and then she gave me a pale lager so I said, "ok." The rest of my story is TV-MA-rated so I can't tell it to you.

4 The Fairy and the Fuzz: A Love Story, Sort of

She saw the lights flashing, the horn buzzing and immediately knew that the fuzzing — or the fuzz — was onto her. The cop was a grizzly looking cowboy, with a Madonna bra strapped to his belt. But she had no time for this balderdash, so as soon as he had opened and shut his door, she took off running, in her car.

The facts were against her, and she knew it was her way or the highway; witch was ironic because she was on the highway and she was also not a witch, but a lovely Fairy dressed in all green with blonde hair, cotton balls on her slippers, and a little Fairy pout.

Then, it happened. The cop shot the tires off of her brand new 1997 Lexus LX, and she knew at that moment that this was the man she would marry.

This time she was forced to pull over, as everyone knows a Lexus without wheels is not a Lexus at all, and she wouldn't be caught dead in anything less than a Lexus, except maybe a Chevy Tahoe, because they drive well, and are lots of fun when a Fairy goes off-roading. But this was the turnpike, and she had to pull over.

As the cop approached, the Fairy became queasy, stricken with the thought that her mother would be disappointed she didn't marry George Michael, Michelangelo (probably not the Teenage Mutant Ninja Turtle), George W. Bush, Geo from Team Umizoomi, George S. Patton, Curious George, George H.W. Bush, Boy George, George Clinton, George Washington, George Peppard, the Madness of King George, George

49

Stephanopoulos, George Stroumboulopoulos, or George Lazenby circa 1977. The fairy had no plans to be married to a Samuel L. Bronkowitz for the rest of her life. But, as her mom always said 'You'll be married to a Samuel L. Bronkowitz for the rest of your life!' The cop was almost to the window, and as he got closer, the Fairy could tell that he was not all that bad, only mostly bad, but very ruggedly handsome in the most extreme, Fairy sense.

"Can I see your license, Miss?"

"What did I do officer?"

"Nothing, I just wanted to see you license."

"Oh."

"Hey, do you have a permit for those wings?"

"No sir, I was born with them, I'm a fairy."

"Oh. Still, I'll have to check on that, it's against California penal code 1.23.22.7.Duck.13 to have wings without a permit."

"Yes, but we are in Canada."

"So we are? I hadn't noticed. Hey, what are you doing for dinner?"

"Nothing apparently; I don't have a car."

"Good, let's go get some food. Hey, what's all that fairy dust doing on your dashboard?"

"It's not doing anything sir!"

"So it is. Well, let's go to McDonald's, they have a new value meal burger of the month."

"Is it any good?"

"I don't know. I don't like McDonald's. They have an apostrophe in their name."

"So is it apostrophes or burgers that you find distasteful?"

"Both."

"Sounds delicious!"

"Well, let's take your car, because a cop car would be to inconspicuous for us."

"All right then." Deep in her mind, she knew that this was

the man she would marry. "Say, you look like the Duke."

"So I do? That's funny. I am the Duke. And I'd appreciate it if you would address me as such in the future."

"Okay, Duke. Aren't you going to ask my name?"

"What for?"

Yes, deep in her most secret and desirous thoughts, she knew that this was her man.

Elsewhere, deep in outer space

Deep in outer space, Borpos, the planet killer, roamed the galaxy, seething with thoughts of revenge. His intelligence was vastly superior to any human, or any other of the billions of alien species he had encountered. But there was always that one time back on Earth, all those years ago...

Embarrassed by his humiliating defeat at the hands of some young punk, he was forced to hide his shame in the vastness of space. Only now, years later, when focus, regiment, and lots of folic acid vitamins had honed his body into the perfect killing machine could he return to face his mortal enemy.

Of course, his body had already been a perfect killing machine, but now it would be even more of a perfect killing machine. It was like a super perfect killing machine, at least for killing planets. It had yet to be determined if his ability to kill planets would also translate into killing people. Or at least one person.

All those years ago...

The cowboy had demolished Borpos in a barroom brawl over a lovely lady that Borpos had put the moves on. Of course this man was jealous. Everyone could see how well Borpos had been doing with her, the way she shouted, "Get off of my foot you imbecile," and "Leave me alone!" But that villainous swine, he had blind-sided Borpos, the way he came directly at him.

Borpos would never forget the beating he took at this man's

hand, the way the cowboy slightly maneuvered Borpos away from the girl. No one ever had maneuvered the great Borpos before, and no one would ever maneuver him again.

But Borpos was ashamed, and so he was forced to vacate the puny planet with the funny looking, slightly sentient life forms. He departed, but vowed to return after he had developed enough power to annihilate entire solar systems, confident that this destructive force would be sufficient to conquer the maneuverer.

Now Borpos could destroy planets, small suns, and even space nuggets (the really big kind), all at the same time.

His final destination was Earth, but first, a little target practice was in order. There, in front of him, was a beautiful cobalt planet. Its vast size made it the perfect choice...

Elsewhere, in the most technologically advanced observatory on Earth

In the most technologically advanced observatory on Earth, the world's greatest scientists met for a discussion on the planet Neptune. Dr. Judy Darwinkly, Nobel Prize winner and snappy dresser, was giving the talk.

"As you can see here, fellow scientists, from this sped up image of the planet Neptune, we can see the 'great black spot' weather pattern rotating in the opposite direction of the planet's revolution around the sun. We here at the institute have plenty of our own theories as to the causes of this fascinating event.

"Dr. Yoglev T. Blindofsky wishes to discuss his personal theory. This is the first time the doctor has been willing to reveal his startling discoveries, so I ask, please listen and be open to his notions and speculations, or he may never again be willing to share them with us. Now please, everyone, give a warm welcome to Dr. Blindofsky, all the way from his homeland in Somethingorotherovia."

52

Dr. Blindofsky was an old man. His beard resembled the prehistoric pictures of Charles Darwin or Walt Whitman. His demeanor was always serious, if also slightly condescending. His work on the planet Neptune had been some of the most widely cited and respected in the field of astronomy. He approached the podium with a solemn look on his face.

"I am quite afraid, to say, that... I'm sorry Judy, I can't do this."

Dr. Judy Darwinkly stood up, to offer her encouragement. She had waited so long to hear this revered man speak. She would not be disappointed.

"Please Dr. Blindofsky, it's all right. You are among friends and colleagues. We all respect and admire everything you have done. What ever you have to say, we will listen." She was quite persuasive.

"Okay Judy, if you think so. I believe... that is to say... I have formulized... what I mean is... I have come to the conclusion... After serious research... that the cause for the reverse rotation of the planet Neptune... is caused by... has resulted from... I think that every so often some little flying people use some strange force, or power at their disposal, to play with the planets. It just happens that the last time this was done with Neptune, the little flying person forgot to spin it back in the correct direction," said Dr. Blindofsky looking out over the crowd with a most inquisitive demeanor.

He started to show signs of a smile when he heard the silence. Perhaps people were finally ready to listen. Yes, perhaps his theories would finally be accepted. Finally Dr. Yoglev T. Blindofsky would have his redemption.

And then, in unison, the crowd gave Dr. Blindofsky his answer:

The lecture hall burst into uproarious laughter.

It was enough to make a grown man cry. But in his enraged state, Dr. Blindofsky was beyond tears. He was peeved, as peeved as Jeeves, as enraged as Armand Assante and Ken Howard fighting over Jaclyn Smith in *Sidney Sheldon's Rage of Angels.*

"You'll all see! You know what else? Can't stop laughing to listen, can you? I will tell you anyway! I think another one of these little flying beings is headed toward earth! I think he may be coming to do something to our planet! If he happens to decide to spin the earth in the opposite direction from its current rotation, you know what that means, don't you? The Continents would topple on top of each other! Massive tidal waves will rain down across places like Kansas! Civilization? What about civilization, do you ask? Okay, you're all too busy rolling around on the floor to ask anything, but I'll tell you anyway. It will all be over! Every living thing on this planet will die within seconds. We would be demolished, if we were lucky. The force of the change in the atmosphere will simply crush most of us. Unfortunately, it seems that the flying men have the ability to control that as well! If they want to torture us, they could do really awful things! For instance, most of us would likely fly around the planet in a matter of seconds as a result of the force of the change. Perhaps a few of us will get lucky and float up out of the atmosphere. Maybe we will even be lucky enough to see our destroyer before we implode amidst the vacuum of space. Maybe some of us might live long enough to see the moon topple into the planet and knock it perilously out of its revolution. I'm not kidding! I have proof! I have the facts! I'm going to find someone to listen to me!" The old man stormed out of the meeting. He punched one little scientist in the face as he walked passed. There was no use talking to these people.

Meanwhile, Dr. Judy Darwinkly and the rest of the scientists were still having quite a laugh. "See, I told you! What a quack! Wasn't that hysterical? I nearly peed my pants. And look at Dr. Male-Pattern-Baldnificent, he got punched in the face!" More laughter filled the room. Only Dr. Male-Pattern-Baldnificent stopped chuckling.

Dr. Butch Wallpaper, a hefty man of about 120 pounds (120 pounds is big for a scientist) finally proposed the continuation of the forum. "Gosh, well, gee, Judy, do you think we should get back to the Neptune thing?"

"Oh Butch, you always know how to spoil a good time. But enough of the comedy stuff. It was funny though, wasn't it? Ha! Let's see now. Oh yes, we were discussing Neptune. Little flying people! Ha! I loved that bit. Oh, next we have some live pictures of the planet, via the Hubble Telescope. Now, it does take a little while for light to travel from Neptune to Earth, so it is technically a delayed feed, but, let's not be too technical, lest we end up like Dr. Blindofsky. Okay Frank, let her rip!"

From up in the control booth, Frank activated the monitor in front of the room. There, before the forum, was the glorious planet Neptune. The color perception of the feed was quite remarkable.

"Okay, as we can all see, reverse rotation can actually occur in our solar system. Unfortunately, it does not seem to be caused by little flying people, playing with the rotation of the planet. No, in fact, the real reason for this planet's opposite rotation is most likely the result of a strong gravitational pull generating from a massive source in Neptune's past. Now, let us begin by examining the 'Great Black Spot.' As I have stated before, this is a weather pattern in the planet's atmosphere that would travel from the right to the left of the planet on our screen. Oh yes, here it comes into the picture, at the bottom right of the screen."

"Dr. Judy? Isn't that the bottom left of the screen?"

"Why yes, I believe you're right! Hey Frank! You're fired! That's right, fired! Unless of course, you want to stop messing around with the picture and get this feed back in the proper order!"

Frank, not understanding the question, but fearful of losing his job, responded in the only way he knew how. "I'll get right on you, Dr. Judy!"

"Frank, you were supposed to keep that a secret!"

The scientists looked puzzled. Frank, who by this point was sweating profusely, tried to recover. "I mean, I'll get right on top of the problem, Dr. Judy! I'll get... Oh my God..."

"Please, Frank, not here. I have my reputation!" Dr. Darwinkly was livid. She was about ready to thrash Frank when she noticed that the view screen had transfixed the scientists. There, on the main monitor, the planet Neptune was in the process of shrinking, expanding, spinning and jumping out of its normal rotation and revolution.

From the small right-hand corner of the screen, a little flying man could be seen moving his hands, seemingly in control of the planet. And then, in one swooping motion, the planet-killing flying man made a crushing motion with his fists. At the same time, Neptune exploded. The blast seemed to shake the audience.

"Dr. Judy, what kind of joke is this? Are you sick? Don't you think you've taken this thing a little too far?"

Dr. Judy was in the most disbelief. This was no longer a game. She wouldn't tell the others. She couldn't tell the others. It was unthinkable. She put her hands over her face. She tried to shake the image from her mind. She opened her eyes again. The little flying man was moving, moving toward Earth...

Act II:
Of Forks & Mojo Cheetos
Ferdinand Franco

The Styrofoam cup never knew why he had been picked, out of all the possible choices. Sometimes you can't choose in life, especially when you are an inanimate object such as a Styrofoam cup. Once, the cup was asked to assassinate the leader of a very prestigious fantasy football league, and the Styrofoam cup really liked the Cowboys a lot, even if they weren't as spectacularly awesome as Eli Manning, Victor Cruz and the N.Y. Giants. Had he failed, however, he wouldn't have eaten that week, so you do what has to be done. This confused the cup, because he was on a strict liquid diet. But then he remembered he did enjoy a nice steak every once in a while. But then he remembered he was a Styrofoam cup without a brain, and he wondered why he was still remembering. Assassination can be a dirty business, and the Styrofoam cup was as unclean as they come.

5 Alien vs. Predator at the O.K. Corral

Cecilia's roommate, now being crushed under Dave's weight, responded in anger.

"I'm angry!"

"Why don't you just leave then, Becky?" Becky was a real fill-in-the-blank. Cecilia had tried in vain to get a new roommate earlier in the semester, but, well, school administrations stink everywhere, especially when they don't wear deodorant.

As usual, Becky shouted incomprehensible nonsense at Cecilia, this time from under the sleeping frame of Dave. Cecilia would normally not take notice, but it was late at night, and visiting hours were over. And so she turned to hear Becky out, shielding her eyes from the detestable sight of her roommate, as the thing from beyond the grave began to speak.

"This is my room too, Cecilia. What makes you think you can just barge in here with some guy you met out at your stupid lodge and take over the place?"

"Oh well, I suppose you are right. I am being extremely inconsiderate by assuming that I have any right to have a guy over simply because you have a different man in here every night of the week. I was just so presumptuous!"

"Get this guy off me Cecilia, and take back what you said!"

"Oh, I am truly sorry, did I offend you again? What I meant to say was a different man, woman, polar bear, otter or manatee."

"His name is Gary and he happens to be a dugong from Australia," said Becky. "I'll make you pay for your insolence!"

58

"Why that is, I think, the toughest statement I have ever heard you say. Let me think about this. No, there was that one time you told me I was 'a mean, awful person.' That was the toughest statement I have heard. I think that 'His name is Gary' would be second, or possibly third, however. So don't fear, Becky, you haven't lost that intimidating touch. Now, would you mind leaving, before I kick the crap out of you?"

Infuriated, Becky finally squeezed out from under the still unconscious Dave. She got up and started swinging, but was unable to connect with any of her uppercuts or jabs. Cecilia, meanwhile, in true Muhammad Ali form, danced around Becky with grace before pummeling her into submission. Cecilia then proceeded to toss the demon-spawn out of the room.

Now she could turn her attention toward her unconscious dance partner.

Dave, finally waking up, reached for Cecilia. "Jane Seymour?" He asked, in a dazed stupor.

"We're back at my place Dave, don't you remember?"

"Oh, my head."

"You didn't get hit there, Dave."

"What happened, Sequentia?"

"It's Cecilia, Dave. Don't you remember?" Cecilia gently brushed Dave's hair. "Well, what's the last thing you do remember?"

"I remember you taking your clothes off and then we were about to..."

"What?" said Cecilia, leaping up from the bed. "The last thing that happened was you got hit by that Nerf ball and then you fell asleep."

"What are you trying to say? You mean you didn't take your clothes off?"

"No!"

"Why not? Will you take them off now? I mean, clearly I'll be able to see better, now that I'm awake."

59

"What is it with you?"

Dave sat up and looked around. There were many posters up along the walls. There were a couple of beds, two dressers, and a couple of desks. There was also a pair of laptops, a little refrigerator, and a television. Dave, putting his most advanced spy techniques to use, attempted to decipher just where he had been taken.

"Yes, it's all coming back to me, now. Clearly we are at your secret headquarters. A wise decision... to take me here," said Dave. "However, your attempt to make this room look like a shoe factory has failed completely. You should know right off the bat that you can't store secret agent footwear in a refrigerator. The laser-guided missile systems will malfunction in a high-humidity, low-temperature environment. Then again, if you kept them in the crisper, that might keep the shoe phone circuitry as fresh as maple syrup-infused asparagus. So you've got that going for you."

Dave began searching the room for other evil secret agent gadgetry.

The elegant Cecilia prepared an equally eloquent soliloquy in response to Dave's interrogation. "What?"

"Come now, Splendorina, the time for games has ended," exclaimed Dave. "I know you're working for these producers. I hope you understand that mass production of fresh produce inexorably leads to one outcome: healthy school lunches and morbid obesity among our nation's youth. Well, you can attack me with laced pastries all you want, but I won't let you poison any more American kids with Brussels sprouts, carrots or cauliflower. You're reign of tyranny is at an end! Now then, I instruct you to take me to your master. We must have words."

"Master? You think I have a master?" Cecilia, puzzled as the conversation drifted from shoe factories to vegetables, was beginning to have second thoughts about her dance partner, no matter how spry he was. "You need to listen to me, Dave, you are cute and all, but that only goes so far. I don't date guys that are stuck on themselves. If that's what you think this is going to be, you have got another thing coming. Wait a minute. What am I saying? We're not dating! I just brought you here because I felt sorry for you. This is all so confusing."

"Outrageous! I can't believe it!"

"Believe it!" Cecilia did not want to get angry with Dave, so soon after he had passed out, but he had left her no choice. But as she spoke, Dave seemed to be preoccupied with an empty jar. "Wait, are you talking to me or to the pickle jar?"

Interrupting matters, Becky walked back into the room. "I mean it, Cecilia! I'll get the R.A., and she'll take care of you. Oh, I see your friend is awake. I can't wait until you-know-who finds out!"

With that last wisecrack, Cecilia dropped her anger of Dave and focused it on the undead creature of the night. "What do you want, Becky? If you don't leave us alone I will be forced to injure you." Cecilia did not wish to make a complete fool of herself in front of Dave, but she would do whatever was necessary to get Becky out of the room and Becky could sense this. But Becky relished in annoying Cecilia, especially in front of company, so she continued to do so.

"Just let me get my shoes out of the refrigerator, and I'll be on my way. Hey, what's that guy doing with my pickle jar? Give it here!" Becky plucked the jar from Dave's hands.
Dave looked as if he was going to cry. Becky smiled at the sight of the distraught secret agent. She then glared back at Cecilia from across the room. Cecilia returned the glare, but proceeded to open the refrigerator door, where an entire stock of shoes was found. She got out the first pair she could reach, and flung them toward the door.

"No, not these ones! The purple ones, with the little bows, those are the ones I want!" Becky had just about caused Cecilia to cross the threshold, which had been her intention all along.

61

But when she saw the fury in Cecilia's eyes, Becky decided that the best choice would be to leave, before she really did get hurt. "These will be fine, after all."

As Becky shut the door behind her, Dave peered up at Cecilia, with a peculiar look on his face. Cecilia was not in the mood for any more looks.

"What? What is it? I'll get you a new pickle jar, I promise."

"Great! Wait, that's not what I was thinking about. I was going to say... No, I won't ask. Perhaps this really is a shoe factory. It would mark the first time that I would have been wrong, but, as the saying goes, 'fools are not particularly the brightest people on the planet, they are only the second brightest.' Besides, being bright isn't all that great if you are trying to be a super agent, because we often have to hide."

Dave arose from the bed, and began examining his surroundings more closely. "I guess it's on to more pressing matters, such as, how did we get here?"

"We took a cab. I had to borrow some of your money, I hope you don't mind." Now that Becky had left, Cecilia was able to relax. She was ready for a flashback sequence...

Earlier that evening

The cold night air bristled through the soft, flowing hair of Cecilia. Dave was hoisted over her shoulder like a sack of Idaho potatoes. But this was L.A., not spud country. She brought Dave right to the edge of the sidewalk, where she could flag down one of the thousands of New York City taxis driving in every conceivable direction.

Just then, an agent of evil leapt out of a fast moving vehicle. He pulled out a large sweet potato, definitely not of the Idaho variety.

The short, red-haired scoundrel was known as O'Grady McGrotton. Yes, the unconscious Dave knew him from his old KGB files. He was an assassin. His fiendish use of vegetable weaponry earned him a reputation as one of the world's most lethally precise professionals.

McGrotton had secretly been working with the 'Producers' to destroy all of L.A., but Dave's actions at *Shorty's* had thwarted his plans, let alone obliterated thousands of perfectly good tater tots.

As Cecilia swung around to see what the commotion was all about, the slumbering Dave struck O'Grady with his sleeping, yet still very deadly left foot. O'Grady hit the ground like, well, a large sack of mushy yams, the imported variety. The sweet potato he had been carrying shot 400 feet into the air, before landing on top of the moose antler club. The explosion made the tater tot incident look like *Breakfast at Tiffany's*.

The cab formerly carrying McGrotton stopped. Cecilia dumped Dave into the trunk, grabbed forty dollars out of his wallet, and then made her way to the back seat as the cab sped away toward the airport...

"A cab? Oh no.. that means the whole mission could be in jeopard... I mean... Did I miss *Wheel of Fortune?*"

"I'm afraid so, Dave. By the way, we came here to my room, not the airport."

"Well in that case, do you think I could use your phone? I have to contact PROTOCOL, um... I mean I have to call my grandma."

"No problem, just dial nine to get off-campus."

"Off-Campus? Off Campus! Off-Campus, you say?"

"Yes, this is my school, Dave. You have to dial 9 to get off campus." Once again, Cecilia seemed to be slightly irritated with all of Dave's undulations.

"I see. Hmm. I sense danger. Perhaps PROTOCOL has been compromised... Well, there is only one way to find that out. Wait! What I meant to say was that perhaps someone came over to grandma's house, uninvited... Yes, that's it! Well

63

then, do you think I could be alone for just one moment?"

"Your not going to do anything weird, are you?" Cecilia still had to think about getting her room deposit back at the end of the semester.

"That all depends," said Dave. "If you could specify your parameters, perhaps I could give you a more detailed answer."

"Just forget it. I'll be out in the hall. It sounds like Becky went to get the R.A. I'll have to do some explaining about you."

Cecilia then departed, and Dave tried to get a handle, for the third time, on his unrecognizable evil surroundings.

He slowly searched Cecilia's room, passing over her books and clothes, her posters and her food before finding that item for which he had been searching: a silver, circular object with an imprint of some peculiar looking man, codename 'quarter' in Dave's spy manual.

Then Dave approached the secret access device known only to Dave and a few other spies, such as Cecilia, as codename 'phone.' To his dismay, however, Dave realized that the quarter did not fit in the slot. In fact, there was no slot at all.

Dave knew right then and there that he was in grave danger. Slowly he picked up the receiver, only to find that unusual noise on the other end. Dave decided to take his chances that the 'phone' wasn't tapped, and proceeded to enter nine, followed by the secret code which would allow him to communicate with his 'grandma.' At the other end, the message was received, and Dave began to articulate according to his secret agent guidelines.

"This is agent AQ169 dash 2 Alpha niner, over, requesting confirmation on the mission specs I have been sent."

The voice on the other line was silent. 'Of course! The old 'repeat your message because they probably didn't hear you' trick!' The 'trick' as Dave called it, was often used in his line of work, as one had to be absolutely sure who one was talking to if one wanted to stay alive for more than one day. Dave, of course, had lived for many one day's, and so he repeated his message: "This is agent AQ169 dash 2 Alpha niner, over."

"Ah, you want a pizza, buddy? This is TACO SUPER BURRITO."

"There's something familiar about that name..." Dave paused, recalling his earlier visit to an eating establishment.

Earlier at Taco Super Burrito

As Dave cut out the ad announcing the sale on booty-enhancing sketchers, several fiendish bad guys from Cobra Kai darted about TACO SUPER BURRITO, furiously seeking to conceal from Dave the fact that they had captured the good guy agents. Meanwhile, Ray Charles, Alan Price and Johann Sebastian Bach conducted an epic organ battle on a set of Vox Continentals, oblivious to the chaos surrounding them.

Suddenly Dave realized that his home base must have been infiltrated. The operative on the other line began responding in the ultra-secret food lingo, which was only employed in moments of grave danger. Always prepared for any contingency, Dave responded in the same food code. "Yes, I see. I will have a New York Strip with a side of mash potatoes, hold the gravy. Repeat: Hold the gravy, over."

"Ah, we can give you a beef chimichanga or something."

"Understood, beef chimichanga is the new call sign. I shall put the operation into effect immediately. This is AQ169 dash 2 Alpha niner, over and out."

Dave reached for his super spy manual and looked up operation chimichanga. To his dismay, he was unable to find it. In fact, Dave was unable to find his spy manual. "It's just as I feared: PROTOCOL has been compromised."

Slowly Dave made his way toward the door. As he listened, he could hear footsteps approaching from down the hall. Dave was certain that the footsteps belonged to his dance partner when he heard Cecilia's voice. Trained, however, to spot a fake voice like a wiener in a pack of hot dogs, Dave decided to look out of the device attached to Cecilia's door, codename 'peephole.' He was aghast, though, when he saw another woman walking behind Cecilia. It was not, much to Dave's chagrin, R.A. Dickey, as he had been expecting. Dejected, Dave put away his Mets baseball card collection.

Just then it hit Dave exactly what 'R.A.' could stand for: Beef Chimichanga! 'Of course, that's it,' Dave thought to himself. After all, Beef Chimichanga meant Indianapolis Speedway in French. Citizens of France were the most diabolical according to the annual diabolical citizenry rankings released every two weeks by PROTOCOL. Considering how much traffic there was at the Brickyard this time of year, Dave was sure that other agents of malfeasance would be arriving shortly. Dave despised traffic almost as much as he despised producers, and produce. But now was not the time to practice his driving skills. It was time to depart. There was only one other exit besides the door, and Dave decided to use it.

As Dave threw himself out the window, he was sure that escape was within his grasp. Unfortunately, Dave failed to realize the window was closed until it was too late. Trained, however, to never take anyone for his or her word, Dave attempted once again to hurl himself out the window, and was again thwarted.

Cecilia, hearing the commotion coming from her room, made an excuse to leave her 'R.A.' in the hallway and hurried inside to find the cause of the disturbance. As she entered, she saw Dave clutching his rear, with a big red mark on his head.

"Did you just try to jump out the window?"

"How did you realize it?"

"Lucky guess. Hey, that's not a very good idea, you know. We are five stories up."

"Did you just say five feet up? But Cecilia, I'm deathly afraid of heights! Five feet..." Suddenly Dave broke out in a cold sweat.

"Five stories Dave, that's about 54 feet, not five."

Dave then slumped to the ground in a mound of Norwegian meatballs and began to make some sort of gurgling sound.

"Listen Dave, you're going to have to get up. My R.A. is outside. I also just got a text that my boyfriend is coming over. Anyway, you're going to have to leave. I'm sorry."

"Yes, I know all about this R.A., as you call her, and she is clearly not capable of throwing a major league knuckleball. Hard to believe after so many missions, it has to end like this," said Dave, wistful as he saw his career flash before his eyes.

Cecilia, super-dancing blue-dress wearing vixen of evil spydom, responded as only a super-dancing blue-dress wearing vixen of evil spydom was capable of responding. "Huh?"

"I mean, after so many women, who would have ever thought you were the one! I've just been a fool, Selma, and I can't hide it any longer. I want you, I need you, I love you. Don't be cruel to a heart that's true. Oh, love me, you hound dog! Viva Las Vegas!" Dave, quickly realizing his blunder of revealing his super secret agent status, tried to cover it up by quoting lyrics from his teacher, the King. Then Dave realized that he may have been singing, and had confused his kings.

"Dave, I'm flattered that you feel this way, but we've just met, and, you see, I all ready have a special someone."

"Of course. I understand completely Sheila."

"That's Cecilia, Dave."

"I see, so we're back to calling ourselves Dave, are we? Listen lady, let's get one thing straight, I'm the secret agent, and you are the lady. I wear the dress and you carry around the secret pocket watch slash ultrasonic super car. Is that clear?"

"Um, I'll be right back," said Cecilia, slowly starting back toward the door.

"I see. In that case, now is as good a time as any for me to depart. It's been a pleasure, Starlatina." Dave could see the

67

effect he was having on Cecilia, and rather than get involved with the beautiful young lady, he decided to take his chances with the window. Besides, what possibility for happiness could she have with a super spy that would be her mortal enemy?

As Dave jumped for the window, and found it still closed, he knew for certain that some evil was afoot. Dave was deathly afraid of feet, almost as much as he was afraid of heights. This only doubled his concern that his mission was in serious jeopardy. Fortunately, the window finally shattered with this last attempt.

Cecilia looked displeased. She had her hands in fists as she put them on her hips. She began to tap her foot. The glass was all over the place.

"Try and keep in mind that we are five stories up. If you need to leave... which is fine by me... please use the door," said Cecilia, as she viewed the broken window. Only the screen remained in place.

Eager to usher the crash-happy dancer from her abode, Cecilia grabbed the doorknob and began motioning for Dave to use the standard exit method. As Dave looked at the door with a perplexed expression, Cecilia felt it best to give him one last word of advice, before saying good-bye forever. "By the way, don't let Winston see you leave, he gets jealous."

"Winston? What's all this about a Winston?" Dave suddenly seemed interested in Cecilia's outside affairs. Perhaps she wasn't the super spy he thought she was. Perhaps she was also just a pawn in this game of death. Dave would not stand for it. It angered him to think that not only was Cecilia not a secret agent, but perhaps she was also unwittingly shielding Dave's true nemesis, and that Dave had not thought of using the word 'not' on more occasions.

"Winston Wallingford. He's my boyfriend, although I couldn't tell you why at the moment. We've been seeing each other for a few weeks now. We met in Munich while I was studying abroad," said Cecilia. "He was supposed to meet me tonight, but he never made it to the bar. I assume he's coming to apologize. In fact, I think that's him outside."

Indeed, at that very moment, a knock was heard coming from outside the room.

It didn't take Dave long to realize that this knock was from a hand in the form of a fist lightly tapping at the door directly outside Cecilia's room. In fact, the door connected to a hallway, and if opened, it might allow the bad guy to enter.

"So *that's* how I ended up in Munich." Dave paused, before continuing. He was slowly putting the pieces of the puzzle together, even if he hated puzzles. "And that's why I met you at the bar and not him. Drat. Once again, I've solved the case backwards. I hate when that happens."

"Well, I tried to warn you earlier. Now let's see if we can hide you under the bed, or something," said Cecilia, attempting to devise a way to conceal her guest. "You're going to have to keep quiet until I can get him to leave."

"No time for that now!" Dave had to react fast. He knew it was a death or death situation. Faced with a 54-foot drop or meeting Cecilia's boyfriend was a difficult decision, but one that would have to be resolved immediately.

The shattered glass on the floor left imprints of Dave's forehead. Winston would recognize the marks. That was all the calling card that Dave felt like leaving. With that, Dave threw himself out the window, right through the screen, leaving Cecilia shrieking behind. At that very same instant, Winston Wallingford broke down the door, by turning the knob.

69

6 Gimpus Foo Foo and the Clash of the Superstars

The sun rose on that first morning of the great journey, although since the journey technically started the day before, albeit in the afternoon, does anybody know if it should be called the second morning or the first morning? Maybe it should be called the first morning of the day after the first day of the great journey. Yeah, that sounds good. The light squeezed its way into the barn of doom and into the steely gaze of Flabius Flaximus. Flabius, however, was ill prepared to receive visitors at that very moment, for he was not what one would call a 'morning Emperor who is just about to lose his kingdom to the evil wizard, Weemus Bobeemus.'

Biffus Palookus was slightly more chipper, however, and when Flabius went for the ancient stapler of Rosco Pico Train to start shooting at stuff indiscriminately, Biffus stepped in his way.

"Sire, we have to get moving if we're ever going to get that 'Great Fork That Has Been Known to Wreak Havoc on Entire Countries' before lunchtime," said Biffus.

"Thanks, my trusted alarm clock."

"No problem, sire."

"Yes, thank you for reminding me of what a dismal failure of an Emperor I have turned out to be. I might as well just throw in my *Action Comics* No. 1 and my *Detective Comics* No. 27! Hey, why not give Weemus my best tooth brush, too, while I think of it, or maybe we'll even give him my wool socks that my grandmother gave me for my fifth birthday." Ever the cheery warrior, Flabius Maximus had, on that morning, the disposition of marmalade toasted coconuts and bad cabbage.

"I sense there may be something bothering you, my Emperor," said the concerned Biffus Palookus.

"Oh, no, I just didn't get up on the right side of the universe this morning. Come on, let's go."

And so the two set out on their momentous journey with the great hope and wonderment of a child going to the dentist, or a man going to the doctor to get a vasectomy. Yes indeed, they were in high spirits.

Meanwhile

The ancient and evil wizard Weemus Bobeemus settled down in the last place Flabius Flaximus would look, the Great Hall of Panzies.

DUNT DUNT DA!!!!!!!!!!!!!!

Weemus looked around to see if he could figure out where the music had suddenly sprung from, but to no avail. There were no musical members in his vast army, known as the Impolitus Guard. Weemus had been in a barbershop quartet once upon a time, but when he and his fellow singers played their first concert, they were applauded off the stage.

Not being able to suffer such humiliation, Weemus executed the entire audience, the pit orchestra, and his fellow singers, as well. The only one who allegedly survived the incident was a Timpani drummer of some distinction. It was only after giving up the search for the wily drummer that Weemus settled down to practice evil-wizardry.

And now, Weemus was on the verge of ruling the world. It had been his lifelong dream. It was this goal that had kept him alive after Flabius had humiliated him in the 'Great Leap Incident.' Now he had two scores to settle. Firstly, he had to beat Flabius. Next, he had to do battle with that mouse and duck duo that had dishonored him as a child. Soon he would

71

have Flabius just where he wanted him. Soon he would be able to return to Disney World, to face his other enemies. But for now, he could sit back comfortably as Flabius retrieved all of the items from the 'Great Set of Doom.' Flabius would never come around to The Great Hall of Panzies.

DUNT DUNT DA!!!!!!!!!!!!!!

This time, Weemus chose to disregard the music.

Yes, Flabius would never come to the great hall of... He would never come because of the stories surrounding the hall...

The Story of Quick McSwivlitz and Sir St. John Don de la Vega Saint John, A.K.A. the story of why nobody ever went to the Great Hall of this word that sounds kind of like 'Pansy' or 'Panzer,' or some combination thereof

Legend had it that once upon a time a great and powerful insomniac knight built the hall with the aid of only a poor old fool who just happened to suffer from a severe case of narcolepsy. The two men formed an above-average pugilistic force, as a pair such as they was indeed a most regular occurrence in any village across the ancestral lands, as well as parts of Nordreisa, Norway.

But when it came time to build the hall, the troubles began. The knight, constantly shouting orders to his servant, failed to realize that only about half of the commands were being followed, which caused some serious faults in the architecture. The knight would ask his servant for a cup of water and a plate of bread, and end up with a poem composed in couplets, delivered on a freight train driven by an engineer named Fred.

These actions caused the knight, who thought he was being toyed with, to run after the fool in a frenzied rage. But, when the fool fell asleep about half way through the chase, the knight continued past until being struck in the head by a meteor crashing to the Earth.

When the fool awoke, he became quite distraught upon

72

seeing his dead master. Believing that he had caused the disaster, the jester turned himself over to the ancient authorities.

Later, the execution squad, which utilized compound bows made from the finest carbon-fiber-reinforced polymers and Lik-M-Aid sugar sticks (this was before the invention of the arrow) thought they had killed the fool when, yet again, the man fell asleep.

Believing their job complete, they sent the fool's remains (although there weren't any actual remains since the fool was still alive) down the river. When the fool awoke he was drifting downstream and out to sea. Then the fool was taken prisoner by a division of Nazi Panzer tanks, aided by several Gypsy flower girls carrying baskets of Pansies. Seeing no means of escape, the fool decided to attack, but fell asleep mid-thrust. The Nazis and the flower girls disposed of the fool, and ever since that time, no man has had the courage to attempt to sleep in the Great Hall of Panzies.

DUNT DUNT DA!!!!!!!!!!!!!

Meanwhile, Meanwhile

Inside the Hall, Weemus began his plans for retrieving the fork. He knew that Flabius, a big fan of sleeping in (except on Sundays when he cheered for the N.Y. Giants, although the Giants' schedule often offered plenty of chances for fans to sleep in when the team played in the late afternoon game, or Sunday Night Football at Cowboys Stadium), would stay far away from the hall and its haunted grounds.

Weemus looked out from high atop the sturdy structure. Within his sight he could see everything from the hall to a piece of marble about six inches in front of him. 'This must be some remnant of the fool's work,' Weemus thought to himself.

Outside the Hall, the wolves began to howl at the moon. What had not occurred to Weemus was that there was no moon, nor any wolves. The howling noise was actually from

73

one of the Impolitus guards that Weemus had been stepping on for quite some time without realizing it. 'Yes,' Weemus thought, 'I'll get you for this, McFly, if it's the last thing... wait... Flabius Flaximus, and your little dog too.' The discombobulated Weemus shook his pirate booty, awaiting the arrival of his most trusted servants.

Finally, they arrived. The first man was an elongated looking fellow, with fat, Marshmallow proportions; the second was some sort of Styrofoam cup, being escorted by a third guy who was kind of unremarkable, except for maybe the fact that his head was shaped like a giant triangle, and he also wore a triangle-shaped hockey mask.

The first man spoke as if he knew Weemus Bobeemus on a personal level. "Good heavens, old man. Don't you realize that I'm supposed to be knocking on a door at this exact moment? I must leave before I am spotted by literary reviewers with a nose for incongruous, incognito characters unceremoniously plucked from the space-time continuum."

Infuriated by the insolent tone of the first man, Weemus displayed his wrath by vaporizing the guard he had been standing on. "What do you have to say to that, boy?"

"Well, you could have at least let me change my attire. I am completely without a decent pair of trousers in this epoch."

"And what about you two?" asked Weemus, awaiting a report from his most sinister henchmen.

The Styrofoam cup, suffering from severe laryngitis, had the triangle head guy speak for him. "Sir, I've been asked to advise you that we no longer deem the term 'henchmen' politically correct. We'd like to be called 'people who are stupid so they do what ever their evil leaders tell them to do.' We feel it's a much less insulting designation."

"Anything else?" asked Weemus.

"Well, now that you ask, the evil henchmen union has requested that I represent them in the next round of contract

74

negotiations, and we've decided that we require a dental plan. Not me, per se, since I'm not sure I have any teeth, or a face, since it's shaped kind of like a pyramid, but some of the other lads could really use a dental plan."

"I thought you had a triangle head," said Weemus.

"No, it's a pyramid."

"Well, what do you think?" asked Weemus, returning to the first henchman who was still concerned about being in the wrong scene in between chapters, even if he wasn't officially in any other scenes yet.

"I brush and floss with great frequency. I don't see what all the fuss is about," said the first henchman.

"Well maybe you would, if you had five kids to feed and a wife who sucks the life out of you every chance she gets." The third henchman was clearly offended.

"What about that Jigsaw guy? Why isn't he your spokesman?" asked Weemus.

"His face is made of plastic, so I'm not sure he needs a dental plan," said henchman No. 3.

"But you've already indicated that you don't need a dental plan, as you don't have any teeth," said henchman No. 1.

"You don't know that for sure! I could have teeth. I said I wasn't *sure* if *I had* any teeth."

And so Weemus used the spoon to vaporize the third henchman as well, leaving only the first guard and the cup, and the third henchman's teeth.

"Unbelievable. I didn't even say 'henchman.' It was simply written into the scene description. Any more outbursts, and everyone, including the writer and readers, will get vaporized. Understood?" Weemus knew he had their attentions.

"By Jove, he did have teeth!" exclaimed Winst, um, henchman No. 1.

"Very well, if you need me to be more accurate in my threats, then I will vaporize everyone, leaving only their teeth

75

behind," said the evil wizard.

"Now you're just wittering on," said the first servant, dressed in slacks that were a far cry from spiffy. "Although I must say I would have thought the spoon capable of vaporizing both individuals and molars."

"That's why we need the entire set, boy. Seriously, does anybody pay attention around here?" Finally assured that both the cup and the remaining henchman were listening, Weemus commenced with delivering his orders. "Okay, now your mission: first, you and the cup will ride out and meet with that wretched Flabius Flaximus. Your orders are to... No, on second thought, I better write them down."

Weemus scribbled down brief instructions for his chief lieutenants. "Now be off with you, and don't forget to take the cup. He is good in a fight."

"But he's just a cup, not a he..."

"Nonsense. That cup is a lethal force of nature. He'll do his job for us, though, I've seen to that," The evil wizard glared at the white inorganic object. "That cup and I have a little agreement. You just do your job, boy, and the cup will do his."

Weemus stared at the pair, before making a motion for them to depart. "Okay, that's enough. Shoo!"

"Wait, that's it? I trudge over mountains, lakes, bangers and mash, glaciers, several BBC broadcasts of *The Benny Hill Show*, and I can't reveal my true personage? It just isn't fair!"

"Who are you, Luke Skywalker? I can assure you that you are no more than an absurd plot device, just as insignificant to me as all of these ridiculous digressions. And speaking of digressions, get moving."

"Yes sir!" And with that, the young man and the cup departed as quickly as they came, which may or may not have been fast. I don't know. I wasn't paying attention.

In another part of the Hall, the beautiful Buffy awaited her Emperor, bound, yet ravishing in a lovely Angora sweater,

76

trying to keep her hair as perfect as possible. She could only hope for the chance to be reunited with Flabius, so they could be married and then she could ask him why she was wearing Angora.

Meanwhile, meanwhile, meanwhile

Flabius and Biffus surveyed the landscape. Upon withdrawing from the barn of dread, with the little evil ducks remaining behind, the two warriors had to pass through a great marsh, known to have swallowed entire armies.

Now that they were in full view of the evil abode, the two men gave a quick shudder before committing themselves to the last bit of land that separated them from Gimpus Foo Foo.

The vast length of the Marsh was estimated to be at least 953 miles. The width, fortunately, was only about two feet. Therefore, if a train traveling 70 miles per hour leaves Chicago at 3 p.m. and Jay-Z devises a secret formula to turn Cristal into a combination of Chex Mix and the Periodic Table of Elements with the noble gases extracted, Flabius and Biffus would find a way to enter Gimpus Foo Foo without taking the despicably diagonalizable detour through Decaturville.

As the two men guided their horses, keeping the beasts from plummeting into the murky mess, they conversed about the previous night's encounter with Weemus Bobeemus.

"Well, your grace, maybe we could find out where he's held up," said Biffus. "I have some sources. We get the fork, take out his Impolitus Guard, and then sneak into his lair and grab Buffy before anyone knows we were there. We may even be able to get the spoon back."

"I know where he's hiding out, my trusted sneaky-pants man."

"Where?"

"The Hall of Panzies."

DUNT DUNT DA!!!!!!!!!!!!!

77

The two men looked around, wondering where the music had suddenly came from. But they had more important matters to attend to: Biffus was curious about how it was that Flabius knew where Weemus had been hiding, and why Flabius did not want to attempt the breakout.

"Come your highness, you don't honestly believe all of those stories about that place?"

"Oh yes, my trusted friend, oh yes I do believe them. Oh yes, I believe all of them. Oh yes, I can't afford not to believe the stories, oh yes. Oh yes, there are too many lives in jeopardy, as you have stated, oh yes."

"Oh yes, I understand, your grace. But we will have to go there eventually," interjected Biffus. "Oh yes, you're going to have to face your fear about those evil sleep demons at some point, oh yes. And, I might add, oh yes, that point will be a sooner point than you think, oh yes."

"Sooner point? Is that right?" Flabius spoke this allowed when he should have spoken it aloud.

"I think so. It's better than saying 'oh yes' 150 times in one sentence," said Biffus.

"It was a paragraph and I only said 'oh yes' seven times. Besides, you said it five times in the next passage."

"Hey, I know what you're trying to do, your grace. I won't let you change the subject," said Biffus, fighting to keep his leader from changing the subject.

"Let's change the subject."

"Excellent idea," said Biffus, glancing forward to find that their path only worsened. "Perhaps we could debate which is the best *Miss Congeniality* movie?"

"You watch far too much television, my trusted boob-tubian," said Flabius, keeping a watchful eye on the trail ahead.

And then, it happened.

Biffus's horse took a misstep and plunged into the ghastly marsh. It must have been unthinkably deep, as the horse quickly became buried up to the shoe. The more the two warriors struggled to free the Mustang, the deeper it sank.

The two men exhausted all possibilities. They tried pulling, pushing, using fiber-optic cables, reciting sonnets, lifting, but nothing would work.

Finally, they had to say good-bye to the drowning steed, now with two of his hooves sunk below the shoe.

"Good-bye my love! I will never forget you," said Biffus shaking his fists, covering his face, and smashing at the ground. He then glanced over at his Emperor. "Sire, I won't leave my horse! He has been my greatest friend for so long! I can't do it! Nay, I won't do it! We can't just leave him! Nay!"

Flabius knew there was but one chance to save the steed, a long shot, but it just might work... He slapped his companion silly, simultaneously preventing Biffus from utilizing another exclamation point and sparking the horse's fury.

The steed jumped from the swamp, ready to charge the slaphappy Flabius Flaximus, which, in all honesty, would have been a terrible idea, kind of like that fan who ran onto the field during a Dolphins-Colts game in 1971 and got leveled by Baltimore's 'Mad Dog' Mike Curtis. The fan would have been the horse, and Flabius would have played the role of Mike Curtis, which, I have to admit, is slightly ironic considering the Colts' mascot is a horse. Anyway, the horse was free, and Biffus had stopped crying. Once again, Flabius had saved the day.

"You truly are the greatest warrior that has ever lived," said an appreciative Biffus. "I will name my first three sons after you. Then I will name one Mojo Frito Franz Francisco, then two more after you, then I will probably have a few daughters who will be called Sprot, Spriff and Splotf."

"That's not necessary," said Flabius, honored by his deputy's praise. "Just name the first two after me and your middle daughter after my father: Fattia."

"That seems entirely reasonable. Thank you, your grace."

Biffus Palookus picked himself up off the ground, and returned to his master's side.

As the journey continued, both men walked in silence. Something was deeply troubling Flabius, however, and he had to speak. "So, my trusted Baby-Name-Dictionarious-Rex, why Frito Franz Francisco? I get the Mojo part, but I find the rest baffling."

"Well sire, my favorite food is Cheetos, my favorite song is 'Take Me Out,' and I had an uncle named Francisco Franco," said Biffus.

"Then why not go with Mojo Cheetos Ferdinand Franco?" asked Flabius.

"Sire, that's an absurd name," said Biffus.

Flabius paused before responding. "Nonetheless I'm glad you are able to dream of the day you will have a child named Mojo Frito Franz Francisco Palookus."

The Emperor was indeed happy for Biffus, who had gotten his love back. But Flabius couldn't help but dwell on his own misfortune. His lost love may never be saved. But then he remembered that his love was a girl and Biffus's love was a horse, so he felt a little better. He remembered his last encounter with the exquisite Buffy...

The Tale of Flabius, Buffy and Boogus MacDoogus

Flabius Flaximus had just taken control of the Rambo Brighteaen lands. He was Emperor. He was the most powerful man in the world, and he was only 25. He was also really looking to get down with an around-the-kingdom girl. But he wouldn't get with just any around-the-kingdom lady-in-waiting. He wanted the type of love Lionel Richie used to sing about (you know, in "Dancing on the Ceiling").

Flabius' father, Fattus, used to say, "An Emperor without an empress is not really an Emperor at all, but more like a Gobot with strawberry or blueberry Go-Gurt."

80

The young ruler could only be reminded of those words as he peered around the tavern where he was celebrating his new title. It was the Pub of Boogus MacDoogus, where Flabius found himself surrounded by members of Boogus's harem. The man must have had at least 30 wives, and he was only an Earl, or some garbage like that. That meant that this man was an Earl[30], which is a pretty high number. Of course, Flabius knew you can't raise titles and names to the 30th power, only to the eighth power or something. He felt obliged to relay this information to Boogus, the next time he saw him.

Flabius slowly made his way around, politely acknowledging his fans whenever introductions were made. Finally, he ran into the Grand Boogus himself, who was, once again, getting stinky-faced at the bar with the other old folks.

"Boogus, I just wanted you to know that you can't raise your title to the 30th power, only to the eighth power."

"Yes, I believe I own three of them, although one might be at the dry cleaners. Sit here, my boy. You're old enough to drink now. Have a beer. Have two. Have three!" Boogus MacDoogus shoved three half-gallon glasses in front of the king. Flabius took about 15 seconds to finish off the mugs, a good 3 to 4 seconds slower than usual. It was at this point that Boogus knew that something was amiss.

"Say, lad, what's the matter? Oh now, don't tell me. It's girl trouble, isn't it? Oh, I know the feeling, dear boy. So many women, there are just too many to choose from!"

Flabius was touched by his friend's interest in the young Emperor's predicament. "Actually, I..."

"Not remotely, but she does know her way around the bedroom, if you catch my drift," said Boogus, elbowing the Emperor in a most irritating fashion. "On the other hand, you're the Emperor, so you only get to marry one. So who's it going to be, anyway?"

"I was thinking of..."

"No, I don't imagine she does, but I'll go ask her for you. Who am I kidding? I'll go ask her for me," said Boogus, rising from his seat. "Say, Buffy, my daughter, had the most peculiar question for you."

"Yes?"

"Good, then you're all set. Here, hold this," said Boogus, handing Flabius a frilly sack as he walked away. Flabius was uncertain who owned the bag, and he became infuriated at having been left with the responsibility of securing the tote.

"What question? Stand still, MacDoogus! I'm the Emperor! Doesn't that count for anything? You know what? Screw you guys, I'm going home," said Flabius, annoyed that a simple message could not be conveyed. He was just about to fling the purse he was holding (which for the record was made from the same material as Liberace's pink tuxedo) through the brick wall across the hall and then through six or seven other castles, as well as Mount Vesuvius, the Conrad discontinuity and the eaten portion of Archie Bunker's final grilled Reuben sandwich when he heard a voice coming from behind him, the most beautiful voice in the whole wide world.

"She wanted to know how your shins were doing." Slowly Flabius wheeled around to see who spoke those words. To his dismay, it was just a large boar.

"Hey, over here!" Flabius wheeled around even further to see it was actually none other than Buffy.

She was radiant. Flabius attempted to form a response, but could only motion with his hands while making whistle-like noises, to go along with a few throat-clearing grunts.

"Pardon?"

"Heaah, a shambee, fodor-rory?" said Flabius, motioning to the dance floor.

"I'm going to assume you're asking me to dance, in which case I'd love to, sire," said Buffy.

"Seah, see-ah, hesta," said Flabius, before clearing his throat and guiding the lovely Buffy to a small vacant area of the floor. "Seah, fodor-rory?"

"Sure... I think," said Buffy, gracefully presenting Flabius her hand. And so the two young lovers danced a dance that rivaled even the great two-steps of Astaire and Rogers, Romeo and Juliet, Riggs and Murtaugh, Dave and Cecilia.

"Say, um, whistle, huh, deep breath, huh, um, say?" Flabius was a master of words around women.

"I've been fine, thank you for asking. I haven't really been up to anything at all, just school, mostly." Buffy seemed flattered by the kind words of Flabius. She batted her eyelashes in his direction. This only proceeded to make the face of Flabius turn a bright vermilion.

"What's the matter, sire?"

"Fodor, seah, um, deep breath, um, hee-ya!" Flabius made a celebratory arm gesture, kind of like the one employed by Howard Dean after he went crazy following the Iowa caucuses.

"Right," said Buffy, in a long, drawn out Dr. Evil-esque fashion. "Anyway, just finished up my senior year at the University of Ancientlandia. I didn't want to bother you in front of all your friends, considering our last encounter."

"Hegaga, hegaga," said Flabius, waving his hand back in forth in a 'No, you're not bothering me at all. Actually, I would very much like to jump your bones,' type of motion. "Hem, hip, ahem, flem. Flem, ahem. Throat clear. Flem-flarn-flem."

"Yes, I think we covered that," said Buffy.

As they danced into the night, Flabius could only think about making this young woman his empress. Unfortunately, before he could ask the question, he was called away, to once again perform the duties of Emperor.

Biffus was the one who had to bring the bad news to Flabius. "Sire, come quickly, floods! Big ones! We can't stop it! The royal palace will be destroyed!"

Flabius looked at the beautiful Buffy. If he only had more

83

time, he could have asked her. "Hegaga?"

"I, um, I know," said Buffy, who didn't know, but assumed Flabius still wanted to tango. "Go, your highness. I'll be here when you get back. We can dance as long as you wish."

And so Flabius and Biffus rushed back to the castle. Biffus was correct. There was a flood, cascading from all corners of the castle: through the windows, out the six doorways, even the ones with sploof holders. "How did this start, my trusted overly excited 76 trombonist?"

"Up there. It was one of the servants. I bet they work for Weemus Bobeemus. I bet he's come back!"

"Calm yourself, my friend. Let me put a stop to this." Flabius approached the staircase. He followed the trail of the floodwaters. They led to... the bathroom. The toilet had overflowed! The damage would have been irreversible if Flabius had not been there to stop it.

Fortunately, not only was Flabius an expert Emperor, he was also a master plumber. Flabius took hold of the handle, ever so delicately, and shook it until the little black floaty thing settled back into place. The flood was stopped.

Now it was time to go back to the party. Flabius raced back to the Pub of Boogus MacDoogus. The guests were still there. The lights were still on. The bar was still open. But Buffy was gone. Of course, all of the old folks were too blitzed to converse. Nobody knew anything. She was gone...

"We've arrived, your grace." Biffus was correct. After an agonizing expedition, Flabius and Biffus had made their way to 'the puddle that never goes away.' It was here where the pair expected to find the 'Fork that has been known to Wreak Havoc on Entire Countries.'

All around the puddle, ancient traps waited for an unprepared fool to set them off. This day, however, they would be the fooled ones, because Flabius was the fool who would set them off, even though the traps were lifeless objects that can't be fooled because they weren't alive.

"Sire, there... Upon that large hill. 'The puddle that never goes away!' The rumors of the fork must also be true," said Biffus. "Although, there's only one thing I don't understand."

"What's that, my trusted Mrs. Featherbottom?"

"If Weemus could lead us to the exact location of the fork, why did he have us find it instead of his dreaded Impolitus Guard? Aren't they supposed to be the most vicious warriors the world has ever seen?"

"Well, my trusted little 'I believe everything I hear' friend, if you had paid more attention in astronomy class, you would realize that the traps that stand between us and that fork are large, as well as being really, really big. So, only a fool would attempt to steal such a device."

"Then why are we trying to steal the fork?"

"That's a mighty good question, my trusted ever-observant comrade! It's like this you see... um... ah... Well I think that should answer your question."

"So that's the end of the story?"

"No, but a sudden plot twist would be good right about now. Come on, let's slowly move toward the fork."

Just then the giant hill turned into a real giant, leaving the fork on the ground behind it. The monster was really big, and it was made from a hill, which made it kind of weird looking.

"Your grace, what'll we do?" Biffus Palookus was slightly less than moderately exasperated. "I thought that the traps were supposed to be lifeless!"

"Do not fear, my trusted sidekick, I have a plan." Apparently Flabius had a plan. And apparently somebody finally solved Fermat's Last Theorem. Cindy and Scott are newlyweds. Whoopity doo!

"Sire, if your plan involves Fermat's Last Theorem, I'm not sure how much help that will be right now," said Biffus.

"Look, my trusted clearly-not-trusting amigo, I know I've told you this before, but only one thing's for sure.."

"Love stinks?" said the fat guy who was going to have a heart attack if we don't eat again soon from *The Wedding Singer*.

"Who's that guy?" asked Flabius. "No, the only thing that is for sure is that cherry cheesecake cupcakes with Nilla wafer crusts taste the best. But woe unto you that useth a graham cracker crust recipe instead."

Biffus and the fat guy wholeheartedly agreed. But the giant, confused by the cheesecake reference, ate the fat guy.

Thus, the brave Wimpole Street warriors prepared for battle. Their enemy was quite enormous; too big to really put into words and do the thing justice, but it was on the larger-than-giant-size side of the giant scale. Ok, if I were to put it into words, I would say it was bigger than Manimal, after he turned into a bear, and at least as large as Grawp. Come to think of it, if it was a hill, it was probably bigger than Grawp. If Grawp had another brother who was as big to him as he was to Dolores Umbridge, that's how big the hill giant was.

Biffus began the fight by flinging himself at the creature, much as Flabius had done during the 'great leap' incident.

Unfortunately for Biffus, the great leap only worked if your last name was Flaximus, not Palookus, as Flabius relayed. "Hey my trusted fling-flang man! That only works if your last name is Flaximus, not Palookus!"

Biffus was not in any condition to listen, however, as he was now being crushed under the weight of the larger than giant-sized giant.

Flabius immediately took off running, not because he was frightened or anything, but because he hoped that the giant, being just a big giant made from a hill and not particularly intelligent, would follow him and leave Biffus alone.

Unfortunately for the giant, he didn't follow and was instead hit by a larger-than-hill-giant-sized meteor, striking him dead on the spot, except that the giant was really a hill and thus not actually alive, so it was struck inanimate on the spot.

Flabius then helped his companion to his feet.

"Thank you sire, I'll remember not to try that leap thing again," said the appreciative squire.

"Don't thank me; thank the digression. But enough of that for now, I have a feeling that a Nazi Panzer Division and several Gypsy flower girls may be close on our heels. Let's grab the fork and get out of this chapter while we're still capable of locomotory movement." Flabius looked around himself, keeping a keen nose out for the sounds of tank engines and Romany singing.

"Yes sire," said Biffus, dusting himself off. "But I still say the leap thing has more to do with weight than last name."

"Please, my trusted 'I-never-took-physics-in-high-school student. If you insist on believing that one's weight or strength has more to do with how much force he or she can apply on an object, such as a giant made from a hill, as opposed to one's last name, you're only showcasing a complete and utter lack of understanding of quantum mechanics."

"I see, sire. My apologies. But I do have another question."

"Yes, my trusted Jungian typology?"

"How can you kill a hill that is made from dirt? I mean, even a meteor falling from space shouldn't kill dirt. It might make a hole or something, but how can you kill something that was never alive to begin with?"

"No, my trusted colleague, 'twas not the meteor that kill the giant, 'twas the digression." Just then, the giant started to reform from the dirt hill. "Or, perhaps I was wrong. Wait, do you hear that?"

Flabius held his ear to the sky, even as the giant began to move toward the two adventurers. Biffus continued to look back at the creature. "Come, your grace, we've got to get out of here! The giant!"

87

"Ah yes, I thought I heard the distinct sound of a 12-cylinder Maybach HL engine," said Flabius. "The Nazis are coming. Damn those Nazis! Damn their tanks! Damn!"

The Nazis were indeed coming. An entire division appeared from around the bend, rumbling toward the mighty heroes.

"Come, my trusted floppy flop flopper, let's get behind this big pile of dirt over here," said Flabius. Of course, the big pile of dirt was actually the hill giant in the process of reforming.

"Sire, not to alarm you, but we have just taken refuge behind the giant hill monster," said Biffus, unsure if his master was aware of their prickly predicament.

"At the moment, I'm a bit more concerned about those gigantic 7.5 cm Kampfwagenkanone 40 guns mounted on those Panzer IVs pointed in our direction," said the Emperor.

"What in the name of all that is Flabian is going on?" Biffus was from ancient times, thus the appearance of Nazis was akin to that scene in *The Final Countdown* where the crew of the aircraft carrier skippered by Kirk Douglas scare off a couple of Japanese zero pilots with their awesome fighter jets, in which case Biffus Palookus represents the Japanese pilots and... actually that doesn't work well because then the awesome fighter jets would be Nazis, and *The Final Countdown*, while mostly a slick advertisement for the U.S. Navy, was also a pretty cool sci-fi/action movie, and it just wouldn't be right to compare Nazis to anything but other evil-doers, like say evil agent Winston Wallingford, or Brussels sprouts.

"You worry about those fighters, I'll worry about the tower," said Flabius, as he jumped out into the open, and flipped up into the air in an incredible jump of incredibly no height. He then quickly utilized Fermat's Last Theorem to build a tricycle capable of breaking the sound barrier. As a result, the Nazis were sent scattering in fear, holding each other's hands and sucking each other's thumbs.

Flabius raised his hands in victory. He had done it. He had

used his keen intellect to scare off the Nazis.

But Flabius had forgotten about the giant, who proceeded to pick him up in a King Kong-like manner. He peered down at Flabius. He began to laugh. He then put Flabius down, turned around, gave him the fork, and sent him on his way.

Then a bunch of Gypsy flower girls showed up and pelted the giant with pansies. The giant exploded into Michael Shannon. Then Michael Shannon exploded into chocolate sprinkles, which were eaten by a nearby pack of tribbles. Next, multiple Klingon warships descended from the skies, firing hundreds of photon torpedoes at the tribbles. Several thousand Klingon warriors wielding bat'leths disembarked, preparing for battle. When it was over, scores of Klingons lay motionless on the ground. Others collected severed limbs and scurried back up onto the warships. The campaign was over, for now.

Flabius and Biffus began their trek toward the next stop on their journey: a meeting with the chief vile henchman of Weemus Bobeemus. Neither man looked at each other as they got on their horses. They rode further into the vile land of Gimpus Foo Foo. The two brave men kept a solemn silence as they pondered the battle they had just won. It was a couple of miles before they would talk.

Biffus was the first to break the ice. "Sire, did you happen to see Miley Cyrus perform on MTV last night?"

"Yes my trusted video music award, after all, Buffy's life depends on it, as well as Robin Thicke's," said the Emperor.

"I heard from some of the guys that Robin Thicke's dad is the guy from *Growing Pains*. Does that make him Kirk Cameron's brother?"

"On the contrary, my trusted Leonardo-DiCaprio-starred-as-a-homeless-kid-in-the-last-season Seattle Supersonic, what you have to ask yourself is 'how hot is Joanna Kerns?' And the answer is, what is the temperature of the sun?" said Flabius.

"I think it varies, sire, but in general it's extremely hot."

89

"Of course, seeing how we are in ancient times, we still believe the sun revolves around the Earth, and therefore Joanna Kerns qualifies as a celestial body," continued Flabius.

Further up the road, the winding lands of Gimpus Foo Foo began to resemble the northern kingdom of Arnor from Middle Earth, or at least that part where Aragorn took Frodo, Sam and company, so you know, like New Zealand.

Soon it was time to dismount and rest their stallions for a while. The pair continued to devise a plan, knowing how critical it was to focus on their mission, and nothing else.

"You know your grace, this reminds me of the story of Nathanus Braytanus."

"Why, I agree my trusted Foo Fooian historian! What an amazing coincidence! And what an exculpatory use of rhyme!"

The Story of Nathanus Braytanus

Nathanus Braytanus was known through out the ancient lands of Ancient-landia as the greatest swordsman who had ever lived. Of course, in ancient times, there had really only been like a handful of 'greatest swordsman's,' and at least three of those were only slightly better than a broom handle-wielding George Michael Bluth, but once upon a time, that level of skill would have been described as *Kick-Ass,* or possibly *Kick-Ass 2,* or maybe a kiss ass. But more importantly, he was a Foo Foo.

The Foo Foos were always considered evildoers, even when compared with Brussels sprouts. Nathanus Braytanus, was honor-bound to kill, maim and otherwise conduct himself in a most dastardly fashion. Ultimately, though, he longed to be something other than the greatest swordsman who had ever lived. But he could never tell the other Foo Foos. They had earned international distinction as tartle tails and gossthrop Shedd's Spreads (later known as tattle tales and gossip spreaders), far worse than Biffus Palookus.

One day, after killing the usual assortment of challengers,

90

Nathanus Braytanus came upon a little girl who had lost her all-pink panda. He searched and searched, but he could not find the girl's panda. He asked her if she was telling the truth. She said it was true. And so he looked even more. Eventually though, he got bored. And so he and the girl sat and had Darjeeling tea and crumpets. Then the all-pink panda bear arrived to partake in the vittles.

After the snack, Nathanus went back home. When he arrived, everyone was gone. The all-pink panda bear had eaten them, too. The bear could eat a lot. He was big. Nathanus was now honor-bound to challenge the all-pink panda.

He practiced for weeks before challenging the bear. Chords of "Gonna Fly Now" paraded his every thought as he marched through the ancient city of Foo-Foopia. Still, Nathanus, the girl and the all-pink panda had tea and crumpets every day. Sometimes they ate crumpets in the shape of English muffins. Other times, they looked like little round pieces of bread with holes in the middle; not a big hole like a donut, but more like the Grand Canyon divided by the weight of a 1987 green Chevy Blazer towing a heath bar flurry.

Finally, the day came. Nathanus Braytanus left early for tea and crumpets that morning, for he would most likely not be returning, and he did not want to miss out on the crumpets, as the all-pink panda tended to wolf them all down, in addition to six or seven packs of timber wolves from nearby Manitoba.

He arrived, ready to challenge the bear. They ate. Then, Nathanus Braytanus spoke. "I hate to say this, all-pink panda bear, but I need to challenge you to a duel... you know, for killing off all of the other Foo Foos from my village. Sorry."

"You're a Foo Foo? Wow. I could have sworn you said you were from Louisville. Man."

"Louisville? Come to think of it, my aunt was on layover there last year, on her way back from Christmas vacation."

"Really? What happened to her?"

91

"I think she was probably one of the ones you ate."

"Oh. Sorry. But at least you don't have to buy her a present this holiday season."

"You know? I never thought of it that way. Say, all-pink panda, what are you doing tomorrow?"

"I was thinking about joining Starfleet Academy. I'd like to work for the Department of Temporal Investigations, or maybe Section 31. I don't have a partner though, so I can't get in."

"Really?" asked Nathanus Braytanus. "That's what I have wanted to do for as long as I can remember. Can I join you?"

"Um, the only thing is, you're a Foo Foo," said the panda. "Starfleet tends to be pretty biased. They also refuse to accept people who consume vast quantities of Cocoa Krispies for breakfast. Man, Cocoa Krispies."

"It's ok, I'll say I'm from Iran," said Nathanus Braytanus. "I think I can get my Cocoa Krispies dealer to deliver, as well."

"Thank God for that!" said the panda.

And so, the two adventurers became partners. The girl grew up and followed in the bear's footsteps. It was pretty much a happy ending until Nathanus Braytanus slipped on a wet floor and killed a galaxy-class starship. Then the bear and Nathanus realized that the method by which the girl followed in the panda's footsteps was not by joining Starfleet, but by eating Foo Foos. She also became an internationally acclaimed assassin, roustabout and Elvis impersonator. Ironically, during her performances, rather than singing "Roustabout," the girl often belted out her own renditions of "Clambake," "A Little Less Conversation," "In the Ghetto," or "Little Egypt."

Thus, things got even better.

"That's it, my trusted cartographer, we'll find Weemus's henchman in Egypt!"

7 Merv Griffin Stars as Rae Dong Chong in: *Abraham Lincoln, his Women, and Indiana Jones Battle Mechagodzilla and Grandma for Super Bowl MCLXVI*

I never believed her when she said that I was acting funny. She couldn't understand my goal to be the first man to walk from New York City to Scranton on my face. I told her I would do it, that I had to prove to her just what a man I was. Then she said something I can't really recall because I was looking at her breasts. Then I understood what the Wizard of Oz had meant when he said he didn't know how it worked.

But Natasha was such a proud lady. She had such vast wisdom and great knowledge and a really big brain and other things that were really big and nice before that one day. The day seemed so long ago that it was like yesterday and that I was saying it was like this other day from before I knew her: The day I went back to the future. But then I found out that I was lied to, and it was only a movie. Natasha told me this. I didn't believe her at the time because I was looking at her breasts. Then she said something like "stop looking at my breasts," but I didn't really hear exactly what she said because my eyes were fixed on her breasts.

After that she removed my head from her chest and told me to concentrate or I would fail the exam. Then I realized I wasn't in Kansas, but at Wichita State University, and my dream of walking on my face was shattered.

We sat there, Natasha's breasts and I, waiting for Natasha to let us play together. But Natasha was selfish, and she said that she didn't want to play. I, meanwhile, was preparing to embark on another of my great conquests: this time down to Mr. Robert's food stand on the corner. I left the humble abode with high aspirations, which were dashed almost immediately when I realized my wallet was still upstairs.

They were up there also, and I knew that if I returned that it would take me a good month or so before any one of us would get out of the apartment, except that isn't completely right because they go where Natasha goes, so I am the only one that could go by myself, which I wouldn't have been able to do if I returned to the apartment empty-handed.

Then I saw this little old lady with $2,000 in her hands, returning from a successful trip to the lottery store. I think she was a big fat liar though, so I stayed away from her. Then there was this priest who walked by with a bunch of nuns or something, but I wasn't in the mood for upsetting the man upstairs, so a settled on a pack of thugs who had been beating up the old lady and the priest and the nuns. They were the perfect choice to hold up, I just knew it!

I said it to them loud and clear that this was a stick up! But then I realized that not only was I still talking to myself, I had left my gun back in the apartment as well. Then I realized I didn't have a gun and I sighed with relief at thought of not telling those guys that this was a stick up. But I said that out loud and they heard me, and they came after me.

So then I told them that they were all a bunch of wussies, and that got them really upset. I guess I shouldn't have kicked that one leader in the family jewels, either.

But men with jewelry are losers, anyway, and I said so, so I kicked him in the family jewels again and said so again because I don't think he believed me the first time. Then they chased me through the mean streets of Los Angeles, which was odd because we were in Manitoba, and then they chased me into a bar, which was even more unusual because I wasn't running away from them.

Once inside we started the battle, except that I forgot to tell

94

them that the battle started so they got upset when I threw the bartender at them. The bartender was mad too, because I didn't even hit one of the thugs.

Then I found out that the thugs were actually undercover police officers. But I said they were stupid because they were not even undercover.

Then they said that they were never undercover police officers, they were simply regular police officers and I said "Yeah, right." And then I said that I ate bad cabbage, once, too. After that I called them all big, fat jerks because they were impolite and were also overweight by a little. Then they said I called them names, which wasn't true but then they blew up, so I didn't really worry about it.

After that I went back to Mr. Roberts and got my food. He's a real mean, awful person, though, and I told him so. Then he said that I hurt his feelings and I said that I meant he was a real mean, awful person, in the good way, and then he said that his feelings were okay. I didn't really care about him, though, so I punched his lights out. He said his lights were really expensive and he wanted me to pay for them but I said his lights were not expensive at all and then he got angry. I don't take a liking to angry people, so I punched him, too.

After beating up roughly half the neighborhood, people started to come looking for the guy that beat up half the neighborhood, so I told them to go look in Las Vegas.

They said that my idea was stupid and I said they just don't know because I saw the guy and he said that he was going to Las Vegas. Then they said "okay" and went to Nevada or something. I felt bad though because I had lied about Las Vegas. In fact the guy said he was going to Hawaii. But I didn't really care because they said my idea was stupid.

Then I went back up to the apartment where Natasha was and I found her with some other woman. Except then it turn out that I just forgot to put my glasses on and it was really just Natasha and another Natasha, so there were four of them in the room with her and her friend. Then I found out that I don't wear glasses and I said so to Natasha. She said that I was drunk and that's why I couldn't see straight, so I said that I didn't drink a thing, but Natasha is really smart and she said if I was honest that she would give me something special. So then I got out the bottle of Scotch that I took from the bar and gave it to Natasha and she said I had to stop beating people up, but I didn't really listen because I was drunk.

Then I realized that I left my hat downstairs, so I had to go get it. But when I got there I found out that I didn't a hat, so I got really angry and took the hat from the guy next to me. He said that he was a police officer too, and then he blew up. Then I left and went back up to Natasha.

When I returned I realized Natasha must be in the shower, so I decided to go look there. But it turned out that she was just making dinner and I got upset. Then she asked me why I was upset but I didn't say anything because I was only thinking Natasha was in the shower because then I could see her breasts. But then I found out that I spoke that out loud again and Natasha got that look on her face.

Then I knew that I was in trouble. The rest I can't really tell you because we didn't have dinner. After that all I remember is that I can't tell you because it's X-rated, so I better stop now. Then I heard they changed it to NC-17, and I said that was stupid and they should stop changing stuff because sometimes normal people like us don't like it when change comes along and does stuff that we don't like, because it's different.

Natasha doesn't want me to worry about that sort of rubbish, so I don't. But I don't say rubbish, except I just did, so I forgot the whole thing again. But I did get a beer from Natasha when we were done and she said I did a good job so I was proud, and then I wasn't thinking about those perfect breasts of hers as much.

8 Vic from Detroit and the Daredevil Bunnies

The Fairy was out on a limb. Not just any limb, mind you, but one way up in the Himalayas, where trees don't grow. The Duke was trying everything he could think of to get her down, but when a fairy doesn't want to do something, no one, not even the Duke himself, could get her to do it.

Their murderous trek across three county lines had led them from their quiet dinner in the Yukon territory to their present location in Tibet. The facts were against them, though, as nobody could prove they had killed anybody. This was the final straw for the Fairy. So, as fairies with attitudes often do, at least, those who know how to fly, she ran away.

"Come on down from there," said the Duke. "I don't care who we didn't kill. I won't stand for your behavior."

"But that's just it," said the Fairy. "You never understood, did you?"

"Yes."

"Yes as in no, or no as in yes?"

"No."

"Okay, I'll come down then."

And so they were back on the case. However, the highly intellectual conversation had been too taxing for the Fairy, and she needed to rest. Her cute little fairy outfit was wrinkled, and as anyone with a large cerebrum would know, a fairy without her cute little fairy outfit is like a football player without his putter, or a cowboy without his breath spray.

"Where are we going now, Duke?"

"The drugstore, I need some more breath-savers."

"You too?"

"Listen, if we are ever going to find that guy we haven't been looking for, we better get moving. The barrel goes over the waterfall at noon and I'm going to be late."

"Don't worry, we'll make it."

"No, I want to be late."

"What about that guy whose been following us?"

"He'd better catch up."

Utilizing an excessively long yellow ribbon, the Fairy and the Duke worked their way down from the snow-covered oak tree, and then traversed several Johnny Weissmuller movies before arriving at the waterfall. Unfortunately, not only had all of Tibet gone to sleep, the waterfall had solidified into some sort of a crystalline structure.

"We probably should have stopped and asked directions from Tantor, the elephant," said the Fairy.

"Do you speak elephant?" asked the Duke.

"Why yes, as a matter of fact, I don't," exclaimed the Fairy.

"Then obviously you should have asked him."

Now, the Fairy and the Duke could only seek the comfort of the Hawaiian inn. Once inside, the hotel lobby attendant realized that something was up.

"Aren't you dead?"

"Yes."

"Can we have a room, please?" asked the Fairy, interrupting the proceedings. "I need to get out of this dress."

The Fairy, by this point, only wanted a nice long hot fairy bath to dry her aching bones.

"All right! But, you'll have to check your wings in."

"What is this, an airport?" The Duke was angered by the innkeeper's suggestive remarks.

"What does it look like, a hotel or something?"

"Yes."

"No."

"Yes."

"No."

"Yes."

"No."

"All right, yes!"

"Then I am glad we are in agreement, sir."

"Then you did lie, before!"

"Listen, do you want the room or not?"

"We'll take it, Mr. Stewardess," interrupted the Fairy. "Come on Duke, stop arguing with the help."

The two found some lodging near the check-in gate for flight 283, departing for Boston by way of Bratislava. They were about to enter their room when Dave crashed through the ceiling, bounced off the Duke and landed on a nearby chesterfield.

"What a fall! Hey, maybe heights *are* good for you."

The Duke immediately began interrogating the mysterious stranger whom he had never met before. "Let's go over this one last time, pilgrim. Alex Karras was an ex-football player turned actor who *played* the role of Mongo in *Blazing Saddles*, not the other way around. And don't call me Shirley."

"So then it *is* safe to eat baked beans. As you can imagine, my main concern was combustible flatulence," said Dave.

"We're going to have to cut this conversation short, pilgrim. Looks like somebody's beginning to take an interest in your handiwork," said the Duke. Sure enough, no one was coming, unless you counted the Imperial stormtroopers from the original *Star Wars* movie, marching side-by-side, unlike sand people, who always ride single file to hide their numbers. Also there were a couple of sand people.

"Drat! I thought I lost those guys in the Jundland Wastes," said Dave. "Well, it was a pleasure meeting you, Mrs. Duke."

"Thank you, the name is Belle. Bell for short; but no 'short' jokes or jokes about short shorts." The Fairy felt it was about

99

time that her name got mentioned, so she did what the writer wouldn't. He didn't seem to care, though.

"Is it okay to sing the song about short shorts?" asked Dave.

"I don't know. How does it go?" asked the Fairy.

And then Dave was off, just as average as he came, with the grace and speed of a saber-tooth tiger caught in a tar pit.

The stormtroopers arrived shortly thereafter, and began their own interrogation of the Duke and the Fairy.

"How long have you had these droids?" asked Gunnery Sergeant Mehmet G. Korkmaz.

"Um, Sarge, they don't have any droids," said Private Kip Langston, who had been stationed with the Tatooine Regulars for merely a month.

Once upon a time, Korkmaz had been like Langston, eager to serve the Empire and ready to tackle any new assignment. He had originally taken great pride in his posting to Tatooine. After all, Korkmaz was one of the elite. But the truth was Tatooine sand found its way into every nook and cranny of a stormtrooper's uniform, and most of the citizens of the backwater planet really didn't seem to like him very much.

One time he got stuck pulling security detail for the Boonta Eve Classic, and he was repeatedly pelted by beer cans and bantha jerky. On another occasion, he and his troops were called in to deal with a domestic dispute between a couple of Sarlacc pits. It was bad enough trying to figure out which was the boy and which was the girl. But when they started throwing the slowly digested body parts of previously eaten pirates who had gotten on the wrong side of Jabba the Hut at each other, he had officially seen enough.

Of course, Korkmaz never officially reported that he had officially seen enough, for fear of Emperor Palpatine either blasting him with force lightning or putting him on bantha poodoo clean up duty. It was unclear which would be a worse fate, so Korkmaz simply went through the motions, ignoring the fact that Tatooine was a sun-blasted rock in the middle of nowhere populated by moisture farmers, giant slugs, scum, villainy and a bunch of noisy Tusken Raiders.

"I knew that, Private," said Korkmaz. "So are they for sale if we want them? Can we see your identification? No, these aren't the droids we're looking for?"

"Um, Sarge, who are you talking to?" said Langston. Sure enough, the Duke and the Fairy had closed the door to their suite, leaving Korkmaz talking to the chesterfield.

"You know, Chip, I envy you," said Korkmaz, taking a seat on the lounger.

"It's 'Kip,' Sarge," said Langston.

"Well now it's Chip," said Sergeant Korkmaz. "Why Chip, I remember a time when this uniform used to mean something. We struck fear in the hearts of rebel scum and pirates alike. Our blast points were far too precise to ever get confused with those of some sand dude with a Gaffi stick."

"I resent that," said Uuurruurr'Rur'Rur'Rur, one of the sand people who had been involved in the chase.

"You guys can talk?" asked Private Langston. "I thought you just made those guttural noises and shot at pod racers."

"Yeah, those guys were my cousins, URoRRuR'R'R and RR'uruurrr. They, um, had issues," said the sand person. "On the other hand, I happen to be an excellent marksman."

Uuurruurr'Rur'Rur'Rur then held up his Gaffi stick and pointed it at Private Langston and Gunnery Sargeant Korkmaz, who raised their hands in surprise.

Just then, Dave came crashing through the same hole in the ceiling as earlier. "Whoops, took a wrong turn."

"You saved us!" said the stormtroopers, peering down at the crumpled body of Uuurruurr'Rur'Rur'Rur.

"Funny you should ask. I am, in fact, equally adroit at hoops and basketball," said Dave. "However, my least favorite expression is 'cold enough to freeze the balls off a brass monkey.' Wow! It's cold enough to freeze the balls off a brass monkey. Where am I, Borneo?"

"We've been tracking you ever since you smashed into that Jawa sandcrawler just outside of Mos Eisley. You left before they could get your insurance information," said Langston.

"Yes, I see how my ultra-powerful skills of deduction could instigate such a fiendish caper," said Dave. "You were right to come looking for me. Now, if we pool our resources, our combined strength should be enough to discover the whereabouts of this dreaded Jawa fender-benderer."

Private Chip Langston, formerly known as Private Kip Langston, scratched his helmet. "I'm pretty sure that's you, buddy. We've got surveillance footage from Watto's junkyard. A person matching your description can clearly be seen smashing into the top of the sandcrawler and then bouncing away. Look, you're even wearing the same dinner jacket. Nobody wears a dinner jacket on Tatooine, well, except if you're eating at Rick's Café Americain. Jackets are always required at Rick's."

"Damn it, man," said Dave, shaking the private. "Do know what this means? If we don't find this guy soon, the entire Rebel Alliance could be at risk. Sergeant, you get on the horn with Captain Renault. Here's the number to TACO SUPER BURRITO. Tell him to call and ask for a Good Golly Miss Molly cupcake with Tutti Frutti frosting, hold the Little Richard. Now this is important! He'll want to hold the usual suspects, but you must tell him to hold the Little Richard. With any luck, we'll have this criminal back behind bars so that Jawas everywhere can get a good night's sleep."

The Duke, hearing the commotion just outside his expensive hotel room, opened the door, ready to deal with the hooligans. "Look guys, we've been on the lam for several chapters now, and I've got to get some shut-eye."

102

Seeing the cause of the disturbance, the Duke grabbed Dave by the collar of his dinner jacket and heaved him back up through the hole in the ceiling.

He then turned his attention back to the stormtroopers. "You can go about your business. Move along, move along."

The phone number to TACO SUPER BURRITO firmly in hand, Mehmet and Chip looked at each other (or at least I assume they did since they were wearing stormtrooper helmets), and decided it best to move along.

The Fairy, meanwhile, had adjourned to the luxury suite of the fine establishment. The room had a beautiful bath, of which the Fairy was making good use. It was difficult, as usual, to wash her wings. And so she called on her mystery date in that lovely fairy way that is known for its ability to attract any man. "Duke, get in here!"

Suddenly the Duke came crashing through the door at low speed, witch made for a most unusual site to behold, especially because he missed the door and instead left a Duke-sized hole in the wall separating the bathroom from the parlor.

"What? Where is he? I'll kill him!"

"Who? I just wanted you to wash my wings. By the way, does anybody still use the word parlor, and are you sure it's being used in the correct way?" The fairy was quite good at making statements sound like questions, and vice versa. "And remember, I'm not a witch. They are ugly and have no fashion sense."

"Oh yeah. No, I can't wash your wings," said the Duke. "We have to be moving again. I just ran into the heat outside."

"But dear, we're in Tibet. It can't be the heat."

"Believe me, it is. I know. I was hot once."

"But aren't you also an officer of the law?" The Fairy was quite upset at the use of the word 'fuzz' in reference to the Duke when it apparently was not appropriate, as if the story had anything appropriate about it.

103

"Clearly, an old west sheriff would not be called fuzz. Maybe Super Fuzz. Witch is why... I mean which is why we must leave immediately."

"I see."

"Come on, I'll pack your stuff while you get dressed."

"Okay, I'll get your hat and breath-savers from the desk."

Then the Fairy got up from her warm Fairy bath, and her wings started to shimmer.

"Ok I can wash your wings now."

"But Duke, you said we had no time!" The Fairy was still, ahem, standing in the Fairy bath.

"So then I will wash your wings." The Duke was resolute that he could wash her wings. Who wouldn't be? I mean, come on, she's freakin' Tinker Bell!

So, like, a few... um... a short time later (maybe an hour, maybe a few days)... Once again they were off, desperate to escape their pursuers. Fortunately, their tracks in the snow were hardly traceable, only around three feet deep.

"Where should we go?" asked the Fairy.

"Well, I always wanted to learn to play the flute. Let's go to a Jethro Tull concert," said the Duke.

"Wait, is that the guy or the band?" asked Belle.

"No, the guy was their gym teacher and the band was the Allman Brothers," said the Duke.

"I thought the Allman Brothers band was named after the Allman Brothers," said the Fairy.

"Look, did you live through the seventies?"

"The 1870s? No, but I do know how to play the flute."

"Then why didn't Fleetwood Mac call themselves Brunning Spencer?"

"I can't believe you would ask me that, after all we've been through," said Belle. "You know how much time and energy I spend each day cleaning and fluffing the cotton balls on my slippers for you?"

"Can I have three guesses?"

"Fine, but I get the first one."

"As always," said the Duke, who then stepped on something lumpy. He picked it up and dusted it off. It was an odd looking device. "I wonder what this is?"

"I don't know, but I wouldn't speak too loudly. There are several creatures, approaching from the southeast."

"Hey, did anyone lose this? It looks like an 18th-century agriculturist, possibly the inventor of the farm seed drill."

Sure enough, some more sand people emerged from behind several snow-covered banthas. They quickly scooped up Jethro Tull and headed back toward the wastelands.

"Well, that was easier than I expected," said Belle.

"Come on," said the Duke, leading his lovely leading lady through the choking blizzard. "Boy, this is worse than a T.S. Eliot poem. Hey, can you do that shimmer thing again?"

"Look, I'm not cracking my wings out here in the snow for anybody," said Bell. "But yes I can do that shimmer thing again as soon as we find me another fairy bath."

"You know a buddy of mine told me that Ian Anderson has a cottage somewhere around here."

"Which buddy?"

"I don't recall," said the Duke. "He was in a Christian band, I think. I know one of his songs was called 'Hymn 43.' Now where was this place? It was either in Scotland or Morocco."

"I don't think either of those places are around here. Aren't we still in Tibet?"

"You know if we went to Epcot we could see them both in about six minutes. Hey, maybe you could get us tickets?"

"I'm sorry? I'm not following you. What is an Epcot?"

"Some people think it's the giant golf ball, but that's just the Spaceship Earth ride. Wait, don't you work for those guys?"

"I'm not getting into that right now," said the Fairy.

"Fine, lets head southeast, instead," said the Duke.

"You mean toward the sand people?"

"Yep."

"But what if they come after us?"

"That'll be the day," said the Duke, slowly scanning the environment. The pair moved on, further into the wilderness.

And then, as quickly as a hippo on dry land, the speedy man who had been on their trail stepped out of the Hawaiian inn and into the stifling evening heat of a Tibetan winter. His moo moo skimmed the snow-covered ground.

The doors closed quickly on the stranger, as people in the town were known for their hospitality. And then the new moon glistened upon his face, exposing the scar running from the base of his left ear to another part of his face some one and a half millimeters away.

The look of a man 'happy to be here' was his expression. It struck fear into all of those who knew that a new moon was the one we can't see, just like this man's face. He set off after the couple once again, waiting for his chance to pounce.

Yes, he knew when he saw them together for the first time those ten minutes ago that his centuries-old pursuit was about to be completed. He quickly overtook them, some two thousand miles away, in a sexy, steamy South China Sea port that looked a lot like Casablanca...

Meanwhile, back at the most technologically advanced observatory on Earth

Dr. Judy Darwinkly looked at the image of Neptune blowing up, again and again. It was getting late. Almost all of the other scientists had left the observatory. They had gotten quite a chuckle out of the explosion, especially after Dr. Blindofsky's little speech.

Only Dr. Judy Darwinkly knew the truth.

And then Frank came out of the control room. "Hey Dr. Judy! Do you still want me to drive you?"

106

"I told you to knock that stuff off, Frank! I'm not losing my job over you!"

"So you don't want a ride home?"

"Oh. Sure, I'll take you up on that ride home. I just have to go back to my office to collect a few things."

Frank was a good boy. He was good in the sack, at least, like a potato sack race. As for the other kind of sack, he was marginally sufficient. Judy knew it wasn't ethical to be 'jostling repugnants' (the scientific term for bumping uglies) with a college boy doing an internship, but it was slightly perspiring.

As she approached her office, she thought about jostling repugnants later that evening. The excitement and anticipation sent shivers through her body. Then she realized that it was not the excitement and anticipation, but the gun buried in her back that was causing the minor tremors.

"Don't turn around, Doc. Just you open the door, here, and we'll have a little discussion about that movie tonight." It was Butch Wallpaper. His voice was immediately unrecognizable. Dr. Darwinkly had her suspicions about the man before, and now they had been confirmed.

But this was nothing to lose her life over, so she obeyed. Either that or she had some diabolical plan where she would lure Butch and Dr. Male-Pattern-Baldnificent into a trap, then Admiral Ackbar would shout, "It's a trap!"

But by that time, Wallpaper and Dr. Male-Pattern-Baldnificent would likely be riddled with either bullet holes or flowering tomato plants. As they went inside the office, a second man (clearly Dr. Male-Pattern-Baldnificent) followed. Dr. Darwinkly quickly switched on the lights and wheeled around.

"Hello boys! What do we have here?"

"That was very foolish of you, Dr. Darwinkly. Now we are going to have to kill you," Butch cocked his gun.

"Wait! You don't have what you came for, yet. You still

107

need to know about our little movie. You said that yourself."

"She's right, Butch." The nasal-impaired voice of the second man could be heard just out of range of the lights. Slowly Dr. Male-Pattern-Baldnificent, the man who was punched in the face, revealed himself to Dr. Darwinkly.

"Thought so," said Dr. Darwinkly. "Queue Admiral Ackbar!"

Butch and Dr. Male-Pattern-Baldnificent looked around for the Mon Calamari naval officer, but he failed to appear.

"Very clever, Dr. Darwinkly! You realize, of course, that we will be ready for any surprises," said Dr. Male-Pattern-Baldnificent.

"Oh, come on, Doc! What good can this lady do for us?" Butch looked back at Dr. Male-Pattern-Baldnificent, while keeping the gun trained on Dr. Darwinkly.

"We have our orders, Butch. Okay, Dr. Darwinkly, what can you tell us?" Dr. Male-Pattern-Baldnificent was obviously the brains of the operation, whatever type of surgery it might have been.

"I should have known that you were not real scientists. No scientist could possibly look like Wallpaper. He's much too strong. And you, Male-Pattern-Baldnificent, you don't look the part, either." Dr. Darwinkly seemed more excited than frightened. She slowly breathed in and out, her chest heaving as a result of the stimulation.

"I assure you, Doctor, that I am indeed a scientist. After all, even without revealing my true physical form, one can ascertain that I have Androgenic alopecia, A.K.A. male pattern baldness!"

"No, I don't quite see how one would ascertain that."

"You know, from my last name."

"A.K.A. is your last name?"

"No, it's Male-Pattern-Baldnificent."

"Well that's what I thought. But how does that explain your

108

male pattern baldness?" asked Dr. Judy.

"Um, because the only difference between 'Male Pattern Baldness' and 'Male-Pattern-Baldnificent' is that one has 'ess' at the end and the other has 'ificent.' Otherwise it's completely the same," said the evil scientist.

"What about the apostrophes in your last name?"

"Those aren't apostrophes; their hyphens, or dashes."

"Well which one is it, hyphen or dash?"

"Hyphen, I think?"

"Well then, perhaps you shouldn't think until thinken to!"

"Can we get back to the story?" Dr. Male-Pattern-Baldnificent started singing scales, and clearing his throat, all in an attempt to get ready for his monstrously magnificent monologue. "Can I have a glass of water?"

Dr. Judy got him a glass of water.

"As for Wallpaper, I have to concede to your powerful skills of deduction," said Dr. Male-Pattern-Baldnificent.

"Whose powerful skills of deduction? Mine?" Butch was confused.

"No, nobody is talking to you. Scientists conversing here!" Darwinkly pointed to herself and Male-Pattern-Baldnificent.

"As I was saying, Butch is clearly not a scientist. However, it's hard to come by a thug that will also fit the profile of a scientist," said Male-Pattern-Baldnificent, quite at ease.

Wallpaper, on the other hand, was sweating bullets. Of course these were not real bullets, or else Dr. Darwinkly would be dead. No, Wallpaper was sweating metaphorical bullets as a result of the situation.

"Well, Male-Pattern-Baldnificent, it looks as though your gunman is about to pass out. Perhaps you should rethink your strategy, next time," said Dr. Judy. "Now, as for tonight's film, let's just say it wasn't a special effect."

Wallpaper began making high-pitched squeaky noises. "What'll we do? We gotta tell the boss!"

109

"Relax, Butch. We've got plenty of time."

"Who is this boss you speak of?" asked Dr. Judy.

"Sorry Dr. Judy, that's privileged information. Come on, Butch, our first order of business is silencing the scientists."

"Yes! Silencing the scientists! You can begin with me. Come on boys!" Dr. Darwinkly almost seemed orgasmic at the thought of getting blown away. "Yes! Come on! Yes!"

"I'm going to regret this tomorrow, lady."

"I think you're going to regret it sooner than that, Dr. Male-Pattern-Baldnificent," At that moment, Frank knocked out Male-Pattern-Baldnificent with a vicious chop to the back of the neck. Of course it was more like a love tap, but that's pretty much all the force required when knocking out a scientist.

Wallpaper turned around to see what the problem was. Immediately, Dr. Darwinkly kicked him with a quick strike to the head, causing him to explode into little pieces of Wallpaper... as in the guy, not the stuff that comes flying off the wall if you blew up actual wallpaper.

"Oh my gosh, Dr. Judy! That guy had a gun!"

"Shut up and get in here, Frank!"

The doors closed, the lights went out, and the noise started. Beakers broke, books flew, and the party began. After it appeared as if all the commotion had ceased, a few quick gunshots pierced the air. The door opened, and out walked Dr. Darwinkly, the gun in her left hand smoking, her hair slightly askew. She whispered something on her lips, almost inaudible:

"Borpos, you have returned to me..."

110

The Elusive Inter-Calorie Cheese Chapter

(To be sung like 'Food, Glorious Food' From Oliver! – that crappy musical movie from the 1960s – although I will readily admit that Oliver Reed as Bill Sikes scared the bejesus out of me – but seriously, what's with the exclamation in a movie title? On second thought, maybe I should have written 'scared the dickens out of me' instead of 'scared the bejesus out of me.' Yeah, that probably would have been funnier, or at least, punnier.)

Cheese! Glorious Cheese!
So glorious it's glorious!
Cheese! Glorious Cheese!
So glorious it's like Glorious!

Wait a minute. If it's only like glorious, then it wouldn't really be glorious, which is not grammatically correct. Well then, here is the story of the farmer and the cheese, the ancient tale of a man from Wisconsin and the evil Gouda that haunted him for all ages. It happened about a year ago, as the farmer tells it...

"It happened about a year ago, a piece of cheese that I just couldn't stand... now mind ye... I ain't got nothin' aginnin' a cheese... but there's something different about Gouda... it's evil... it has a mind of its own. I try ta escape it but... you can't... he's fast... faster then you would ever expect a cheese ta be... that fast. I came home from the factory that day and there he was... sitting on the couch staring at me with those evil

111

Gouda eyes of his... cheese and all... I knew right away that I'd have ta leave. I can't fight a cheese! I won't do it! I won't, I tell ye!

"But first, I had ta do battle with Vic from Detroit and the Daredevil Bunnies: a secret, as well as covert, organization bent on world domination. The clandestine society was known for launchin' attacks from their underground base, somewhere in Michigan. But not that cheese!

"I left that very day ... went ta Nebraska... any man'll tell ye... cheeses don't like corns... they hates each others... But not this cheese! There he is sittin' there when I gets ta the motel, like he belong there! And I gots nowhere ta go... Well, I'd eat 'em but he's an evil one... fights ye with all he's got. I got the better of 'em though! He followed me out ta the highway that night... and that's when it happened: a Lexus with no wheels come and run 'em over! Well, I ain't got no legs but that cheese... he's gone fur good, he is! No, no wait. He's back! How now brown cow? He's comin' ta git me! I'm outta here!"

Act III:
Where Butter Knives Dare

fine had she brought enough for everybody. Instead, we were forced to grab the nearest battleship (I believe it was the *New Jersey*, a.k.a. Big J) and shake it upside down until we had enough spinach to build a new black Taj Mahal for Shah Jahan. We had a brief meeting with Henry Marmaduke Marduk, an insurance adjuster from Borsippa, who essentially informed us that a mausoleum constructed entirely of Amaranthaceae plants would only be covered by our policy if we used either beets or Quinoa. Ed Clementine, a flight attendant from Philadelphia, suggested toothpaste, but that was before Marie Curie began her pioneering research on radioactivity, thus only the Minoans were willing to financially support such an absurd venture. Oh, and some venture capitalists from Skokie, Illinois. So it became Barbara Billingsley's responsibility to set up a small working group to study the dentifrice concept. All eyes were on Barbara at Elevenses. Little did we realize that Bingo and Bungo Baggins had already devoured her special recipe breakfast sausage, which would have been

9 Toofy and the Banana

Dave crashed through a barrel of marshmallows, bounced off a herd of roaming C. Thomas Howells, flipped through three consecutive Bananarama CDs, blew out of the luggage hatch of Northwest Orient Airlines Flight 305, before landing softly on a pile of *Game of Thrones* fans waiting outside HBO's Walla Walla, Washington headquarters for no apparent reason.

Confident he had alluded his archenemy, Dave picked up the shattered remains of his *True Confessions* vinyl when he discovered that not only had his prized compact disc collection been transmuted into old-school records, but it was entirely likely that the man whose vertebrae he had shattered when landing could very well have been a conveniently disguised Winston Wallingford, or at the very least, an evil agent of his arch-nemesis. How's that for a sentence?

"So! I have found you at last, evil villain who I have not been looking for!"

"My back! I think you broke my back," said the glitter-covered 40-year-old dude wearing Westerosi pants with a Qartheen gown and a ponytail.

Dave figured he had mere moments to elude this villain and rescue Cecilia, before Winston K. Wackywallibee... no, Willowackerby... Dave had forgotten his mortal enemy's name!

"Ah man, you seriously broke my back! What'll I tell my mom?" Qartheen gown dude remained on the ground while his fellow thronies started throwing thickets, thrushes, thimbles, thalli, theropods, three-toed sloths, Lion-O from *Thundercats* and the moon Thalassa at Dave.

114

Unfortunately, most of the items missed their intended target, instead striking the Ponytail guy wearing Westerosi pants and a Qartheen gown.

"You think just because you allude someone you can also elude him? This won't be the last of Ponytail Westerosi pants Qartheen gown dude!" However after being crushed under the weight of a slightly oblong thimble, it was indeed the last of Ponytail Westerosi pants Qartheen gown dude.

Alas, Dave knew he was definitely in enemy territory.

He searched for his spy manual, but it was nowhere to be found.

It was time to employ his backup plan.

Instinctively, Dave quickly started doing jumping jacks, shouting, "Who wants to meet Barbarella?"

Just then, a woman came screeching towards Dave at full force, carrying a large kitchen utensil, codename "spaghetti drainer," in her hand.

Dave disarmed the woman with a super mega karate toss that sent the utensil hurtling through space.

The woman lunged again, however, crying something along the lines of, "You're ruining my son's birthday party!"

Dave, a master in the art of retaliation, responded with "Whether 'tis nobler in the mind to suffer the slings and arrows of outrageous flatulence, Aye, there's the rub." And when the monologue momentarily halted the attack, he added, "Your mother is so fat that she's a very large person!" Dave followed this with a mega fresh roll that knocked several nearby vegans into a vat of meat sauce, chunky style.

"It's in my brain!" shouted one sauced Walla Wallan, unable to extricate himself from the meat due to poor bone density.

At last having subdued the crowd of thronies (in addition to the pack of vegans), Dave quickly grabbed hold of a passing two-toed sloth that was headed back to its natural feeding grounds: Hollywood. Behind him, he could hear the police collecting a report on his escape.

"He just appeared out of nowhere. Then he started quoting Shakespeare and beat me up," said the chief vegan, still stuck in the congealed Bolognese.

The police, ever vigilant in their efforts to rid the streets of Walla Walla of crime, requested more information. "What did he look like? Where did he go? Did anybody see which direction this guy was headed?" Chief Dusty Mantooth had more than 30 years on the force, and he had never witnessed a scene of such violence and devastation.

"Yeah, he's right over there, sitting on that two-toed sloth," said the congealed vegan.

"Clearly it's too late to get to him now. One can only hope that our all-points bulletin will track the sloth down," said Mantooth.

"No, he's literally like right over there: Six feet away from us, okay now more like six and a half feet away, on top of that sloth. You could probably just reach over and grab him without actually moving."

"Look buddy, I got three weeks to retirement. You think I'm going to risk it all to try to bring down some whacked-out super-spy with an appetite for destruction?"

"Man, that was a great album. Although I still don't get the 'Rocket Queen' song."

"You know who could have answered that?" asked the chief. "Ponytail Westerosi pants Qartheen gown dude!"

"Man, you're right! I bet he could," said vegan congealed man.

The voices of Chief Mantooth and vegan congealed man slowly faded as the sloth continued on its course for southern California.

Dave got out a fruit roll-up he had been saving for a snack, as his thoughts drifted back to Cecilia...

116

Meanwhile, back in the Present-Tense Batcave

Batman's plans to foil the evil scheme of Winston Wallingford have failed. He quits and lights up a stogie and watches Monday Night Football. Robin calls him a big fat loser and Batman responds by opening a beer off Robin's head.

Meanwhile, back in Cecilia's room

Cecilia continued to shriek, peering out of the window as she had all of those chapters ago. Dave was gone. He had jumped out of the window and vanished. There was no blood or anything. Cecilia was disappointed. From behind her, Winston strode forth, with a little white liquid holder in his hand.

"Cecilia darling, what the devil is the matter?"

"Oh Winston! It's awful, just awful! He just jumped out the window! I... he hit... but it was there. What happened?" Cecilia paced around, trying to piece together the events that led to Dave's plummet. "I should have stood in front of it. I knew he was afraid of heights. Oh, this is all my fault!"

"You mean he just vaulted out the window? Afraid of heights and he bounded out? What about the glass?"

"Glass? He broke... and then... and he had a mark on his head and clutched his bottom." Cecilia pointed as she spoke, trying to diagram what happened. She even grabbed her own bottom, which was quite nice (actually that's an enormous understatement: it was really nice. Like J. Lo circa 2002, or maybe even better).

Then Cecilia continued with her story. "I thought if Becky saw that she could... Well, now it's all for nothing. He's dead and it's my fault! Oh my poor Dave! You poor lost little man!"

"Darling, control yourself. Wait, did you say Dave?"

"Yes, I mean I think his name was Dave. He... Oh, what happened?" Cecilia sat down on the bed. She then glanced over at her boyfriend, noting the filthy condition of his shoes and the little white cup he held in his hand. "Did you just go somewhere?"

"What the devil are you referring to? I only just opened the egress to your flat and you were carrying on quite loudly."

"No, I could have sworn that you left in between chapters. You can't just get up and walk out like that. I'm pretty sure there are rules against that sort of thing."

Winston's face began to show the most peculiar of peculiar expressions. But he was the evil Winston Wallingford, and he couldn't let anyone catch onto his evil scheme. "Darling, I would never dream of departing without alerting you. I simply ingested some bad cabbage."

Cecilia sneered in the direction of Winston. "You're lying. What about that ancient dirt all over your shoes? And that cup. Where did that cup come from?" Cecilia was furious.

Quickly, Winston hid the liquid holder behind his back. Then he began to speak in a most suspicious manner. "I don't recall hearing anything about a cup. In all honesty, I simply arrived to converse with you about our appointment. I apologize for my failure to attend."

Cecilia, not yet trained in the ways of super-spydom, didn't catch the ultimate magic trick of evil performed by Winston. "Oh, I don't know. I must have been seeing things. But it wasn't very nice of you to have stood me up, again, I might add." Cecilia was still furious.

"Well, darling, the cabbage was indeed putrefied."

"This all seems very fishy to me."

"Brilliant! I adore fish and chips. We'll do lunch then," said Winston, his evil super spy jargon having served its purpose.

Now it was time to get information from his girlfriend, having used her as bait to lure his archenemy out into the open. "Let us get back to this Dave character. Did you inform him I was to momentarily arrive, by any chance?"

"Why? Did you know the poor man?"

"No more than a water-logged sandcrawler."

"Huh?"

Winston had all of the information he needed. "I'm thrilled we were able to get that out of the way, darling. I must depart, presently. If this Dave individual contacts you, you are to ring me at this number and we'll get this all sorted."

Cecilia took the card from Winston. "Wait, is this a pager number? Do people still use these things?"

"Yes, my employer is a devout adherent of ancient technology," said Winston.

Cecelia was still concerned about her boyfriend's behavior. She kept thinking back to their first encounter in Germany, when after a brief courtship they made plans for a night out on the town. He arranged for her to get escorted to the finest establishment in the city, only to end up in the seediest of locations. He then paid for her to fly first-class back to the U.S., and then invited her for another night of dancing out on the town. But once again, her boyfriend failed to show. But she didn't have any proof of wrong-doing on his part. So she simply acquiesced to his request for the time being.

"Winston, where are you going?"

"I'm off to collect an ancient device known to... Rather, I have an appointment with a tooth physician."

"When you get back, I'd really like to have a discussion with you about our dates," said Cecilia.

"Dates? Cecilia, my dear, you know I'm allergic to Fig Newtons," said Winston. "Now darling, if this Dave fellow contacts you, you must ring me immediately."

And with that, the vile, despicable, evil, narcissistic, slightly waify Winston Wallingford left Cecilia's room.

"Fig Newtons?" Cecilia said to herself, bouncing lightly on her mattress, in an excessively awesome manner. You know, when they playfully bounce up and down while wearing totally sexy light blue retro dresses, pondering deep thoughts? Ok,

119

maybe I'm the only one who finds that completely sexy.

Cecilia placed her hand on her chin, tapping her finger gently against her lips. "Fig Newtons." Cecilia couldn't figure out what it was about the Nabisco cookie that was so puzzling. Why had Winston mentioned cookies? Sookie? Snooki? Nookie? Snooker? Was Winston really interested in her, or was he just using her to snooker Dave's attempts to thwart the destruction of the planet? That would be ludicrous, Cecilia thought, as that would mean Dave was indeed the rumored lost member of Milli Vanilli, and Winston...

Cecilia began to ponder all that had happened to her in the past hour: The dance, Winston, Dave, beating the crap out of Becky, Dave's spy manual, Winston's unusual expression after she told him about Dave, the broken window, and... Wait a minute... Dave's spy manual? What was that little black book still doing here? Dave must have left it! Now if it only had an address, she could find out where Dave lived. Unfortunately, Cecilia was unable to decipher the code. But one number looked promising.

Quickly Cecilia reached for the phone, remembering just as she had told Dave to dial the all-important nine to get off campus. Then came the ringing. Finally, someone on the other end picked up, but did not say anything.

"Hello! Hello! Is anyone there?"

"TACO SUPER BURRITO!"

"Oh, sorry! I must have the wrong num... Hey, you wouldn't by any chance have a guy name Dave working there, would you?"

"No, no Dave's... we do have Beef Chimichangas, though."

"Beef chimi... No, forget it."

"How did you get this number, lady?"

"My true love, Dave, poor, poor Dave. He fell out the window and left his spy manual behind. It had this number under the heading of 'Grandma.'"

"Has your friend perished?"

"Aren't you a little more than generally concerned for a fast food place?"

"Answer the question! Has the man called Dave been eliminated?"

"I'm not sure I care for your tone of voice! What was it he was saying as he left the room? 'PROTOCOL has been compromised.' Yes, that's it! Then he really is a spy! What did you do with my Dave?" But it was too late, TACO SUPER BURRITO had hung up.

Cecilia stumbled around her room. What did it all mean?

Then, a light tapping was heard from her window, which was unusual since it wasn't really there anymore. Cecilia approached the opening, only to see Dave clutching the side of the building, wanting to get in.

"May I come in?"

"Yes, come on in. Hey! What are you doing out there? Have you just been hanging there all this time?" A wave of joy and dread swept over Cecilia. She was happy to see her true love, but was angry with him for jumping in the first place. She was also worried because of her phone conversation with that nacho place.

"I'm sorry Celestina, I *never* should have gotten you involved in this."

"Hey, you remembered my name, um, at least almost!"

"Of course, Guantanamera. Why wouldn't I?"

"But it's... no, forget it. What did you do?"

"I jumped out the window and landed in... Come to think of it, maybe we should just forget that, you wouldn't believe me if I told you."

"I'd believe quite a lot of things, my dear, dear Dave. I just got off of the phone with that taco place and..."

"TACO SUPER BURRITO! You called them?"

"Yes! They wanted to know if you had been eliminated."

121

"Eliminated? I? Dave? I, Dave, the master super spy for all time, eliminated? If they could be so unlucky. I mean, if I could be so lucky. I mean, if they could have luck I would be unluckily determined to..."

"I think you mean, if they could be so lucky."

"Please don't interrupt, Santana, this is very important. I'm sorry to have to be the one to tell you this, but your boyfriend is a nefarious evil spy, most likely bent on world destruction, or domination. One or the other. Now, where did he say he was going?"

"Something about a tooth physician."

"I could have guessed as much. 'toof beautician' is secret evil-agent code for 'diabolical scheme.' It likely means he's preparing some nefarious plot. Did he give you any means by which to contact him?"

"He gave me his card. Maybe this will help?"

Dave peered down at the device, code name 'calling card.' It had some funny looking characters on it that Dave wasn't able to make out.

"It appears as though this Wigglesnots fellow is also incorporating evil-spy code. If I only had my spy manual I could try to decipher it," said Dave.

Cecilia picked the card back up. "It says, 'WB & WW Inc.,' and there's a pager number under it."

"Hey, I wonder what it stands for?"

"Well, WW is probably Winston Wallingford. Maybe the WB is a relative," said Cecilia. "Perhaps it's his father?"

"Yes, that's probably this toot fizztrician we keep hearing about," said Dave.

"I thought you said that stood for 'diabolical scheme?' Come to think of it, you said 'toof beautician,' but I think you have an issue with names."

"A diabolical scheme? Where?" Dave began looking under Cecilia's mattress.

122

"Weren't you about to page somebody?"

"People still use pagers?"

"That's what I said!"

"And you, without any kind of super spy training. Your skills are growing by the minute, Shakiranina," said Dave, as Cecilia returned the card to him. "Still, we'll have to devise a strategy to thwart Wartleflutton's nefarious plants. Also his evil plans. Get me the number to TACO SUPER BURRITO!"

"Here it is," said Cecilia, as she handed Dave his spy manual, open to the appropriate page.

"Hey, this is really cool! Where did you get it? I used to have one just like it," said Dave, thumbing through the book.

"Yeah, that's yours. You left it here when you jumped out of the window," answered Cecilia.

"Really? So I can keep it?"

"Sure, why not."

"Thanks. I promise not to ruin it. At least not intentionally. Yeah, I'll probably ruin it." said Dave. He then started to dial the number of TACO SUPER BURRITO, using the secret access code nine. This time, Dave would incorporate evil super agent lingo into the conversation. "I'd like a Beef Chimichanga hold the guacamole! Repeat, hold the guacamole!"

"What's your number agent?"

"Today's Date is the thirteenth, repeat, today's date is the thirteenth!"

"Winston, is that you sir?"

"Winston! Winston you say? Why, I'll kill him! That's right I'll..." Suddenly Dave felt an unusually sharp pain in his shin, as if some force of nature had struck him in the form of a kick.

Then Dave realized it was just Cecilia, trying to get his attention. "Oh yeah. That's right, I'm supposed to be Wins... I mean... Yes, this is Winston!"

The super agent of evil at the other end gave his report to the 'Winston' impersonator of great skill/super agent of death,

123

Dave. "I think we could be in trouble, sir! Dave knows we have overtaken his base."

"The base? Overtaken?"

"You know sir, I tried to tell you what would happen if we didn't change the phone number of Dave's headquarters. You can't just take over the enemy's HQ and expect them not to know it. Once we started using Dave's base for our own purposes of evil and destruction, we should have changed the phone number. Now, Dave knows."

"Knows what?"

"That we, the secret forces of bad guys, have taken over Dave's 'Grandma.'"

"Gram Gram? What's all this about my grandma?"

"You know, PROTOCOL's secret codename, 'grandma.' It's the term all of the good guy PROTOCOL agents use to secretly talk about their headquarters."

"Well why didn't you just say that in the first place? All this time I've actually been looking for my grandma and I should have been trying to contact PROTOCOL? Unbelievable."

Dave turned his attention to Cecilia. "You know, they should really rewrite this super spy manual so it's a bit easier to understand. I mean, what if I really had to contact my grandmother? And what's all this about swamps and TACO SUPER BURRITO? I stopped there earlier and all they had on the menu were cookies."

Cecilia gasped. "Like Fig Newtons?" she asked.

"Do they have fruit in the middle?"

"Yes, it's a fig paste. Winston's allergic, so he only eats apple or blueberry."

"All of this talk of food is making me hungry. Do you want to go get something to eat?" Asked Dave.

"What's that, sir?" The agent on the other phone thought Dave was speaking to him.

"I'd love to," Cecilia responded.

"Oh, this guy wants to come now too, should we invite him?" asked Dave, putting his hand over the receiver so as not to make the same mistake twice.

"Does he have to come?" Cecilia wanted to go out on one date that did not involve moose antlers and multiple suitors.

"Ok, I just felt bad because he heard me ask you," said Dave, although at that point he had taken his hand off the receiver, and the agent at the other end once again thought the statement was addressed to him.

"Ask me what sir?" The agent was beginning to get suspicious of the conversation, as if the man on the other end was not Winston at all, but an evil, yet good (because they already were the bad guys) 'Winston Impersonator.'

"What's that agent? You dare mock the great and powerful Winifred?"

"Sorry sir. Wait, do you mean Winston?"

"Yes, that one."

"Well, you better not let your father hear you talk like that. I think he's the only guy allowed to be called 'great and powerful.' By the way, does our insurance policy cover evil agent/Jawa motor vehicle accidents?"

"Why do you ask?"

"Some guy from the Imperial Stormtrooper Barracks on Tatooine just called and said one of our agents smashed into a Jawa sandcrawler, then left without providing any insurance."

"Well, who was it?"

"I honestly don't know sir. He said something about Little Richard and then hung up. It could have been an agent of good."

Dave began rubbing his chin, like Sherlock Holmes. "Well, this is a mystery. You know, I just ran into some stormtroopers. Ironically enough, I too smashed into a Jawa sandcrawler today... This is just bizarre. Two agent accidents involving sandcrawlers on the same day? What are the odds?"

"Considering Tatooine is a fictional planet from the *Star Wars* universe and the story happened a long time ago in a galaxy far, far away, I'd say the odds have to be at least 2 to 1."

"Yes, like a two-for-one special," said Dave. "Are we having any of those this month?"

"At TACO SUPER BURRITO?"

"Well, yeah, why else would I be calling?" Dave turned his attention back to Cecilia. "You know, we might want to try something other than Tex/Mex. I don't think these guys know what they are doing. They're also saying they won't honor our two-for-one coupon."

"Aren't those the bad guys you're talking to?"

"Right! Well done, Santa Medulla Oblongata," said Dave, before addressing the bad guy agent, once again. "So, my girlfriend says if you don't honor our two-for-one coupon we're going to skip dinner and just get dessert."

"I'm sorry sir, was that dessert or desert?"

"Desert? As in the Sahara? Is that where the evil base of Wullerton Wendelfrath is located? That's in Egypt, right?"

"You know, that reminds me sir, our evil band of vegans also just called, and it seems Dave trapped them in some high viscosity liquid."

"Hey, I know Dave!"

"That's right sir, he's your archenemy. What'll we do?"

"Dave, that great spy that he is, he will probably defeat each and every last one of us. We better turn ourselves in immediately to PROTOCOL's secondary headquarters in Washington D.C. Maybe we can plea bargain. Now, here is the address... Listen now man! Are you copying this all down?"

"Yes sir, we turn ourselves in at the backup headquarters in Washington. Wait a second. If you have headquarters, wouldn't a backup location be called something other than 'backup headquarters?' That's highly irregular," said Winston's evil TACO SUPER BURRITO henchman/cookie distributor.

"We've had this extensive conversation and the only thing you find highly irregular is that PROTOCOL calls its backup facility 'backup headquarters?' What about the band of vegans trapped in meat sauce? What about Ponytail Westerosi pants Qartheen gown dude?" Dave was incensed.

"Wait a minute, we didn't mention anything about Ponytail Westerosi pants Qartheen gown dude. All I wrote was that we were going to turn ourselves in at the backup headquarters in Washington. How did you know that Ponytail Westerosi pants Qartheen gown dude was terminated?" asked the evil agent.

"Washington D.C. man! Do you have Fig Newtons in your ears? How you ever got the phone job at Wingnut-Moonbat's evil agency, I'll never know."

The voice on the other line trembled as Dave chastised him. "Sorry sir. We've all been under standing orders to place Fig Newtons in our ears. I'll remove them immediately," said the phone operator.

"My apologies," said Dave. "I was unaware that Wibbingfrung made you guys do that. That explains quite a bit." Cecilia was about to strike Dave in the shins again when the super spy sufficiently recovered on his own. "I mean, I, ah... Winston... do hereby decree that evil agents no longer have to put Fig Newtons in their ears. Now, can we continue?"

"Yes sir, I'm ready for the rest of the information."

And with that, Dave single handedly used his secret good spy trickery lingo to fool the bad guys into surrendering. Dave hung up the phone, certain that the enemy agents were on their way to jail.

But his task was far from over. After all, Winston and his father, whomever he may be, were still out there, somewhere, waiting to take over the rest of the world, and only Dave stood in their way. Cecilia was getting anxious, listening to the conversation between Dave and the bad guys. She couldn't stand the thought of losing Dave, once again. She needed to stay with him.

"Winston? Is he in the Sahara? Maybe Egypt? Oh Dave, take me with you! Between the two of us, we can stop him!"

"I've involved you too much already my dear, I'm afraid you'll have to be eliminated. You know, we super agents have a code to uphold. It's the whole secret spy stuff and all that."

"Eliminated? Doesn't that mean you'll have to kill me?" Cecilia fell to the bed, her blue dress lifting slightly into the air before settling. She looked up at Dave, holding her hand over her heart.

"Um." Dave paused for a moment or three. He thought to himself. Cecilia started gently bouncing on the bed again. "Let's skip the 'eliminate' part. You can come with me. But promise me you'll take this blue dress wherever we go."

Deep in his mind though, Dave knew he was betraying every super spy code for which he had ever taken an oath. But, he wasn't thinking with his head. No, instead he was thinking with perhaps his right earlobe, one or both pinky toes, his stomach (which was barely satiated after the fruit roll-up), and maybe something else.

"You know, I could probably draft some new secret-spy legislation that waves the elimination procedure if the intended target is wearing a blue dress. That seems fair, right?"

"Um Dave, shouldn't we be going?" Cecilia, with her awesome J. Lo circa-2002 booty in tow, was ready to depart.

"What? Go where?" Dave was still watching Cecilia gently bounce up and down on the mattress. So that makes at least two hombres who find girls gently bouncing up and down on mattresses to be excessively awesome.

"To go catch Winston and stop the forces of evil?"

"Yeah, let's do this thing!" Dave was about to jump on Cecilia when he suddenly realized that when Cecilia said 'stop the forces of evil,' she didn't mean 'jump on me.' Slightly distraught, Dave prepared a more appropriate retort. "Fine, I guess we can do that, too."

"Wait, were you just about to..."

"Of course, not, Se, Sa, So, Sa Sa... I... merely... was... um... Exactly. So, we should probably get going," said Dave.

"Dave, I only said that because we could probably do that later. I just thought we might want to save the world first."

"Right you are," said Dave. "Save the world." Dave began whistling. "Ok. Save the world. Right. How, how, how do I do that, again?"

"We call Winston?"

"That guy again." Dave knew now that Winston was the bad guy that he should have intercepted at that gin joint. Winston had set in motion the diabolical plan whereby Dave met Cecilia. Actually, that turned out to be awesome for Dave, but the concept was diabolical, as it would force Dave out into the open. It also put Cecilia at risk, which heightened the diabolicability factor by at least five. So it was a factor-five diabolical plan, but also slightly awesome. In addition, Winston had infiltrated and destroyed Dave's base, so that was kind of bad. He had also taken Dave's 'Gram Gram.' Now it was going to be Dave's turn. With the aid of Cecilia, he could bring down the whole operation: Winston, his dad, some Nazis, the evil flower girls, a few ducks, animal crackers, and all of those damn coffee stir things that had foiled Dave in the past.

"I could, of course, just page him," said Cecilia.

"Who?"

"Winston. Winston Wallingford. The bad guy."

"Right." It was time to set their plan in motion. It was time to page someone...

129

10 The Strange Man from Beyond the Gimpus

They met up with the Styrofoam cup in the shadow of the Theban Necropolis, near modern-day Luxor. The ancient burial ground of the Pharaohs dominated the snowy landscape. But a sightseeing tour was not on the agenda for Flabius Flaximus. He had to deal with Weemus's evil henchman.

The cup rode with a partner. Biffus and Flabius began to address the little evil white being, but to no avail, as the cup refused to respond.

When he had no luck with the mug, Flabius began to look at his travelling companion, an oddly dressed, shaggy-looking knight. "I see! You must speak for your leader. I suppose you will have to do."

"Leader? Nonsense, gentlemen. This device is simply a beverage repository. If indeed it is your intention to converse, I am the one to address," said the peculiar-looking man.

Flabius looked around himself, puzzled. "A dress? I see no women."

"No, address."

Flabius again gave the second henchman an odd look. "Yes, I believe we covered that already. There are no dresses, or women in the immediate vicinity," said Flabius, before glancing at his comrade, Biffus. "What's with this guy?"

"No! If you wish to converse, I am the one with whom you must speak. This goblet of alabaster has mislaid his voice."

"Do you need any help finding it?" said the ever-concerned Emperor of everywhere.

"Yeah, we're really good at finding things," added Biffus

Palookus. "One time, the king forgot his spandex bike shorts before the start of the Tour de France, and then we all had..."

"Please, my trusted never-talk-about-my-favorite-spandex-bike-shorts squire, we have more important things to deal with right now." The Emperor would get to the bottom of the mystery surrounding the cup's missing voice if it was the last thing he ever did.

"Gentlemen, I believe we have more pressing matters," said the man holding the cup, clearly growing impatient.

"Well then, if it's that important, I guess we should talk to the cup instead of you after all," said Flabius. "Now, my little white acquaintance, perhaps you can use another form of communication to converse?"

"I'll jolly well encase myself in carbonite at her Majesty's pleasure before I let you strategize with a bloody cup. You're off your trolley, you," said the weirdo.

Flabius had heard enough of the gibberish. "You know Mr. Styrofoam, you should really get your servant to behave. He tends to interrupt. It's just a suggestion though."

The man holding the cup became increasingly irate. "Enough of this nonsense. Look here, it's only a cup. It can't talk, it can't communicate; it doesn't even bloody well hold any liquid of late. It will, on occasion, enjoy a nice steak and potato dinner, but otherwise, I am in command!"

"Don't you mean Weemus Bobeemus is in command?"

"Precisely," said the mystery cup-wielding man, after a long pause. "In all honesty, should you speak with Weemus Bobeemus, I would find myself in your debt if you were to refrain from discussing our little conversation about my being in command. Yes? Smashing. On to business, then?"

"And why should we do anything to help you, Mr. sidekick-of-a-Styrofoam-cup man?" Flabius wasn't averse to doling out a little charity, but he just wanted a little explaino, amigo. Speaking of Dole Whips, I'm wondering right now if the Dole

131

Whip at the ice cream store down the street is as good as the stuff in Adventureland in Walt Disney World. That stuff is good. You can also get it at that Polynesian hotel place, where they have this pretty cool-looking pool with a volcano slide. It doesn't really erupt, but it looks like it could. I say cool-looking because I've never actually swam in the pool, only looked at it. Speaking of awesome, I hear that the turkey leg is also pretty cool. Again never had it, so I can only 'hear' rather than 'confirm.' I can confirm, however, that Pirates of the Caribbean is still a sweet ride, if a bit scary.

And speaking of volcanoes, the name Krakatoa is still wicked sweet. That was this really big volcanic eruption that happened in 1883... look it up. It wasn't as big as this other one from 1815 called Tambora, which was even bigger, but Tambora clearly does not sound as awesome as Krakatoa, even if Krakatoa just might be a spelling error from the first reports of the volcanic eruption in 1883. How do you make a spelling error on a telegraph anyway? Dot-Dot-Dot-Dash instead of Dot-Dot-Dash-Dash? How would you then tell the guy at the other end of the telegraph that you screwed up and needed to start over?

Boy, the telegraph must have been awesome.

"But, I am second-in-command," continued the Styrofoam cup-wielder. Or would that be welder? Probably not. "And since Weemus is not here at the present time, I do the talking for him. The cup is just a cup. Now, if the issue is settled, we have business to attend to. The item, do you have it?"

Flabius looked over the exasperated young man wearing the strange clothing. Apparently, he would be doing the talking, as the Styrofoam cup wished to maintain his silence. 'Perhaps,' Flabius thought, 'the cup must be a Buddhist, or a Pastafarian. They never speak.' But there were more pressing matters that needed his attention. Flabius had to get back to the case of the speckled band.

Just then, Biffus spoke up. "No sire, not the case of the speckled band, that was Sherlock Holmes. We need to solve the case of the evil super dinnerware set of utensils."

"Oh yes. We solved that speckled thing for Holmes last week! Now, where was I?" said Flabius, returning his attention to the henchman. "You asked for an item, strange man carrying the Assassin Styrofoam Cup of Construction. The item you are looking for, is it the 'Great Fork that has Been Known to Wreak Havoc on Entire Countries?"

"Jolly good. Let me peruse this catalogue for a moment." The man peered down at the one item that was written on a small piece of paper titled 'Things to Get From Flabius.' Sure enough, the item mentioned was the same article that Flabius held in his hand. "Look here, did you say the 'Great Fork that has Been Known to Wreak Havoc on Entire Countries?'"

"I think so."

"Well then, yes, that will be all."

"Hey wait, what about the next item? Where do we go?" Biffus was anxious to get moving as he had not relieved himself and was, at present, hopping and running in place.

"Excellent question. Who shall we ask?" Yes, this man with the cup was a shrewd dealer.

"Stand still my trusted private dancer, we'll stop at a nearby restaurant," said Flabius.

"TACO SUPER BURRITO?"

"Oh, you've been there?" asked Flabius.

"Awesome! I can get some Fig Newtons," said Biffus.

He then returned his attention to the pair of villains, both the cup and the guy. In case you haven't picked up on it, the cup is also a bad guy. I probably should have said the bad guy cup and the bad guy cup-holder dude, that would have made more sense. "You there man! Did the evil wizard, Weemus Bobeemus, give you any other piece of paper? Or perhaps he wrote something on the back of that one. He can be a tricky man, you know."

"Of all the absurdities," said the henchman. "But if you insist, I'll proceed. I must tell you, however, that the concept of utilizing both sides of a ledger for the purpose of inscribing directives is quite the foreign concept."

Nonetheless, the man complied. Using virtually all of his strength, the henchman successfully flipped over the parchment, revealing additional instructions. The evil Weemus had written down 'Things to tell Flabius once the Fork That Has Been Known to Wreak Havoc on Entire Countries has been retrieved.' And underneath this was written 'Go to the Ancient Tower of People Who Were Not Particularly Nice to retrieve the Plastic Butter Knife of Wonder.'

The three men and the cup stared in amazement at Weemus's cleverly hidden message. A few days later, suffering from severe dehydration and a bit of sunburn after their Coppertone ran out, the adventurers rose, having sufficiently pondered their amazement at the hidden message. The group then visited a nearby alchemist to restock on sunscreen, dined and danced at a Spanish Discoteca, before entering a regional World Series of Poker tournament. After the cup swept through to the national championship to earn the first of a record 56 WSOP bracelets, the quartet entered several Midwest singing competitions, before being summarily discharged for missing a bass voice.

"I thought the cup was supposed to sing bass," said Biffus, who mostly sang countertenor or falsetto during the group's performances.

"He was," said Flabius, the owner of a rich baritone voice often likened to Jim Morrison or Frank Sinatra, depending on the source material.

"Gentlemen, I am entirely insulted at the accusation that I had anything to do with this failure," said the henchman, who somehow possessed the most elegant tenor voice since Jussi

Björling.

"Look, we all know your pipes are quality. Maybe not Enrico Caruso quality, but quality, nonetheless. Still, if we can't find your friend's voice by the time we arrive in L.A. for the *Celebrity VoiceFactorIdol-X-Men* tryouts, we're going to get booed off the stage," said Flabius. "Wait, that reminds me of something... Something about the cup and his voice..."

"Yes sire, I tried mentioning it back in Skokie," said Biffus. "We were going to search for the cup's voice."

"Ah yes, and also something about saving the world from imminent destruction," said Flabius.

"I feel it prudent to point out that I, in fact, am not trying to save the world... at least in the traditional sense... but am in fact aiding an effort by my fath... ahem... assisting in a plot of global conquest," said the henchman.

"Look, we already told you we're not doing *Dancing with the Stars*," said Flabius. "Once you make that leap you're signaling your career is officially over."

"Sire, I believe he was talking about the plot by Weemus Bobeemus to conquer the known universe. And Disney World. Although I'm still confused why Disney World doesn't count as part of the known universe," said Biffus.

"I believe it's because nobody knows about it yet. Hey look, we're back in Egypt," said Flabius. Apparently they were back in Egypt. "Back to work then, I suppose."

The men then bowed their heads at each other, riding off in separate directions, when Flabius shouted, "We shall see you again. You haven't seen the last of us!"

"Of course he hasn't seen the last of us, sire, we're supposed to give him the butter knife after we rescue it from the Ancient Tower of..."

"Yes I know, my trusted redundant man, but we're obligated, as the good guys, to deliver histrionic statements that attest to our prodigious might and exceptional bravery," said Flabius.

"I see," said Biffus, who really didn't see. "Sire, what does histrionic mean?"

"Theatrical, dramatic, unrestrained..."

"Like, exaggerated, over-the-top, melodramatic?"

"Exactly."

Biffus and Flabius rode on a bit further, away from the Theban ruins. "Your grace, aren't we going the wrong direction?"

"Going in the wrong... fudge. I mean applesauce. I mean, of course, I was just testing you on the finer points of navigation, my trusted navigational device that is similar to a compass." And so the two men turned around, where they did indeed meet up with the messenger from Weemus.

"Sire, you were correct!" exclaimed Biffus.

"Yes, thank you, trusted prognosticator. You know, that skill would have been slightly more helpful when we were losing half of the Rambo Brightus treasury to that cup back in the poker match."

"It's not my fault sire," said Biffus. "Do you know what a Texas is, or what the proper method is for holding it?"

"Of course not. It won't exist for another 5,000 years."

Flabius and Biffus slowly crossed paths with the cup and his sidekick. The teams gave each other the evil eye for three or four seconds before returning on their respective paths.

"Sire, do you know anything about the 'Ancient Tower of People Who Were Not Particularly Nice?'" asked Biffus.

"Only that it's back in Gimpus Foo Foo. Why did we have to trek all the way to Egypt, again?"

"Something about Elvis and a pink panda, sire."

"Ah yes, and the book cover."

"Pardon, sire?"

"Never you mind, trusted 'legally obligated to have at least one scene of the narrative take place in Egypt since the author used a photo of the pyramids as the cover image for the book' sidekick," said Flabius.

At this point, the legend behind the Ancient Tower of People Who Were Not Particularly Nice was discussed between the two weary travelers, so that it could be decided by the author on what to write about once Biffus and Flabius got to the tower.

The legend of the Ancient Tower of People Who Were Not Particularly Nice

The tower had been abandoned for centuries. No one dared to enter its hallowed Formica and sheet-rock walls. As many a bold adventurer could tell you, the closer you got, the louder it all became.

First came the howls, which were not so bad if you enjoyed that sort of thing. If you were hard of hearing you might not be able to discern the howls from too far away.

Next, however, came the screams and shrieks that could stir Beethoven from his grave. Except, of course, that this story is set in the times before Beethoven, so the screams and shrieks would awaken some other famous earlier composer who was legally deaf. But that wasn't the worst of it.

If you were one of the few brave warriors who could stand the screams and shrieks and still keep moving toward the tower (or just some wackadoo who enjoyed shrieking) the final, horrible sounds that came from the tower would surely finish the job.

The sounds were so awful that not a single adventurer was capable of describing them. The warriors would come back, with the most horrific of horrific expressions, mumbling the most mumbled of mumbled words and making the most unusual of unusual sounds. It was quite obvious that something had gotten to them, something evil, and destroyed their brains so that all they were really good for was to look at and say, "Hey look, he must have really destroyed his brain." Or "Wow, he must have been one of those warriors who went to the Ancient Tower of People Who Were Not Particularly Nice and got his brains fried by some really horrific of horrific sounds that has caused irreparable damage to his aural nervous system and maybe even his cerebrum."

Doctors usually said the warriors were "not talking normally for some reason," or "I don't know what the heck is the matter with this guy because I'm only pretending to be a doctor."

Yes indeed, things were looking up for Flabius, Biffus and the Beaver as they were about to collect the third item on their list which would cause the extermination of all life on the planet as we know it, or rather they knew it, since, once again, their story is set in ancient times. Then Wally came early to pick up the Beaver, who was late for dinner.

"Sorry guys, maybe next time," said the Beaver.

"My liege, it looks as though our friend Weemus Bobeemus may be leading us into another trap," said Biffus.

"They are all traps, my trusted Smarties man. It just so happens that we are stuck dealing with all of them."

"But we certainly can't trust that evil wizard."

"Trust? I wouldn't trust Weemus as far as I could throw him, which is pretty far, I might add."

After this comment the two riders rode on for a while. Biffus looked over at Flabius, slightly confused, as if about to ask a question. Flabius beat him to the punch. "What I meant to say was, I can throw the man far, and so I shouldn't trust him... No? Come to think of it, I could probably throw you pretty far and I trust you, so that doesn't make much sense, either. No, I could say that judging from the distance I have thrown Weemus, I can honestly say I cannot trust the man."

"Your grace? Did you ever actually throw Weemus?"

"No! But what does that have to do with it? Okay, fine.

138

How about this: I can throw Weemus as far as I want, but chances are he'll move when I try to record an accurate measurement. Thus, I cannot trust the man."

Biffus thought about it for a moment. "I don't see why it wouldn't work. But it still doesn't sound quite right."

"Don't you see what this man is doing to us, my trusted complicating servant? I can already tell that this one is going to be impossible to figure out. I guess that's because we can't trust Weemus Bobeemus, even when there is no issue that we are basing this trust on."

"Basing? Is that the right word, there, my liege?"

"Basing? I think so, my trusted thesaurus. Well, what else could I have said?" As Flabius peered over at his companion, he could tell that Biffus was not buying into any of the conversation. "All right, but this is the last time. You can't trust a man who rhymes his last name."

"So you can't trust Peter Parker?"

"No, that's alliteration, not rhyme. You can trust Peter Parker; you can't trust Peter Peeper or Peter Tweeter."

"And who are they, sire?"

"It was an example, my trusted not-up-to-date-in-his-literary-terms friend."

They rode further down the sacred path of the evil lands. The winds began to stir all around them.

Biffus was still confused. "Okay, can we trust Marco Polo?"

"I don't know what kind of a name that is. It's not really a rhyme, because only the last two letters are the same. The stress of each word doesn't really rhyme. It would be like rhyming... let me think of some words... um... rhyming and timing, for instan... no wait... that was a rhyme. Forget that last one. Okay, how about this: rhyming and coordinating. Yes, that's it. The words rhyming and coordinating do not rhyme. Which brings us back to... to... where the heck was I?"

"The digression?"

139

"Yes, the digression. Now what about the digression?" Flabius anxiously awaited his captain's next question with patience and despair.

"Is that digression going to have a great impact on the story, as well, my liege?"

"What a silly little question my trusted little-and-yet-quite-large-as-they-really-go school boy. Of course it will be important. Now we have an idea of what to look out for, you know, in case anyone, or anything, starts howling." Just then a howl was heard in the cool night air. "Why, that's very fine work, my trusted ventriloquist. And what a great range you have in throwing your voice. I could have sworn that it came from over beyond the second ridge which I can't really see because it suddenly got dark."

"That wasn't me, your grace. Someone really did just howl."

"Of course. Once again you have passed my test. It was designed to see just how observant you are. I would say you have been very observant. But not totally, for you failed to realize that it has also gotten dark all of the sudden when I stated such was the case a few moments ago."

"Sorry, sire, I didn't know you wanted..."

"That's just it, you never know! You must practice harder if you are ever to be Emperor some day, my trusted next-guy-to-be-Emperor guy."

"Yes, but isn't your child going to ascend to the throne?"

"You knew about that?"

"Knew about what?"

"Um, who were you talking about?"

"The child that you and Buffy will have once we defeat the evil Weemus Bobeemus and his henchmen. These stories always work out in the same way: you take back your kingdom and marry the girl, then nine months later comes Jr. It's how all of these novels finish."

"J.R. from Dallas? The devil of deviousness himself? Why

140

would he come and visit us after nine months? Is there some strange mystic symbolism to that length of time? If he did show up, do you think I would get to meet T.J. Hooker?"

"Why would J.R. know T.J. Hooker? They're in completely different shows. No sire, nine months is how long it takes for a baby to come along. Jr. is short for junior." Biffus seemed a little cranky to everybody, even though Flabius was the only one there. But, his name was Flabius Flaximus, so he could be referred to as 'everybody.'

"Are you okay my trusted cranky-wanky sidekick? You seem very preoccupied, all of the sudden. A baby you say? Buffy's and mine? Excellent! At first I thought you might have been talking about that little incident I had with... Of course, Buffy. Yes, that's right. Once again you have seen through my deception, trusted gumshoe. We must be getting closer, the fog is starting to roll in."

And like clockwork, the screams and moans in the background started getting louder. The haze was on every side. It was getting eerie.

Of course the two travelers paid no attention to the scary things happening all around them. I can tell you I would have been scared. I don't even think I can write anymore because I am so frightened. Woo. Scary stuff. Okay, I'm good now. I'll attempt to continue the story.

Biffus glanced over at his mighty Emperor. Flabius had a strange look on his face, as if trying to hide something. "Sire, what was it you were just talking about, back there?"

"Buffy, of course."

"Come on, sire, tell the truth, your nose is growing."

"Not my nose, I love my nose!"

"No sire, your nose isn't growing, it's an expression. It means you are lying."

"Once again you have..."

"Yes my liege, seen through your deception? Yes. Anyway,

141

what about this girl?"

"Let me see, how did it go? Oh yes, I remember. I was a preacher and she was a married woman with no husband. Then everyone gave her a big letter and I didn't get one which I thought was totally unfair, and then I..."

"That's a different book, sire."

"Oh. All right, how about this: she was a girl and I was a padre. Then her head spun around and I knew it was over. No? I've got it! She was a... tiger cub, and I was a wolf boy. We thought it could... work... but... This isn't working. I can't concentrate with all these interminable howls."

"Try to concentrate sire. We must fight the sounds. We must fight if we are ever to free the girl and save the kingdom!" Biffus fought the sounds valiantly. He was a true warrior on that day.

Flabius was not really paying any attention to his sidekick, however. He was too busy trying to remember some story of great importance to himself. "No wait, I remember, there was this vile evil woman who seduced me one night while I was sleeping. I'll never forget it as long as I live. I was there, sleeping, and she came in and seduced me. I slept right through it. None of the guards saw anything. It was horrible. I didn't even get to see her. That's the worst part of it. Weemus Bobeemus told me the whole thing."

"Are you sure about this, sire?" asked Biffus. "Weemus could have lied to you."

"He wouldn't be lying about that, would he? I am, after all, quite a 'ladies' man. The whole Emperor thing has nothing to do with it, either."

"Right, my liege." Just then the two warriors heard the loudest scream in the history of the known universe up until that time.

"Quick my trusted eh... eh... eh... put something in your ears!" Fortunately Biffus was able to respond in time as both

142

men plugged their ears with their trusty 'things that plug ears,' forever known after their battle as 'ear plugs.' The screams could still be heard.

Finally, the evil sound that had petrified so many heroes before them came rumbling through the mist. Two beautiful seductresses, nearly perfect in the eyes of both men, with great figures, charming personalities, and cute little ancient outfits that were quite revealing, summoned Flabius and Biffus to take off the ear plugs.

"Resist my friend, we must resist!" said Flabius.

The temptation was great however, and worsened as the women began to speak.

"Do you remember me Flabius? Bethsheebaboobooboo? Does it sound familiar? I remember you! You are such a ladies man, after all."

Flabius peered over at his petrified sidekick. "See, I told you. Ladies man! And you thought Weemus was lying."

"What?" asked Biffus, unable to hear over the screams, moans, and the mysterious temptresses.

"Come again?" asked Flabius, also unable to hear over the screams, moans, and the mysterious temptresses.

"Huh?"

"What?"

"What are you saying?"

"I can't hear you," said Flabius. "Can you speak louder?"

"What?"

This went on for two or three more pages, but I thought it best to shorten the conversation. Biffus was drawn to the second seductress. She had his complete attention. She spoke as well, but only to Biffus. Actually, it was more of a horse sound than talking. To Biffus, the second woman looked exactly like his first filly, a pretty pony by the name of Wendy.

Flabius and his sidekick gazed at the enchantresses as if brainwashed. The two glanced at each other, with happy faces.

143

And then things went from bad to worse when the whole fight became a musical...

Musical fight at the Ancient Tower of People Who Were Not Particularly Nice

Bethsheebaboobooboo took the first verse.

FLABIUS! CAN YOU HERE ME?
MY LOVE FOR YOU IS LIKE A DERBY
I WANT TO BE YOUR EVERYTHINGY
I NEED TO FLOAT ON YOUR DINGHY

(Next, a whole group of women dressed in green tights and men in pink tutus came dancing through the mist, singing the chorus.)

ONE... SINGULAR SENSATION! EVERY LITTLE MOVE SHE...

Just then, a man dressed in a black leotard came from out of nowhere. "No! That's the wrong musical. Try again! From the top, please! Can we get the playback?"

Flabius could barely hold out. "Excuse me? Yes, I just wanted to say that I am pretty sure that 'everythingy' is not a word. Well, it isn't a real word anyway. I just felt it necessary to add that point at this juncture."

The director seemed to take personal offense. "Do you know anything that rhymes with 'Dinghy'?"

"Wait, did you say 'dinghy' or 'dingy?' Because if it's 'dingy,' you could have used binge-ee, fringe-ee, or hinge-ee, whereas, if it's 'dinghy', you could go with bing-ee, bring-ee, wing-ee." Flabius was a master lyricist, as well as all-powerful Emperor.

"Who are you to judge me? Can you not see the artistic genius that stands before you?"

144

"Where is this genius? Is he evil, like you and your chorus?"

"That's right. CHORUS!"

(The singers came back, this time, in proper step, singing the proper words...)

FLABIUS
FLAXIMUS
HE'S A MAN!
THE MAN WITH THE GIGUS TOUCH!
A TIGER'S CRUTCH!

Biffus was the one to interrupt the proceedings this time. "My liege? I could be wrong, but I think I've heard this all before. I just had this sudden, uncontrollable urge for a martini... shaken, not stirred. We've got to get out of here before we become inebriated."

"You are right my trusted state-the-obvious colleague. But we must not leave, even if it means we will get sloshed. Of course that might take several hours in my case. Regardless, if we cannot get past this strange musical troupe, we could be in for a great deal of difficulty. The earplugs aren't holding up to the onslaught of horrible music. Another bad lyric, and we could be done for..."

(Then, after a quick dance number in which the women in the green tights carried off the men in the pink tutus, Bethsheebaboobooboo came from out of the woodwork to continue with the next verse...)

I AM SINGING IN THE MIST
AMIDST THIS BAD PLOT TWIST
MY BLOUSE IS SOAKING WET
AND NOW YOU CAN SEE MY—

"NOOOO!!!!!!!!!!!!!!" Flabius could take no more, and began

to take off his earplugs when a tiny Styrofoam cup abruptly tackled him. They looked at each other, and Flabius understood. The cup no longer wanted to be on the side of evil.

The shot knocked Flabius out of his trance.

As he turned to see the women who had been courting him as well as courting Biffus Palookus, Flabius was shocked to discover they were actually evil super witches, who on top of being not particularly nice, were not particularly a pleasure to look at.

The backup dancers and the director were even more horrific. Biffus was still in the trance, however, but before Flabius could react, the cup had already taken the initiative. He once again hurled himself through the air to knock Biffus to the ground and to his senses, all at the same time.

But then, right before Flabius and Biffus could turn to defeat their enemies, a little evil Dixie cup appeared, putting the Styrofoam cup into a trance, and the Styrofoam cup without any 'things to plug his ears with!' Flabius knew he had only one chance, and he took it. Once again, the 'Great Leap' was in full effect...

"Go for it, my liege!"

The evil witches shrieked in agony. They were helpless to prevent the final curtain from falling on their quickly plummeting plan. Flabius partially succeeded. It wasn't a full 'leap,' but it was enough to destroy the evil Dixie cup and bring the Styrofoam cup back to his senses.

Angered by the deception, the Styrofoam cup took matters into his own little Styrofoam hands once again, and annihilated the witches and backup dancers, to the shock of Flabius and Biffus, who were stunned by the fact that he could take matters into his own hands without actually having any appendages.

They were also kind of upset that he killed the witches, since the side of good only kills and maims as a last resort, or if it helps fill a gaping plot hole, like in *Man of Steel* when

Superman, who never kills, decides to whack General Zod. I mean, that was pretty stupid. What if they wanted to bring General Zod back for a sequel? You could have just sent him back to the phantom zone, which is what I thought Jor-El and Lois Lane were scheming at, anyway. That's why I liked *Smallville* so much better than *Man of Steel*. While not "great TV," like say, *Game of Thrones* or *Avatar: the Last Airbender*, it was pretty darn good TV, minus the eight-year yearning/ heartache thing between Lana and Clark, or that Jor-El spent virtually the entire time putting Clark through inexplicably complicated trials. He also came off as a total tool.

But Lois Lane was awesome in the show, and Lex was pretty sweet, and for that matter the guy who played Zod was also more awesome than the guy from *Man of Steel*, even if he did speak in utter fatuities. BTW, *Avatar* really was a kick-ass show; I'm not just saying that.

Then, after it was all over, the cup explained that he only sent the witches and the backup dancers into another super evil dimension, where they would be forced to participate in a never-ending, atrociously horrific musical, making them pay for their past atrocities. Of course, in some respects that sounded worse than just exterminating the witches and dancers, thereby putting them out of their misery. But after that, the cup was on his way, and sequels were still there for the making.

"It's amazing how he gets around that well, without a horse." Biffus was always the astute observer.

"Yes, my trusted das wunderkind," said Flabius. "It's also amazing how he told that story so well, with out actually having any ability to speak."

"Why do you think he turned to evil in the first place?"

"Perhaps his true love is also a prisoner of the evil Weemus Bobeemus. I should have said something back there when we met with that henchman before," said Flabius. "We shall have it out with that strangely dressed man after we retrieve the

'Plastic Butter Knife of Wonder.' Come now, my trusted sidekick, let's get that knife and save the universe."

"Just one more thing, sire. Was that the same witch who seduced you?"

"Yes, I am afraid so, my trusted bringer of bad memories. It's over and done with now, so let's get moving."

"What did you ever see in that evil witch?"

"I actually never saw her, I was sleeping," said Flabius. "Don't you remember me telling you all of this? Really, you must take better notes. So anyway, don't blame me."

"It just doesn't fit sire." Biffus was still confused by the story his master had told him, a story apparently originally relayed through Weemus Bobeemus.

"Okay, I admit it. I have never been able to get anywhere with the ladies."

"So that's what Buffy must have seen in you." Biffus was on to something, now.

"Can it, my trusted jerk-face face. Guy. Stuff. You've done no better," Flabius was quite angry with his helper.

"Have you tried alfalfa sprouts?"

"Let's just forget the whole thing my trusted annoying assistant," said Flabius. "What-not."

"Speaking of forgetting, where did that director fellow go?"

As the two warriors looked around through the mist, they could see a tiny old man dressed in that same black leotard heading for the hills. "There he goes, my liege. Let me take care of this!" Biffus chased after the man, running incredibly fast for someone wearing armor. The director was getting away.

Then Biffus remembered an ancient saying, said to stir even the most frightened-running-away-in-a-black-leotard of directors. Biffus decided to find out if the proverb would succeed. "Cut! Cut! Cut!"

Sure enough, the director heard the shouts of Biffus Palookus, and turned around to face his adversary. "Only the director says cut. Don't you know that? What's the matter with you?" The audacity of Biffus had angered the director.

But Biffus had one more trick up his sleeve. It was a strange looking piece of paper. He handed it to the tiny man, and the old man's face froze in fear. It was... a diploma from the Franklin K. Wabash School of Directing.

"I've been deceived! I've been beaten. No!"

"I'll tell you what, Mr. Leotard, if you tell us how to get into the Ancient Tower of People Who Were Not Particularly Nice, we might just let you go."

"I'll tell you. You go over to that tower over there..." The old man pointed off toward a little Lego structure about the size of the Empire State Building. "You go over there, and you... you..."

"Tell us, or you will never direct another musical as long as you live," demanded Biffus.

"You walk in. There, I said it! Why? Why must I be so quick to give in to the forces of good?" The director began sobbing at a highly uncontrollable rate.

"You walk in? That's ingenious. I must relay this to the Emperor. All right, Mr. Leotard, you may go on your way. But remember, if I ever catch you using musicals for the forces of evil, I'll be back to... Well, you know what I will be forced to do," said Biffus. "Now get going."

"But, you don't know how hard it is for a guy in a black leotard to get a good directing job these days. I needed the money. How else can I afford to pay for my very expensive clothing habit?" The director apparently had a very expensive clothing habit, by ancient standards, anyway.

"You know, Mr. Leotard, they have places where you can go for help," said Biffus Palookus, in a most understanding tone. "Such as Underwear Shopaholics Anonymous, or the Unicycling Society of Ancient-landia. Ok, be seeing you."

The old man was on his way. Biffus returned to Flabius

149

with the information. "Well, sire, it's as we thought. You walk in. How dastardly."

"Come on my trusted fooler-of-old-men-with-forged-documents Captain, let's get this over with."

And with that, the two men entered the ancient tower, which actually turned out to be a lot nicer than most people thought. It had a really nice bathroom for Biffus Palookus, with nice towels and even those little tiny shampoo bottles.

However, they did not have time to stay and relax. The travelers collected the knife and were on their way. As they went back outside, the sun was out, and things were starting to turn around.

Then they realized that they simply had walked out the back door and things were not really turned around, but they were looking brighter.

No, maybe it was just that they had awoken early by accident. It might be that.

Then again, it could just be that Biffus and Flabius were from Rambo Brightus, the capital city which had a reputation for the night life, with car hops, malt shops, brothels, beauty salons and casinos, while still maintaining a disturbing lack of gin joints. Biffus and Flabius may have had an unusual sense of what was bright. I don't think that it is any coincidence that they are from the "dark ages," either.

11 Borpos of the Nether Regions

Where did he come from? The hugest, most powerful, frightening, macabre, unsightly, insightful, obsequious, omniscient, ossified, overwrought, quixotic, reflective, useless, oozy, woozy, wiggly, psychotic, redundant, quixotic evil being in the universe had to have a mother at one point.

Well, he did.

Her name has been lost to the eons of time, but I bet it was something along the lines of Frigga Frick-Frodenburg Lugalbanda, from Ulysses, Pagliacci, on the planet Chinchilla. She was always proud of her boy, even when Borpos didn't win the Olympic gold medal in 1896, or the Pulitzer Prize in 1932, or the Nobel Prize in 1945, or the third grade spelling bee in 1984. The fact that none of these events took place on the planet Chinchilla, but occurred instead on a bluish, water-covered rock in the middle of a star system galaxies away may have had something to do with his repeated failures. The planet Chinchilla, obviously, was covered in billions, or possibly trillions of crepuscular rodent turds. As you can imagine, air fresheners were at a premium on Chinchilla. But through it all, Frigga Frick-Frodenburg Lugalbanda remained a devoted mother.

It was this devoted maternal affection that provided Borpos a spectacular upbringing. The gods were envious of him, mostly because his mom was so great. In all honesty, that was the only reason that they were envious of him. After all, he lived on a planet covered in rodent droppings. The gods were probably pretty stupid to envy the guy at all. Either that, or his mom must have been really awesome. Probably both.

Still, Borpos also had some good points. He could... and he was also really... and then there was the time... Okay, forget that. He was pretty much all-bad. But which one was it? Pretty much all-bad or completely all-bad? Can someone actually be 'pretty much' all-bad? Ode to a cornballer, fro and to, overly blue, what welcomes glue and is made from...

So Borpos started hating the color blue. And also Earth.

Then Borpos started killing planets. He started with small ones, roughly the size of Pluto, but that was before he found out that Pluto had been plutoed. Which totally blows, for the record. I mean, come on! How can they take away Pluto from being a planet? Do they want to kill of Mickey's dog while they're at it, or charge volunteer firefighters extra for their license plates? I got a good one: Let's also cancel the tax breaks for organ donors. They don't deserve any special credit. Borpos eventually moved on to Mars-sized space nuggets. Mind you, I mean Mars bars, not Mars the planet, because that would be totally ridiculous. Then Borpos developed the ability to annihilate Mars-sized planets (as in Mars the planet), and Earth-sized space nuggets (as in Earth the planet, not the dirt stuff that can be found on the planet).

Borpos had developed powers greater than Spider-Man, Thor, Hulk, Avatar and Manimal combined. He was almost as strong as Superman. Well, he was way stronger than *Man of Steel* Superman, but not quite as strong as *Smallville* Superman, since he couldn't throw the planet Apokolips out of the solar system like Tom Welling does in the series finale. Although he could probably have either eaten or blown up Apokolips if he wanted to, just not heave it like a shot put. But he was definitely more powerful than Manimal. And also probably Simon MacCorkindale.

It was at this juncture that Borpos journeyed to our solar system for the first time.

He came forth from the Nether Regions of deepest space around the same time that Glork of the Clan Tog was learning how to use fire on our planet. He had journeyed from the furthest of the far nether-regions. He hadn't spoken to his mother in eons. But it was time to come back to his place of origins. When he couldn't find his place of origins, he went to Earth instead.

It was 1928, and it was a roaring age. Utterly malevolent and looking like the love child of Ricky Spanish and Richie Incognito, Borpos strolled down the street, the center of nobody's attention. The gangs in Chicago were rough at that time. Everyone knew who to look out for, though: It was this new hepcat, Borpos. Yes, Borpos was all that and more. He was also just Borpos, which means I lied before, sorry.

When he arrived on Earth, Borpos knew that his super powers would be of great use, so that he could win some popularity contests. Unfortunately, Earth was one of the few planets that didn't belong to the intergalactic confederation of popularity contests league, as opposed to planets found in the Grumpleot, Grembleo, Gregameem and Blurnu galaxies.

When news of this hit the front page, and then Borpos, as he was still walking in the center of the street, it made him angry. He used his planet-killing powers to destroy the stack of papers that had collided with him. When he caused all of the city's manhole covers to blow as well, people took notice of the dude who could blow stuff up with his mind, like Criss Angel on Blue Sky, Soma, the Spice Melange and Substance D all at the same time and followed by a Pan-Galactic Gargle Blaster chaser.

Soon a showdown was in the works. Crime boss Al Capone wouldn't stand for this new guy invading his turf. He set up a meeting with Borpos at his headquarters in the Lexington Hotel. The meeting did not go well for Capone. First, Borpos shot a glance at Mr. Capone that gave him a scar down one side of his cheek. Then he ate the entire contents of Capone's secret vault, guaranteeing Geraldo Rivera's nationally televised humiliation 58 years later.

Victory secure, Borpos left town and headed toward the real place to be: Hollywood. Tinseltown was calling, "BORPOS! BORPOS! BORPOS!"

Now Borpos could confront his greatest adversary: Glork of the Clan Tog. Glork was the one and only challenger that the planet Earth could offer up against the mighty Borpos.

Borpos made his way out to the great cave of Glork. All of the townspeople came to witness the battle. It was set to be a shootout at high noon. Borpos called to Glork. Glork would not come. Borpos called again, but still no Glork.

And then Borpos called for any representative of the Clan Tog that could explain the situation. No member of the Clan Tog would show himself or herself.

And so Borpos did the unthinkable: he entered the cave. The television cameras followed, which was kind of unusual, considering hardly anybody owned a TV in 1928, except a few folks in Schenectady watching pink fuzzy snow on GE's WRGB. Inside, Borpos discovered the problem: no Glork. In fact, the entire Tog Clan seemed to have disappeared.

Borpos called for a scientific team of experts standing nearby to carbon-date the cave. It turned out that the Clan had been dead for thousands of years. So much for the great threat to Borpos.

Borpos was hailed throughout the world as the conquering hero of everyone. He was Borpos, the Planet-Killing-Glork-Defeating-Planet-Conquering-Hepcat-Dancing-Planet-Saving-Savior with a Pan-Galactic Gargle Blaster chaser.

One of the members of the scientific team standing by was a young and hastily attired Judy Darwinkly. The 8th grader was conducting a school project. But from the moment she saw Borpos, she knew that someday they would be together. And so she followed Borpos around town that night, as he worked

154

his way from party to party, each in his honor. It was the era of prohibition, so naturally everybody was getting tanked.

And Borpos was the man of the hour, with one exception. There was one party that wasn't being held for Borpos. It was a cast party for a movie that had just finished shooting.

Imagine, a movie without Borpos! It was okay when movies didn't have sound and Borpos had not yet appeared on the scene, but this was entirely different. Borpos was very angry. But he decided to use his powers for other things that night. He wouldn't destroy the infidels just yet. Instead, he would infiltrate the party, being held at the underground pub with the funny-sounding name. Once there, he would put his super-suave Rico Suave skills to good use.

Borpos walked in, and all eyes turned his way. Little Judy followed the action from across the street. She was sure that her mother was furious with her, considering she didn't punch in at nine o'clock, her bedtime. So be it. Judy was going to watch her beloved hero clean up these foolish humans that were not paying the proper tribute to Borpos.

As he approached the bar area, Borpos noticed a lovely young lady enjoying all the attention. Borpos knew what to do. He put his bootsies into motion and starting working it. She was like pudding in his hands, they way she yelled "Get away from me," at the top of her lungs. Borpos knew this to be one of the highest compliments a gal could pay a guy, and so he gave her the old' smoochy face. She was falling for it. Borpos was the champion of everything. And then, he showed up...

Yes, that little tiny man that towered over Borpos. Borpos started with the threats, trying to scare the man off.

And then, it happened. The man put his hand up. The audacity of the rogue. And then he moved his hand forward at a fairly brisk pace, directly toward the shoulder of Borpos. He wouldn't. He couldn't. He did. He slightly maneuvered Borpos away from the girl. Borpos shrieked, clutching his shoulder in excruciating pain. He made his way out of the swinging doors of the pub. He looked up to the sky. It was time to depart. He couldn't handle the insufferable agony. He wanted his mommy. And so he flew up into the air, out of the Earth's atmosphere, out of the solar system, past a decent-sized collection of space nuggets, back to the Nether Regions of space.

Across the street from the bar, Judy Darwinkly screamed. Tears filled her little eyes as she saw her hero ascend into the skies.

And out of the door came the man who was responsible, the one known as the Duke. Someday, he would pay for his insolence. She would study the heavens, and wait for the sign. Someday, Borpos would return. Someday, they would destroy the man responsible for Borpos's defeat. And after this Duke was obliterated, she and Borpos would be together forever...

Somewhere, Frigga Frick-Frodenburg Lugalbanda, from Ulysses, Pagliacci, on the planet Chinchilla shed a tear. It was most likely because she had a paper cut. She also might have eaten some flammable chili. I'm guessing she had just watched the end of *It's a Wonderful Life*.

Nonetheless, somewhere, the mother of the great Borpos of the Nether Regions, Borpos the Planet Killer, Borpos the guy more powerful than Manimal, Borpos the Conqueror of Glork from the Clan Tog, shed a tear...

12 Stu and Gaffy Graduate from Dentistry School

Back in Casablanca, things were finally quieting down. The war was over, and people were free to go where they wanted. It was boring.

Back in the Chinese South Seas Seaport that looked like Casablanca, things were starting to come to a mild simmer. The Duke had been out eating snow cones again, and the townsfolk were not beginning to whisper. And so the Fairy and the Duke came out from undercover, to avoid detection from all of the people that were not looking for them.

The pair sat in an outdoor restaurant, awaiting a waiter. They could absolutely eat nothing more, after traveling for so long. As the Fairy glanced at the menu, the Duke looked about, to see if there were any bad guys after them. Over at one table, three men sat in a heated discussion.

"Both of you are *acting* ridiculous."

"Damn it, Jim! Make him admit that he's wrong. Let me take a closer look. Maybe his brain is gone again."

"Hardly, Doctor. I see that you still subscribe to the outmoded notion, promulgated by your ancient Greeks, that what is delicious must also be unfit for consumption."

"I told you both already. I don't care. Whether you choose to consume these fried slices of potatoes with this onion paste is completely your decision. You want the dip? Eat the dip. If you don't want the dip, don't eat the dip. Gentlemen, there are more pressing matters requiring our attention. Now remember, I heard from a good source that Khan is coming to this restaurant, and when he does, I'll squash him like a bug!"

157

"Captain, where exactly did you receive this information?"

"I'll tell you where, he got it in bed! That's where, damn it! He got it while he was bangin' some..."

"That's quite enough out of you, Doctor."

"I concur with our illustrious physician, Captain. After all, history tells us that some of your planet's most critical intelligence reports were assembled during coitus: Helen of Sparta's secret correspondence with the Greeks during the Trojan War; Dolly Madison's classified ice cream recipes; the National Interstate and Defense Highways Act of 1956..."

"You're telling me that Dwight D. Eisenhower signed the Highway Act of 1956 from the Lincoln Bedroom?"

"No, I'm conveying to you that the 84th Congress of the United States of America drafted the legislation during coitus."

The conversation trailed off into incoherent gibberish.

The Duke then decided to get back to his own heated debate with the Fairy. "I say no, and that's final."

"Yes dear. Do you think we should order the shrimp?"

"The Mexicans have a phrase, 'Feo, fuerte y formal,' which means he was ugly, strong and had dignity. Or maybe it was ugly, stupid and dainty. No? Maybe it was the Semaphore Version of Wuthering Heights."

"I know you do, dear, that's why I'm asking you if you think it's okay to have the shrimp."

"I don't know any off hand. I knew a man who did, once."

"Did you kill him?"

"Look, if someone throws a chair at you, hell, you pick up a chair and belt him right back. I'm a man who gets dirty, who sweats sometimes, who enjoys kissing a gal he likes, who gets angry, who fights clean whenever possible but will fight dirty if he has to, and sometimes use an Aldis lamp."

"Well that's good, Duke."

As the peered down at their menus, the couple realized that they had been spotted by the waiter. They both knew if they

158

delayed any longer it could mean the destruction of humanity.

With so much at stake, they started a barroom brawl like none that had ever been started before. The Duke went after the attendant, first, who had all ready rolled to the ground as if he were struck. After that, the fight went berserk, with people throwing punches at nobody and people diving without really moving out of their seats, and bottles being broken while still retaining their structural integrity. It was unqualified madness, which is really saying something. Then again, maybe I should scribe "which is really writing something." Yeah, that would sound kind of stupid, which is the last thing I want. So maybe it was like this really big fight I saw in this movie with this guy named John Something-or-Other, and it also had Randolph Scott and Marlene Dietrich, and there was this awesome barroom brawl at the end of the movie. Yeah, it was like that movie. But I can't remember the name of the main guy in the movie. Bruce Wayne? No that's Aquaman. It'll come to me.

As the Fairy and the Duke recovered from the fight, they decided that before things got any worse, they should leave the restaurant, so they sat back down again.

Then, the man who had been following them for so long came over to take their orders.

"I'll have the shrimp."

"That's what I was going to order! Now I will have to pick something different." The remark seemed peculiar coming from the waiter. But when the Fairy didn't say it, she got upset.

"Why don't you just take your beard and get it out of my face, waiter-boy, the Duke is mine!" She was very protective of the Duke. She stared down the waiter with the evil 'Fairy Death Look,' which was almost as bad as the 'Fairy Look of Death.' Only fairies understood the difference, however.

The waiter slowly moved his writing tablet from its position of covering his left ear. Immediately, both the Duke and the Fairy didn't recognize him. They even shouted out his name at different times:

"Dr. Blindofsky!"

"Please my children, not so loud. We don't want to attract any more attention to ourselves." But Dr. Blindofsky's warning had come too late. A little hedgehog some 12,000 nautical miles away in the Northwestern United States had picked his head up, and spotted them.

"We've been made. Time to run." The Fairy was the first to move. The Duke and Dr. Blindofsky followed, as they entered a waterfront hotel across from the restaurant. They approached the front desk, held the manager at needlepoint, and got a room unnoticed. They then made their way to the elevator.

They were three floors up when the Fairy recommended they take the stairs. Both men agreed with her keen insight. And so they got off at the 10th floor and walked up to their room in the basement.

"Dr. Blindofsky, what are you doing here?"

"I've been following you ever since Tibet. Duke, we have to talk," said the astronomer.

"Where to begin? Well, I'm not playing the oboe anymore. My mom thinks that next year I might be able to cross the street by myself. One time I was in a movie where I played a guy called 'Singin' Sandy Saunders.' I rode around on a white horse, in a black hat, strumming a guitar and looking like an ignoramus. That's why I refuse to sing in movies, or books, or any other form of entertainment. Also, I think that Friday is not the best day of the week, because there isn't anything good on TV on Fridays. Not like the days of *The Dukes of Hazzard* and *Matt Houston.* And why did they cancel that singing cops show? It was incredible. Maybe not as good as *Double Trouble,* but pretty close, considering there were no dancing twins."

"*Matt Houston* was on Sunday nights, dear," said Belle.

"*Miami Vice?*"

"Yes, that works," said Belle.

"I appreciate the update, but we have more important issues to discuss," said Blindofsky.

"Well then, what about you, Doc?"

"I have a hangnail. Look, it's a real bad one!"

Both the Fairy and the Duke looked at the gruesome wound. The Duke couldn't stand the sight of it. It was up to the Fairy to ask the big question.

"How long do you have?"

"They think it might be operable, but their best estimates are only thirty, forty years, at most."

"Why, it couldn't have been more than a decade ago when we celebrated your 110th birthday," said the Duke. "What an unfortunate fate it is, to be cut down in the prime of one's life..."

The memories seemed to strike a chord among all three of them, especially considering they had never met each other before their encounter in the restaurant. Unable to cope with the emotions, the Duke ambled down to the hotel's classy brasserie and started flicking dry roasted peanuts at the bar, like evil Superman in *Superman III*.

Several Metropolis residents peered inside at the distraught western hero, as he gulped down a Guinness extra stout, and then poured himself a glass of The Macallan 60.

"Wow, that's ridiculously good," said the Duke.

"So, can you stop flicking peanuts at the bottles, now?" asked the bartender.

The Duke could only manage a massive eructation, before stumbling out into the streets.

"What are you looking at, huh?" said evil Superman, who happened to be nearby, using his heat vision to fry some plantains. Unfortunately for evil Superman, the Duke slammed into him at the exact same time, splitting him into evil Superman and good Clark Kent, and sending them both flying into a nearby junkyard. Didn't you always wonder how evil

161

Superman got split into evil Superman and good Clark Kent in *Superman III*? Well, now you know.

"Too bad, I was going to let him try The Macallan," said the Duke, suddenly getting a whiff of something scrumptious to accompany his delectable Scotch. "Something smells like cooked bananas. Look, fried plantains! My favorite."

The Duke had a light snack of yummy fried plantains, before returning to the hotel room, where the Fairy rested her head on a pillow.

Finally, Doc Blindofsky fessed up.

"There's something else."

"No."

"Yes. And, there's also something else."

"All right Doc, out with it," said the Duke. He had known Dr. Blindofsky since before the war, when they worked together on the first rocket prototypes. Belle was just a little sprite then, with a hopeless crush on a young lad named Pedro.

"Ok wait a second, you said earlier that we didn't know this guy, even though we were pretending like we did," said Belle.

"What's all this about a guy named Pedro?" asked the Duke.

"He was a mail plane that I dated back in the early forties. He was quite brave. He even took on Aconcagua when his father came down with the sniffles," said Belle, reminiscing about somebody totally different than whom I thought she was going to be reminiscing about. "I don't see what the big deal is, we both knew how to fly. It was a natural pairing."

"Wait, wasn't he in *The Three Amigos*?" asked Dr. Blindofsky.

"Listen Dusty Bottoms, that'll be enough out of you," said the Duke, just as a guy who looked like a middle-aged Chevy Chase motioned as if he were about to speak.

"Perhaps Pedro was one of the prototypes we developed," said Blindofsky.

"Does this have anything to do with those gigawatts you wanted?" asked the Duke.

Finally, Dr. Blindofsky confessed. "You're right Duke. I must confess. He's back, and he's coming for you."

"Come on, old man, that was nothing. Why, I shot the hell out of that federal marshal a long time ago. They covered the whole thing in that Matthew McConaughey movie, you know, the one starring John Sayles. His bones have been laid to rest. Let's just keep it that way." Both the Duke and Dr. Blindofsky give Belle a quick look, puzzled by her comment.

"No, not you Belle. This guy is after the Duke, here. It's that guy from the bar fight."

"I don't know what you're talking about. Which bar fight? The one I just had with evil Superman, or the one Belle and I had right before that?" The Duke didn't know what Dr. Blindofsky was talking about.

Dr. Blindofsky tried to explain it to his young friends. The Duke and the Fairy were exceptionally brilliant, especially when paired together, or with Greg Marmalard, who occasionally chaperoned their dates. But Dr. Blindofsky would have to fight through their genius brainpower and explain it to them in more complicated terms. "Do you remember that guy you pushed?"

"Oh, that guy. Why didn't you say so in the first place?" The Duke's tone changed, as he finally realized which one of his numerous enemies that the Doc was talking about.

"Anyway, that's the reason I'm he..."

"Well, that doesn't make much sense, now, does it? Okay Doc, the game's over. Why don't you get up off the floor, and stop pretending you're 'he.' Sorry don't get it done, Doc. Doc? Doc?" The Doc was dead.

"The Doc is dead, Duke," said Belle, searching Blindofsky for a pulse. "What happened?"

The Duke looked over at his dead friend as Belle went to the window of the room. Out on the streets, no one looked suspicious. Everyone looked suspicious. What was going on?

"He's been shot, that's what's going on."

"I'm sorry, dear?"

"You asked what was going on. Well, he's been shot."

"I didn't ask what was... I think we should leave, Duke. It's your hot friends. Look over there!" Sure enough, there was nobody there. "No, look over there! We've got to get going!"

Sure enough, there were several sizzling-looking people. Some of them were apparently officers of the law, out in search of a steak dinner covered in doughnuts. I'm serious, that's how you spell it, not 'donut.' Although that's apparently allowed now, too. Whatever.

"Looks like the cops," said the Duke, peering out the window. "Come on, we'd better get moving." The Duke knew it was time to depart.

"Didn't I just say that? Don't I get credit for anything?" The Fairy was furious, because she was a big baby when she got jealous, except really pretty because she was also a fairy dressed in green with cute little fairy slippers with little furry cotton puffs on them. Well, technically she had taken her slippers off when they got to the room, so that last part is totally inaccurate, but an essential plot point, as you'll soon see.

"Sure lady, I'll give you some credit when we get moving. We don't have time for anything else," said the Duke.

Belle quickly gathered up her belongings, which was mostly just fairy dust and her fairy slippers, which as I just mentioned she had taken off when they got to the room.

As Belle leaned over to gather her slippers, the Duke wheeled around to see what was taking so long. "What's taking so long?" said the Duke, spotting the, ah, backside of the fairy as she searched for her slippers under the bed.

"I'm just looking for my..." The Duke interrupted the fairy before she could finish the sentence. They got some, um, last minute exercise in before leaving the room. Although, they also took a nap, then did some more exercises, then took another nap, followed by a second fairy bath, which then resulted in at least one more round of exercise and another nap. By the time they awoke, they were famished, and decided to go back down to the brasserie in the hopes of getting something to eat.

"What happened here?" asked the Duke, noticing the broken glass and dry roasted peanuts all over the floor.

"You broke all of the bottles by flicking the peanuts at them," said the bartender.

"Can we get something to eat?" asked Belle.

"Sorry, we're in the middle of remodeling," said the bartender. Devastated by the news, and also famished from all of the... ah... exercise, the Duke and the Fairy left the hotel in search of mouthwatering vittles...

Elsewhere, only really close, as in a few feet away

Dr. Darwinkly stepped out from behind the street corner in the Old South China Seaport. Her aim had been deadly. Dr. Blindofsky could never reveal the secret, now. It was only a matter of time before Borpos was back. He would take care of the Duke, once and for all. Payday was coming for that vile cowboy...

Elsewhere, only really far away

Deep in outer space, a big space nugget floated in the path of Borpos as he made his way through the asteroid belt that separated Jupiter and Mars. With one swift motion of his hand, he caused a spontaneous overflow of emotions from within the nugget, recollected in the tranquility of space. It was all the nugget could take. Only one woman could feel the explosion back on Earth...

"Right Back Where We Started From" by Maxine Nightingale

"Duke? Did hear that?"

165

"Please, Belle, I'm trying to think. Someone has just shot my dearest and oldest friend," said the Duke, even though the death had occurred quite some time ago as he and Belle had conducted several exercise sessions in the interim. "These things tend to be important."

"I heard something. I know I did. It sounded like someone blowing up a space nugget," said Belle. "But, who could possibly do such a thing?"

"Space nuggets? What the heck is a space nugget? Come on," said the Duke. "We've got to find out who killed the Doc, and why. Also I could go for a hoagie and some cookies. And maybe some chocolate ice cream. And another Guinness. And maybe some chicken tenders. Oh, and pepperoni pizza."

"Yes, dear." Belle was anxious, however. She knew something else was definitely wrong, but she could not guess what. It would have to wait. Also she was hungry, but her diet consisted of pine nuts, wheat, maize, cherry blossoms and rose petals, with the occasional exotic dish thrown in.

The two exited the hotel room through the window in the roof of the basement. That is to say, that the window was sort of in the roof of the basement. Okay, that was a bad description as well. It's like this: the cellar was almost completely underground, and only nefarious things happen below the surface of the Earth. Therefore, the train arriving in Chicago will reach its destination before Greg Marmalard and Gaffy graduate from Dentistry School, although by that time Jay-Z would likely have finished his secret Chex-Mix formula and completed his revisions of the Periodic Table of Elements. Anyway, the window that connected to the outside was the exit for the Duke and the Fairy.

They looked around themselves. Suddenly, a bottle could be heard rumbling down an alley near the hotel. As they approached the corner, Duke and Belle came to the sudden conclusion that who ever killed their friend, did it from the corner on which they were now standing. They were about 62 percent sure of the accuracy of their assumption. On the signpost, a note hung, addressed for Belle and the Duke. It was an exceptionally long epistle:

"Dear Belle and Duke,
If you want to catch me, follow me to America.
Love,
Dr. Blindofsky's killer"

This was all the Duke needed to know to set him into a rage. Fortunately, Belle was there to calm him down.

"Calm down."

"We've got to get to America. Any ideas?"

"We are not flying, so don't even think about it."

"Think about what?"

The two of them stood there, concentrating on nothing. Then, the sirens started humming. The cops could be seen from the corner entering the hotel. Soon enough, they would find Blindofsky's body. The Fairy and the Duke were in a foreign land, with nowhere to hide. The cops had them on a murder charge that they could not defend. It was just one more to add to the already multiplying list. No one else was seen with Blindofsky. They had to get out of the country. They had to get back to America.

"I want to live in America," sang the Duke.

"Vamonos, muchachos!" shouted George Chakiris.

"And the sunlight streaming!" sang Rita Moreno.

Then a bunch of sharks showed up and started dancing.

"Great, another dance number," said Belle, under her breath.

The music to Bernstein's "America" started blaring, and several *West Side Story* dancers started popping out from various objects in the alley, including, but not limited to, a

167

cardboard box, a large dumpster, a discarded egg roll, the Duchess of Cambridge's Bugaboo baby carriage, an abandoned Cadillac, seven distinct types of Bavarian chocolate-covered pretzels from Bavaria, by way of the Bronx, and a four-slot toaster.

The women were the first to sing...

"I like to be in America

Okay by me in America

Everything free in America..."

"For a small fee in America," responded Chakiris.

The music and singing continued, as Belle's close friends Iridessa, Rosetta, Silvermist, Fawn, Vidia, Periwinkle, Bobble, Clank and Cheese showed up. Unfortunately this attracted the sharks, who stopped dancing and started swimming after the fairies.

Fortunately, all of the fairies could fly, so they took off as fast as they came.

Cheese, on the other hand, a small field mouse, was pretty much left to fend for himself. He hid in the discarded egg roll as the sharks attempted to gobble him up. When they couldn't reach the rodent, they ate the backup dancers.

"Muchacho, it is time for me to depart," said Chakiris, patting the Duke on the shoulder as he jumped inside the cardboard box.

"I don't know about any of you, but I was in Oz, as in the scary prison show, and I gotta tell you, it looks like it's about to get real," said Moreno, who promptly followed Chakiris into the box.

"Duke, do something," shrieked Belle.

"Fine," said the Duke, sighing with disappointment now that the musical number had ceased. He then whistled that really loud whistle when you put your fingers in your mouth,

168

which I imagine would come in handy if you, or one of your closest friends was about to get eaten by sharks.

Then, from out of the blue, several killer whales appeared and slammed into the great whites, causing them to flip over. The orcas then proceeded to eat the livers out of the sharks, leaving the rest of the carcasses behind.

"I did not need to see that," said Belle.

"Well, you asked me to save your friend Cheese..."

"And now the cops have more to pin on us: First Blindofsky, then the sharks. This day just can't get any better," said Belle.

Then it started raining.

Elsewhere, with Dr. Judy

Dr. Darwinkly had already left the street corner. She was on her way to that forgotten place of so long ago, the pub where the first fight had taken place...

Written by Pierre Tubbs and J. Vincent Edwards, and, for some bizarre reason, the theme song to *Slap Shot*

The Duke and the Fairy raced to catch a Chinese Junk. It was the last boat leaving for the west coast for the rest of the week. Planes were still out of the question, as Belle suffered from a fear of heights that put Dave's phobia to shame. The heat had been getting worse, almost spicy, almost Sausalito Spice Girl Scary Spice spicy.

As Belle and the Duke raced down a shady back street toward the port, the cops roamed the main roads, looking for the two people last seen with the murdered scientist. By the way, that's shady as in 'he's a shady character.' Not that the Duke is a shady character, but that the street was mysterious. Come to think of it, I guess the Duke could qualify as mysterious. Although, I still wouldn't say 'they raced down the Duke-like street.' You could say it, though, if you really wanted to. This is, after all, a free country. Also it might actually have been shady, like when the sun starts to dip in the afternoon. Although it was also apparently raining, so that seems less likely. The Duke and the Fairy could not afford to be taken until they had proven their innocence, and found the real killer.

"If you don't hurry up, we'll miss the boat. Come on!"

"You don't know how hard it is to run in these high heels!"

"Listen Duke, just because you put lifts in your boots is no reason to complain to me," said Belle.

"Hey, 76 inches, baby. That's right. The lifts are just for comfort," said the Duke.

"Well, I have wings, and I can run despite the wind resistance."

"Of course," said the Duke. "Your model was specifically designed that way."

"Oh. Well, there it is."

"Yes, there it is. Your model was specifically designed to be wind resistant. I know. I knew a wind once," said the Duke. "It was a real bad one, too."

"No, I meant there is the boat. No, wait... Don't go yet. Here come the police," said Belle, grabbing the Duke's arm as he was about to go traipsing over to their escape vessel. Unfortunately, the heat had just gotten hotter, not nearly as hot as the Fairy, but still hot enough to cause issues for the Duke and Belle as they plotted their escape.

"They must be searching all of the escape routes out of the country," said the Fairy. "Now we'll never make it."

Belle gazed out of the back street to the Chinese Junk they were to depart on, in less than five minutes. It was docked at a small port. The police had guards all over the place. They had men stationed at the entrance to the port. A group of donut, ah, doughnut munchers patrolled the waters of the harbor on inflatable tubes.

There was also a cop giving passengers the once-over at the

plank leading onto the boat. I'm actually not sure what a once-over is though. A dirty look? Maybe a close shave? A makeover? Ok, so the cop at the plank was giving people a fill-in-the-blank.

"Quick, over here." The Duke pulled Belle into a little alley, just before a squad of police officers passed by. "We've got to find another way. Wait, I've got it, disguises!"

Hurriedly, Belle and the Duke switched outfits. People had been searching all over for a cowboy and a fairy. What would they say to a fairy and a cowboy?

The two made their way out to the main thoroughfare, just across from their boat. It was now time to see how well their costumes would hold up. They walked arm and arm passed the guards at the entrance to the port. They began walking down the wooden dock. They had made it to the boarding ramp unmolested. Now was the real test, as the patrolman waiting at the entry plank looked them over. The keen deck officer was ready for anything. He would be tough to fool.

"One fairy, one cowboy. Hmm. Let me just check this." He peered over to his snapshots of the convicts. There he saw the cowboy and the fairy that the police had been after. These two were definitely not the right couple. He let them go. And the Duke and the Fairy had escaped. They quickly made their way onto the Junk as the officer in charge of the investigation appeared, and headed over toward the policemen at the plank.

"What does the ship's passenger list look like so far?"

"Five ducks, three nuns, a chiropractor, a philologist, a dentist, a mental patient, three serial killers, two donki, a fairy and a cowboy."

"What? What was it that you said? Let me see that list!" From the boat, Belle and the Duke started to get nervous.

"Donki? Donki!"

"Plural of donkey?"

"Oh, of course. I knew that. Really! I did! Good work,

171

officer. Carry on. Remember, we've got to find that cowboy and the fairy. If they get out of this city, it will be our heads. Be on the lookout for anything out of the ordinary." The officer took a quick glance at the passengers, his eyes darting left and right, not in opposite directions, but first to the left and then to the right. Otherwise he probably wouldn't have been able to actually see anything. Then again, I'm not certain since I can't cross my eyes. I suppose it might be a neat party trick but I'm not sure it would help if your goal was to pick up the ladies.

The cop peered toward a group of passengers at the bow of the boat (that means the front). "Those super killers could be in disguise. On second thought, you better get those ducks off the boat. You never know."

"Yes sir, we'll grab the ducks. I bet you're right. They must be the duo. We'll get them."

A group of officers made their way onto the boat, where they took the five mallard ducks into custody. The ducks resisted, saying they were being falsely accused, but when murder weapons came flying out of their pants, the police figured they had their killers.

Greg Marmalard was at last safe. He loosened his sixties-era tie and patted the Duke and Belle on their respective shoulders. "Ok kids, looks like we've made it."

"Have you been here the whole time?" asked the Duke.

"Of course, I'm chaperoning. Didn't you hear the deck officer mention me?"

"Are you the philologist or the chiropractor?"

"Neither. I'm the dentist. Didn't we go over this already? Gaffy and I graduated from the Faber College School of Dentistry decades ago," said Marmalard.

"What the heck is a Gaffy?" asked Belle.

"Damned if I know," said Greg. "Probably a Delta. I do remember a guy delivering an entire truckload of Fizzies to the swim meet last year."

172

"Ah, good times, good times," said the Duke, a card-carrying Delta House alum.

"You know, we had them on double secret probation all last year and we still couldn't get them booted from campus," continued Marmalard. "By the way, have either of you seen Mandy? Last I heard she was running all over town, visiting lodges and dance clubs, and calling herself Cecilia."

"No, but what about Commander Skywalker?" asked Han Solo, hopping onto the Junk as the Millennium Falcon sat dry-docked nearby with John Entwistle onboard, furiously tried to repair the damaged hyperdrive system.

"I haven't seen him," said Marmalard. "It's possible he came in through the south entrance."

"It's possible? Why don't you go find out? It's getting dark out there," said the Duke.

Fearing for Commander Skywalker's life as the sun set on the horizon of the ice planet Hoth, Marmalard raced off to find the deck officer and a tauntuan.

Back on the boat, the Fairy and the Duke made their way to a secluded stateroom where they could continue their exercise program.

The boat set sail for the new world, only not in the usual direction that boats traveled to the new world back in the day, an expression that might actually be out of date now but used to mean at a time when stuff was really neato and important, you know, like when Columbus sailed the ocean blue. I'm pretty sure he sailed from right to left on the map. So, if one travels forward but moves right to left on the chart, does that mean you can move left and forward at the same time, without sidestepping or skipping? And what if you're on a boat? Did Columbus have to skip all the way to America, back when he didn't know it was actually America? What if it had actually been some other place, like Cleveland or something?

Anyway, the Duke and the Fairy switched back into their

173

respective cowboy and fairy outfits, but not before doing lots of other things that I can't get into here, and then discussed plans to find Blindofsky's killer.

Still really far away in terms of miles, but a lot closer than earlier

And there it was... Earth!

Borpos had returned.

He spotted the continent where the incident had taken place all of those decades ago. The Duke would be there. Borpos could feel it, in his Borpii, a.k.a. feet, that may or may not have looked like feet. I'm not really sure since I've never personally seen a Borpos, but I think they can make themselves look like humans, which would probably make them harder to spot than say, if they made themselves look like giant stalks of broccoli. This time, it would be victory for Borpos. As he passed by the satellite known to these puny earth people as 'The Moon,' Borpos took one last practice shot, crushing the barren, lifeless world with one swoop of his hand.

The moon shattered.

On the tiny planet below, chaos ensued...

Act IV:
The Final Napkin

So I was reading in the paper the other day that skim milk is now called "non-fat" milk. I loathe decals. But I do enjoy a good episode of *Fraggle Rock*, so I guess that makes us even.

13 No Bedelia, There Really is Something in the Basement

Biffus and Flabius had not slept for twelve days, even though they had only been on their quest for about four hours. Neither man was near sheer exhaustion, they were actually right on top of it. What could go wrong did go wrong, except that nothing had really gone wrong, so they didn't say anything like that.

The legendary journey was coming to a close, and all that was left was to find the Paper Napkin of Doom.

"Where do we go from here, my liege?" Biffus was anxious to be done with the evil affair.

"How about Jamaica? I hear the desserts are fantastic."

"No, not the Jamaican desert!"

"I was referring to rock buns."

"Say no more, sire, we shall comb the Jamaican desert for rock buns. I shall put my most trusted lieutenants on the case."

"And what of the *French Lieutenant's Woman*, will she be invited as well?" asked Flabius.

"I am unaware of any French lieutenants in the Rambo Brightus army," said Biffus.

"Oh, that reminds me. If we're going to have enough dessert for everyone when they return from the desert, we should probably pick up some napkins," said Flabius. "Jamaican desserts can be messy."

"Sire, that reminds me," said Biffus. the worry showing on his face. "Where do we go to get the Napkin?"

"Oh, of course my trusted question man, I understand."

"Then we go where?"

"Exactly." Flabius glared at his foolish comrade. Of course Flabius knew what he was talking about. He was the Emperor. Biffus was only a Captain of the Guard. Besides, you had to feel sorry for him, considering his last name and all. "Now, as I was saying, the... refrigerators... sample... of... Alabaster... and... What was I saying?"

"Something about Jamaica."

"Ah yes, the paper napkin. Well, I can guarantee that we will find our last item to form the Weather Dominator by daybreak, before the evil purple fortress disappears."

"What was that all about, sire?"

"I think it's pretty self-explanatory, don't you?"

"No, not really sire."

"I am glad we are in agreement, then, my trusted untrusting comrade. Now, we can finally get down to business," said Flabius, as he once again surveyed the dreary winter landscape of Upper Egypt. Just then, the stranger who had collected the fork from the mighty duo approached from the distance, only this time, he traveled alone. "Hey, here comes that man again, and look, our good friend the cup is goon."

"Don't you mean gone, sire?"

"No, I don't think so, my trusted lexicon," said Flabius. "Well now, what do we have here?"

The man from the earlier chapter approached on his horse, sporting a large welt on his forehead.

"What's that?"

"It is in fact, a large welt on my forehead, courtesy of my former partner," said the henchman. "He threw a wobbly and knocked me from my horse."

Flabius again pointed to the man's head. "No, that!"

"Ah, yes, that is also a large welt on my forehead," said the henchman. "The dastardly fiend. Apologies for my utilization of unpleasant language, lads, but I am quite cheesed off. I fully

177

intend to repay the favor. It won't be pretty! You hear me, it will not be pretty!"

Flabius's confusion was growing. As he glanced over to Biffus, he could see that Biffus was equally puzzled. "Well?"

The henchman was now confused. "Pardon?"

"You said it 'won't be pretty.' Then you said it 'will not be pretty.' Which is it?" Flabius wanted answers immediately.

"What the devil are you nattering on about?" Winston did not understand the question, but nonetheless attempted to clarify. "To be clear, gentleman, it is not going to be pretty."

Flabius and Biffus looked at each other. Flabius had to respond. He was offended. "Why not?" Flabius was quite intrigued with this man's apparent lack of taste for the fine arts. "Do you take issue, sir, with the writings of Shakespeare? Do you find the *Mona Lisa* offensive? Should we start burning the collected works of the Brontë sisters?"

"All right, if you must know, I have Flibbertigibbet's disease. I... I... I am unable to read."

"I don't buy that for one minute. You read the instructions to us during our last encounter," said Biffus.

"My, we're quite the Johnny on the spot, aren't we? Nonetheless, I trust you'll believe me, now!" The henchman stared at Biffus, his arm raised out in front of him in a pointing motion. He then took his thumb and pinky finger and pressed it against his head, and then again extended his arm in front of him in the general direction of Flabius's sidekick.

"Is that a Jedi mind trick?" asked Flabius.

"Quite right, old bean."

"How do you do it?"

"First, you make this motion with your hand," said the henchman, showing Flabius the proper thumb and pinky finger alignment. Then you do this thing where you point to your head, then at your prey, and Robert's your mother's brother."

"How did you know that Bob's my uncle?" asked Biffus.

"Ingenious! Do you mind if I requisition your expression?"

"That entirely depends on what condition his condition is in. It's also likely that Kenny Rogers and The First Edition will be required to drop in," said Flabius.

"Will they also require weighing in?" asked the henchman.

"Doubtful. Kenny is as an island in the stream, setting out to get us like a fine tooth comb, requiring dedication, no conversation, a sail boat and Dolly Parton."

"Like in the America's Cup?"

"More akin to the Bee Gees. Although my grandfather did at one point consider presenting a deed of gift challenge via the Rambo Brightus Yacht and Beach Club," said Flabius.

"What happened?"

"Those shortsighted New Yorkers refused to race catamarans," said Flabius. "Look whose laughing now, eh?"

"Your grandfather?" asked the henchman.

"So, it is you, the son," said Flabius, astonished to learn that the henchman was Winston Wallingford all along.

"Um, my liege, you can't use that line. It's been done before," said Biffus, no longer under the effects of the Jedi mind trick or classic 1980s adult contemporary music.

"Where?"

"This awesome Jean-Claude Van Damme movie. It had this totally wicked theme song. Come to think of it, Van Damme doesn't even win," continued Biffus.

"Who, then, is the victor?" asked the wizard's son.

"I don't know his name," said Biffus. "It starts out where he's like this red belt and gets beat up, or his dad gets whooped by JCVD, and then Bruce Lee trains him, even though it's actually some other dude who's actually from Korea."

Flabius and the stranger looked at each other, comparing notes. "So it's a mystery?" they said together.

"No, no, I just thought I should clarify. Anyway, in the end, JCVD gets beat up by the kid who was trained by the Korean

Bruce Lee and then this other kid says 'No retreat, no surrender!' and then there's this awesome theme song. That's pretty much it. I don't remember the name of the movie."

"Well, that being the case, clearly we shouldn't use the line," said Flabius. "What about this, 'No. I am your father!!!!!!'"

"Sorry, that's been used, too. And that wouldn't be grammatically correct, either. Try this: 'Hey, I didn't know Weemus was your Father!' Or: 'Hey, Weemus is your Father! Did you know that?' Or: 'According to a recent biological survey we have come to the conclusion that your parental unit supplying the Y-chromosome half of your zygote is none other than Weemus Bobeemus.'"

Flabius and Winston kept jotting down the suggestions, trying to keep up with Biffus. They whispered to one another, in a slightly combative tone of two people who couldn't agree on the next thing to say. Finally, Flabius stepped forward.

"It's okay, I got it, I got it," said the great warrior, hushing the stranger. "Ok so this guy over here and I both agree that those phrases don't have enough of a dramatic impact. You've really got to come up with something that sounds really regal. Like more regal than William Regal." The Emperor glanced over at Winston, who nodded in agreement.

"And when you become Emperor, you'll learn that you have to speak in an authoritative, commanding tone, at least mezzo-soprano or contralto," concluded Flabius.

"But sire, your son is going to be the next Emperor."

"You know, my redundant friend, it just so happens that Buffy might have a girl. And by the way, don't yell at me like that. It scares me."

"Oh. In that case, I must tell you that you were the one who said to speak in an 'authoritative, commanding' tone, and it wouldn't make much sense for Buffy to have a girl if she is still a virgin, because then she wouldn't be a virgin and it would mean that I am becoming just as bad as the rest of you with my run-on sentences."

"Very well, my short-lined friend, I think we shall just not get into it at this juncture," said Flabius. "But don't blame me when you're shooting for Giuseppe Di Stefano and end up sounding like Rolando Villazón, or Vanilla Ice. One or the other. Or maybe Snoop Lion. Actually I kind of liked that *California Love* song."

"That was Tupac," said Biffus.

"Where?" asked the henchman and Flabius, in unison.

"I was just pointing out that Snoop Lion wasn't in *California Love*, although he was in that *Turbo* movie about the wicked fast snail. That was a particularly ludicrous film, if you ask me," continued Biffus.

"Nobody is asking you," said Flabius, clearly disappointed to find that Tupac was nowhere in sight.

"Yes, sire, and of course *Mad Max Beyond Thunderdome* did have Tina Turner in it, and you've always spoken highly of her vocal prowess," responded Biffus.

"Tina Turner? She is hardly the vocal equal of the great Bette Midler, or Sir Barbra Streisand." The man without the Styrofoam cup appeared to be getting more and more distressed. He looked like a man who thought that the moon was falling out of the sky. What a silly man.

"Obviously this guy has no idea what he's talking about. Both their names start with the letter B. How could they be gifted songstresses? And when was Barbra Streisand knighted?" Flabius returned his attention to the villain. "Okay, here's the knife."

After handing the small object over, the Emperor noticed Winston's agitated state. "I see you are getting extremely nervous. Perhaps you shouldn't be handling that fork like that." Flabius saw the son of Weemus put the knife in a little satchel with the fork. It was time to take the advantage, and so, the Emperor attempted to employ a super secret spy technique he had learned in summer camp, but to no avail. The man caught on too quickly.

"On the contrary, I refuse to be a party to any tomfoolery, or fooltommery for that matter. Next you'll be telling me that plastic butter knives of wisdom will induce scurvy."

"Plastic? No. But you really should be using some low calorie non-fat butter substitute."

"Then why the bloody hell should I keep this knife on my person?" The all powerful Flabius succeeded in tricking Winston into throwing away his knife, but Flabius, in turn, forgot to pick it up, causing mass confusion, even though there were only the three individuals present. Then Biffus made an astounding discovery.

"Sire, your shoelaces! Hey look, there's some knife on the ground over there." Biffus was no fool; he knew how to take matters into his own hands. "I think I could use one of these things for butter, maybe."

"Do you realize what you've done, my trusted I-am-going to-add-multiple-question-marks-at-the-end-of-this-sentence-for -dramatic-effect man???????"

"No."

"Oh, me neither," said Flabius, before returning his attention to the guy without the cup. "Okay, we'll be seeing you later then, 'Mr. I-Have-No-Styrofoam-Cup-Man.'"

"Hey, sire?"

"Yes, my trusted fireman?"

"Ah, oh yeah. Shouldn't we ask this man where we are going?"

"Why?"

"Just in case, my liege."

"All right my trusted little social worker. Hey kid, where's the next item supposed to be on that super secret list of your father's?"

"At the bottom of the list. That's where the next item is."

"Oh." Flabius had to think about that one for a moment, as did the writer. "Oh, yeah. Okay, what does the next item say? What are the words? Could you read them to us?"

As he rode off, the Un-Styrofoamed man shouted back the instructions. "Take the trail leading south. Then head to the evil 'Purple Fortress of People Who Were Not Particularly Nice' before it disappears. Make sure you are there before dawn, or else..."

"Or else what?"

"I'm not quite sure. But in *Krull,* this similar-themed mountain of dread kept disappearing until the heroes wedged this giant Cyclops under the door, and then they were able to get in. You might want to look into procuring one of those Cyclops wedges," said the Styrofoam-cupless man. "Nevertheless, after you have retrieved the napkin, we shall be waiting for you at the secret hideout."

Biffus wanted to clarify a few things. "But, didn't we just go to the Tower of People Who Were Not Particularly Nice?"

Before the henchman of Weemus Bobeemus could answer, Flabius Flaximus jumped in. "Yes, but this is the Evil Purple Fortress of People Who Were Not Particularly Nice."

"Thank you, that clears it up," said Biffus.

The henchman was getting confused. "Is that a good thing?"

Flabius knew it was his turn to answer the man. "It can be."

All three men were overjoyed as a result of the conversation. They shouted together, "All right!" and started giving each other high-fives whilst singing "Stayin' Alive." Then the three guys finished off a keg of ginger ale. After that, they missed on most of their high-five attempts.

It was up to Biffus to make a point. "I'm sorry sire, but they only sell half kegs now, and it isn't even really ginger ale anymore."

"Well, no reason for you to stick around for such a snooze

of a party as that, henchman-slash-son guy!"

"By Jove, I believe you're spot-on. Make haste, my friends, and we will soon reunite." The mystery man seemed overjoyed as he departed. By the way I hated *Mystery Men*. And Riunite on Ice. Although Susan Lucci's Riunite commercial from 1977 is pretty nice. And so is Susan Lucci.

But as the party friends went on their separate ways, each knew all too well that the next time they were to meet, death and destruction would also be invited to the party, even though nobody liked them.

Death and destruction had a habit, in ancient times, of boring the pants off of everybody at a soiree. Therefore, most people really got aggravated when they found out that death and destruction were coming over. Mostly because they wanted to keep their pants.

As the un-cupped henchman continued on his way, the two weary travelers pondered their misfortunes. Biffus was curious about something.

"Didn't that guy say that he didn't know how to read?"

"You know, my trusted guy-that-catches-on-to-neat-stuff-really-quickly sidekick, I believe you may be correct in that assessment."

"I have one more question, sire. Why did that man keep looking up at the sky? He seemed so nervous. What could possibly be the matter?"

Flabius patted his companion on the shoulder. "I see, my trusted can't-tell-a-time-traveler-when-they-are-stared-in-the-face-by-one captain. That man appears to come from a different era than ours, judging from his strange clothing. Maybe where he comes from, the customary greeting is looking up at the sky." Flabius made perfect sense.

"That makes perfect sense, sire. Thanks."

"Then again, the moon might just be falling from the night sky. Oh well, let's be on are way." After this last comment of

184

Flabius, his trusted comrade looked a little piqued.

The two soldiers quickly surveyed the landscape. After a while, they stared up at the sky as the Un-Styrofoamed man had done.

They continued on their way toward the dreaded purple fortress. After about a good two or three yards of travel, their stallions got tired.

Just then, the evil beautiful mares that they had seen earlier reemerged. They both returned to looking at the sky, then to each other, and finally they returned their eyes to the mares.

"Things sure are looking up, Sire!"

"You said it, my trusted can't-trust-a-gift-horse-in-the-face companion!"

The pair returned to Gimpus Foo Foo, continuing on their path toward the purple fortress, hoping to spot a Cyclops wedge along the way. Evil was again afoot, although this time it was on the other shoe.

Elsewhere with Dave and Cecilia

It was time for Cecilia to call Winston. Dave waited, dancing around the room as the super phone served its purpose, once again.

"Well, Sextilla, what news?"

"One moment, Dave. These things take time," said Cecilia, listening for the cue to type her number in for Winston's pager.

"Come on! Call back Wenceslas! We've got to find that hideout before it's too late!" Dave started breakdancing to pass the time. He was gifted at windmills, but not at head spins. Don Quixote freely mocked him in both Castilian and Andalusian Spanish. Meanwhile, Sancho Panza detailed his logistics for crossing the Delaware with General Washington.

"Panza, my good man, you'll go down in history for this. After all, many a mickle makes a muckle," said the mostly dashing General and soon-to-be first U.S. president (mostly

185

dashing since he had donkey teeth... Look it up! At least, that's what MSNBC says and everything they say is totally truthful).

"I'm fairly certain those mean the same thing, Don Washington," said Panza, a master of 18th century American English and frequently misquoted Scottish proverbs. "Still, I'm glad I could come to your aid, Señor. I trust you will relay my role in this important endeavor to those who write your official biography?"

"Of course my most excellent gimcrack. Despite your frowzy appearance, you are clearly in possession of the greatest strategic mind I have ever witnessed." Washington, of course, had no intention of honoring Panza for his work, but it was critical that the New Jersey campaign succeed, and thus he was forced to continue with the deception.

"Why, that blackguard Henry Knox up and left right in the middle of preparations, claiming equipage failure," said Washington, furiously pacing back and forth as his troops readied for battle with the Hessian villains now occupying Trenton. "Of all the crapulous habits, his fondness for huskanoyed huzzies is second to none. I seriously have no patience for the man. Not to mention, he's a total fatty."

Just then, the page went through, and Cecilia hung up the phone.

"Is that it, Sestina? Did you get through to Wadleigh?"

"No Dave, he calls us back after we hang up the phone. It should only be a matter of seconds now."

"Wow. You mean, you have to hang up the phone when they say they are calling you back?"

"Ah, I think so, but I'm not really sure what you just asked me," said Cecilia.

Just then, the phone rang. It was... TACO SUPER BURRITO! "I just wanted to let Winston know that we turned ourselves in. Tell him we did what he wanted. Agent 77 refused to turn himself in until somebody bought him a spa

186

treatment to get rid of the meat sauce smell. We took it out of petty cash. (By the way, the moon just exploded.) The odor was quite nasty, so I hope you don't mind. Agents 432 and 433 went for some ice cream. They are coming in a little bit later. So now that we are here in Washington, what are we supposed to do? There isn't anybody here."

Dave, hearing the man's error, decided to take the phone himself. In his best Winston voice, he responded to the evil agent of darkness and doom. "Washington, D.C.! What's the matter with you guys? That's why there is nobody at the headquarters. You must be in the wrong place. Now get moving. Make sure you pick up those two that went for ice cream on your way out, as well."

"Oh yes, sorry sir. Washington, D.C. it is. This is TACO SUPER BURRITO, over and out for good." Dave returned the phone to Cecilia.

Cecilia was so nervous that she nearly ripped the phone out of the wall when taking it from Dave. She was able to return it to the receiver with out any serious bodily harm, however. "At least that's taken care of... What was all of that moon stuff? You spies speak in the weirdest code. The moon exploding? Does that mean we have to diffuse some sort of nuclear weapon or something? Do we need to steal ultra-covert data collected by the Huygens probe as it descended onto Saturn's moon Titan? Or do we need to apprehend WWF announcer Sean Mooney's evil twins Ian and Betty Mooney?"

Dave's eidetic memory skills flashed back to a previous mission: January 19, 1992, Albany, N.Y., the Royal Rumble at the Knickerbocker Arena.

PROTOCOL Mission XJ7: The Royal Rumble

It was the late afternoon in Albany, or nearly the witching hour in Munich, and probably about 5 a.m. in Rarotonga. Disguised as the Million Dollar Man, Ted Dibiase, Dave had entered the ring second after the British Bulldog, intent on making a quick exit so that he could track down the villainous Ian and Betty Mooney. Unfortunately, Dave got caught up in his role, so much so that he quickly threw Davey Boy Smith over the top rope, showcasing his wrestling prowess.

Dave failed to realize, however, that you need to make sure your enemies hit the mat outside the ring during a Royal Rumble. Simply dumping them over the top rope is insufficient. The end result meant Davey Boy had the opportunity to sneak up behind Dave and throw him out of the ring. The furious super spy tried to fight past some fake referees, including Dave Hebner and his evil twin Earl.

On his way back to the dressing room, he caught Ian and Betty Mooney scheming to undermine the event: they had kidnapped and merged evil Nasty Boy Brian Knobs and smelly Nasty Boy Jerry Sags, thus creating an evil smelly Nasty Boy named Brerian Snobs. Snobs would have easily defeated the great Ric Flair, thus destroying the hopes and dreams of the billions who tuned in to watch the Nature Boy defeat 29 other wrestlers and rightfully claim the WWF Championship.

Dave, still disguised as the Million Dollar Man, performed a perfect 'Million Dollar Dream' on the pair of villains. He turned them over to special agent Robert Remus, a.k.a. Sergeant Slaughter, who handed them over to his subordinates from the G.I. Joe team stationed nearby, Barbeque and Spirit.

Next, Dave had to halt the attack of Brerian Snobs before he had the chance to enter the ring and carry out his malevolent scheme. Snobs prepared to hoist Dibiase over his head for an evil suplex, but Dave quickly changed out of his disguise and revealed his true nature to the fiend. Snobs was horrified, thinking the Million Dollar Man had been cannibalized by a weirdo in a tuxedo who then started wearing his epidermis like a suit.

Alarmed, Dave tried to explain to the evil creature that he

was not, in fact, wearing an Edgar Suit, but was simply borrowing Dibiase's costume. However it was too late: Brerian Snobs exploded from the shock, bursting into two pieces that looked roughly like the original Nasty Boyz, except that Knobs was now smelly and Sags was evil.

"Close enough," Dave said to himself. Then he went to return Dibiase's outfit to the actual Million Dollar Man. It was at this point that he realized he had in fact pulled an Edgar Suit on Dibiase, who was running around like Frank Cotton in *Hellraiser*, looking for his skin and hoping not to run into Pinhead.

"Whoops, sorry about that," said Dave, helping Dibiase put his skin back on.

Mission accomplished, Dave headed for the nearest exit, only to walk into a broom closet by mistake. It was there that he found Sean Mooney, who had been tied up by his evil twins after he apparently tried to stop their scheme.

"Sorry to bother you," said Dave, closing the door.

Little did Dave realize that the true mastermind behind the scheme was the maleficent Todd Pettengill, who had escaped years earlier from Arkham Asylum. With Batman hot on his tail, Pettengill disguised himself as an Albany-area radio host, and began searching for any opportunity to break into the über-wealthy world of professional sports.

When he saw Mooney for the first time on *Prime Time Wrestling* with Bobby "The Brain" Heenan, he found the perfect target. Pettengill would replace Mooney, and begin his pursuit of global conquest through the announcer's chair of the World Wrestling Federation, where he could use his public speaking skills to warp the minds of trillions.

Unfortunately for Pettengill, he was unaware that a secret agent would be there to thwart his plans.

Still, Dave was only on temporary assignment. He wouldn't aid Batman in the final defeat of the criminally insane Pettengill

189

until the "Case of the Hitman, the Anvil and Bigfoot vs. Lawrence Taylor, Honky Tonk Man and a Banjo..."

"I mean, that would be really scary if the moon ever exploded," said Cecilia, still unsure of the code utilized by the TACO SUPER BURRITO drive-thru attendant.

Dave walked over to the window and peered out. "The moon exploding. Hah! Yeah, those guys don't know what they're talking about, saying the moon exploded. My grandmother's sister exploded one time. I also saw Brerian Snobs explode into Brian Knobs and Jerry Sags. That was an explosion. Not as big as my grandmother's sister, mind you, but pretty decent. I mean, with the moon, you can still see plenty of pieces burning up in the atmosphere. That's nothing. It's more like chunks of moon. Or Chunky soup. Chunks don't equal exploded. At least not in my math class."

Dave then paused, before asking, "Do you by chance have any Chunky soup?"

This didn't seem to improve Cecilia's agitated state. "I'm pretty sure we don't have any Chunky soup. Anyway, now that the Burrito people have turned themselves in, the next call should be from Winston." It was.

The phone rang. "Cecilia, dear, jolly good to hear your voice," said Winston, barely audible over the winds echoing through the receiver.

"Winston, it sounds as if you are in a blizzard. Where are you, Egypt?"

"Highly perceptive, darling. Good show. I am, indeed, in the ancient city of Thebes. You might know it as Luxor," said the evil wizard's son. "Dearest, I must first deliver a few utensils to my father, and then I will return to your flat without delay."

Dave looked over to Cecilia as she talked to Winston. Dave made a strange head tilt motion in her general direction, giving her some sort of super signal that can only be described by secret agents, as the mysterious device known as 'the nod.'

Cecilia knew what to do. The first spy trick Dave had taught her was 'the nod.' This meant that their plan was to be put into action. It was all up to Cecilia, now.

"Winston?"

"Yes, darling?"

"Don't bother coming. I'm leaving you."

"Simply because of a little ginger ale? After all we've worked for?"

"What have we worked for, Winston?"

"A great deal, I would argue. Actually fairly little, if one ponders the question. Do you mind if I contemplate your query for a moment?" Winston could be heard counting to himself. "Right you are, darling, what have we worked for? But just imagine if I had been there all of those times I utilized you as a decoy to lure my archenemy from hiding. That would have been a significant consignment of cargo. If such were the case, then I would be able to answer in the affirmative, as has been my strategy from the beginning."

It was time for Cecilia to go in for the kill. "Huh?"

"Right-o, my dear. You're too clever for me. I have been ignoring you of late. But I promise that will all change."

"Then tell me where you are, Winston. If you let me talk to you in person, I might just reconsider." She waited. Dave waited, staring at her from across the room. She was going to make a great super agent. Under Dave's guidance, who knew how far she could go?

"All right. Meet me at the following address..."

Cecilia scribbled furiously on a passing saber-toothed Uintatherium. "Okay, I've got it Winston. The Hall of the Panzies."

DUNT DUNT DA!!!!!!!!!

"What was that?" asked Cecilia, alarmed at the sudden

cacophonous chorus echoing throughout her erstwhile domicile.

"Never you mind, darling, just come quickly," said Winston, before breaking into a mildly entertaining rendition of Helen Reddy's "Candle on the Water."

Cecilia, no fan of *Pete's Dragon*, did her best to end the conversation. "Fantastic! We'll beat you up when we, I mean, I'll meet you there. I've got the directions. Okay, I hate y... you know the rest. Good-bye, Winston." With that, Cecilia hung up. She began to shake. Dave went over to calm her.

"I'm sorry, my sweet Sandrine. You did good, though. Real good. I would have totally stumbled over *Ferdinand the Bull*. That was my dad's favorite cartoon, let alone 'I am woman, hear me roar.' Say, you don't really love him, do you? I mean, I'm just asking... for... um... security's sake... Yes, that's it... For safety reasons."

"How can you ask me that, Dave?"

"Well, first I usually breathe in, and at some point while I'm doing that I start to formulate these intricate patterns with my mouth, and when I expel the air, it creates different sounds that your brain identifies as words, usually in the form of a sentence." Dave said this while throwing popcorn kernels at the Uintatherium.

"Actually I was referring to the... Forget it. I don't know what I want. He always seemed so... so... lugubrious. And now you come into my life... You... You're always in control, always on top of everything... What could I ever offer you? Oh, I don't know. What am I supposed to think? Please Dave, let's just go. I don't want to talk about this anymore."

Dave, preoccupied with the Eocene herbivore, was totally paying attention. Except he wasn't, and clearly he should have been. That was probably kind of rude. I don't really think I need to make excuses for the guy. Seriously. But as it turned out, Cecilia was looking down the whole time, so she didn't notice that Dave wasn't paying attention either.

Then Smaggles (the Uintatherium that Dave had just named while we were discussing his failure to pay attention) ran back into Fangorn Forest, never to be heard from again. Like the Entwives.

Cecilia looked at Dave, waiting for his response.

"Excellent! You're right, as usual, Saffronna. We should get going."

"Yes. It's not important..." Cecilia was upset, though. She was afraid Dave couldn't see it. He couldn't understand.

"Then we're off," said Dave. A bit flummoxed at the loss of his pet Smaggles, Dave was sad to leave without the chance to say goodbye.

But now was not the time to shirk in the face of danger. It was his job to straighten his tie and put on a brave face for the fair Cecilia. "I know this must be devastating for you, Shania, but I promise that tomorrow will bring rainy skies and frosty weather. It'll be like Christmas, but with poisonous dust clouds instead of snow."

When this didn't brighten Cecilia's spirits, Dave turned to a different subject. "You say it's called the Hall of the Fannies?"

DUNT DU, oh, sorry.

"NO. Panzies, Dave."

--NT DA!!!!!

"Excellent! I love Edvard Grieg! *I Dovregubbens Hall* is the greatest piece of orchestral music ever composed." For those of you without a Norwegian dictionary, that's non-translated *In the Hall of the Mountain King*. So it would be funny if you were Norwegian. Also that book *Snow Treasure* was pretty awesome. Then again, I read it like 30 years ago, so maybe it was crap and I just thought it was good at the time.

Apparently the movie version has James Franciscus in it, which is one of the most awesome actor names ever. He was also in *Beneath the Planet of the Apes*, which was pretty good, and then got awesome when Charlton Heston shows back up again out of nowhere.

Also Linda Harrison is really hot.

In the meantime, Dave and Cecilia went looking for Winston.

Elsewhere with Weemus Bobeemus and Buffy

Weemus awaited the entrance of his son, who by now had two of the four sacred elements in his possession. Soon the game would be over for Flabius, and there would be a new reign of terror to be swept down upon the world as never before. With victory only one step away, Weemus decided to take a moment to gloat over the poor, helpless, Angora sweater-wearing Buffy.

"You see now that you can never win. Your hero is out now, getting the last element in the weather dominat... Ah, I mean the last element of the set of destruction. And when he has given my boy that final napkin, I shall be the ultimate master of everything and your boyfriend will be dead. So you can see Flabius is done for. I am the master and he is deceased! Washed-up! Yesterday's news! No, make that two days ago news!"

The lovely Buffy was more bewildered than upset. "But if he's deceased then he can't get the napkin, which means he's alive since that's what you said he was doing. So there!"

"Yes, but he will be dead. That's what I meant. Yes, he will be dead," Weemus was unequivocally equivocating.

He pranced about the evil lair, flexing his woebegone musculature for the petite beauty tied up at his feet, just like Princess Daphne from that video game with the lair and the dragon, *Dragon's Hideout* or something like that. I don't know. I never played video games. Ok, I did play *Space Rogue*, which was awesome. Except the freaking Commodore 64 disk drive took a freaking eternity to freaking load. Seriously, you could run to the freaking store, or to freaking Saskatoon, or join the freaking Carthaginian army under freaking Hannibal, serve two freaking tours in the Second freaking Punic War as an elephant dung removal expert, and still be waiting for the game to freaking load when you got back to your freaking desk.

But the evil wizard cared little for the C64, or the VIC-20. "Anyway, let's not harp on old news. Let's get hitched. Come on, me and you!"

"I don't really feel that would be appropriate while I'm still in mourning for the death of my fiancé," said the stunningly beautiful Buffy, her hair slightly askew in a super-groovy sexy way, unlike View Askew, which is Kevin Smith's production company and therefore not likely to be super-groovy sexy.

Unless, Buffy was sitting in the View Askew waiting room, if there is such a place, in which case View Askew Productions would also likely be super-groovy sexy, although not because it was sexy, but because of the aforementioned Buffy with her Angora sweater, which, for the record, also made her super-groovy sexy, not just her slightly askew hair. I'm also going to assume that Kevin Smith is a mammoth Vince Askew fan. And a fan of mammoths. But getting back to Buffy's sexy factor, did you ever see Marilyn Monroe in *How to Marry a Millionaire?* Like that.

Weemus sought to clarify his remarks. "No, you don't understand, he's not dead yet. He will be, in the future."

"Flabius is in the future? I just can't believe it!"

"What? How did we get to the future?"

"I hope you're happy. I liked living in the dark ages. Even if I have a glamorous, carnation pink Angora sweater."

"That's from the 50's, though. That's also in the past, or something."

"Yes I know, but it's still the future if this is the Bronze Age."

Weemus glared at the infamous behavior of his captive. Wait, he glared at his captive, who was behaving in a most

195

infamous manner. Not infamous like *Three Amigos* infamous, but like El Guapo infamous, so yeah, like in the *Three Amigos*. "There's nothing dark about it. It's all out in the open. And that's not all!"

"What are you talking about? First we were in the future, and now we're in the past, and now you're asking about a 50's convertible? Did they even have cars like that in the 50's? Besides, you can't 'glare' at infamous behavior."

"Good point."

And as their disconcerted conversation went from bacon to Barbasol, Winston Wallingford entered the room. "Guess what father, I invited Cecilia to join us for tea. She'll be here presently. Now you can finally meet my girl."

"What girl, son?"

"Oh, that's right, I didn't tell you, yet. Smashing good story. I have a girlfriend. I think we're going to be married. I've asked her to visit."

"You did what? Do you know what you have done?"

"No."

"Excellent. Well, at least that's taken care of," said Weemus. "Come. We have much to discuss. Where's my stuff?"

"I am thrilled you approve. I shall go and fetch her. Hey now, by Jove, who is this stunning beauty in the rose pink sweater?" Winston was staring at the beautiful Buffy.

"That's Buffy, the Flaximus boy's girlfriend. Or was... now she's mine, and I'll thank you to unhand my fiancé." The evil sorcerer gave his son the evil eye, in a most evil manner. Nice *Searchers* reference, by the way. Or BTW. Either one.

"I wasn't handing or handling her, honest," said Winston.

"Well then, I'll thank you to unstare my fiancé."

Winston and Buffy could only offer Weemus puzzled looks. Then Buffy spoke. "Actually, my sweater is 'carnation pink,' not 'rose pink.' There's a difference, and I'll thank you to learn your colors of the rainbow."

196

"I have a rainbow? Smashing! This day keeps getting more jolly by the minute..." Winston then wheeled back around to finish the conversation with his father. "I should mention, on a brighter note, Cecilia (that's my fair lady) says she observed my archenemy Dave jump out of a window. I looked at the marks he left on the glass. They indeed match Dave's forehead. He's likely to attack at any moment."

"Then again, I ask, where's my stuff?"

"I'm sorry father, butter isn't good for you, especially with the amount of weight that you've put on in the past few months," said Winston, gesturing toward the spare tire around Weemus's midsection. "Therefore I can provide you with the fork, but I dispensed with the butter knife."

"I'm working on it," exclaimed Weemus, patting his belly, which was not a gut. It's called a 'beer belly,' not a 'beer gut.' Wait, apparently it's also called a 'beer gut.' My mistake. "Come on, we'll have to go retrieve it... Then again I could go for a grilled Reuben, or maybe some olive tapenade. Or maybe a grilled Reuben with olive tapenade. Let's go get lunch."

Weemus and Winston prepared to leave, their collective stomachs growling in unison. Then the wizard realized that trickery was afoot. "You idiot, Winston! They tricked you, didn't they? Now I'll never know the whereabouts of the missing evidence to clear... um... I will be late in returning my Judy Bloom book to the library... ah... bad cabbage."

"I believe, father, that you are trying to detail how your plan to rule the universe is in elevated jeopardy due to my miscalculation," said Winston.

"Yeah, that one," said Weemus. "Well, I guess we don't need the Emperor's girl anymore. After all, she can't do us any good if she doesn't know how to prepare a grilled Reuben."

Winston cast a stark gaze toward his father's prisoner. "Yes, or olive tapenade..."

"Actually, olive tapenade can be a little tricky to make, so

197

that would be a little unfair," said Weemus.

"What about biscuits? What if she didn't know how to prepare buttery biscuits?" asked Winston.

"Wait, you're talking about cookies, right? Isn't a cookie a biscuit in England? Why do you speak with a British accent, son? We're from Gimpus Foo Foo by way of Motown," said Weemus. "Then again, I do love cookies. Okay, new plan: let's execute the princess and then go score some Shasta and Hydrox. I know a guy who knows a guy who knows Kevin Bacon."

"Yes, or maybe, Fig Newtons?" asked Winston.

"Why Fig Newtons?" asked Weemus.

Buffy, who had heard the entire conversation, was quick to react in the defense of her true love, Flabius Flaximus. "On second thought, Weemus, marriage doesn't sound like such a bad idea after all."

"No, it's too late for that now, my pretty." Weemus approached Buffy. His menacing expression caused Buffy to shrink back in her seat, or the ground, you know, since she was kind of bound up like Princess Daphne.

The wizard cracked a wicked smile. His eyes widened. "Besides, I could never get over the rejection from the last time I proposed. There would always be that doubt between us. There would always be that hesitation in your step. I just couldn't handle going through it all again, after it ended so quickly. I want to be alone," said Weemus, beginning cry, mascara running down his face as visions of Greta Garbo danced in his head. Then Weemus began dancing along, humming "The French Mistake."

"But father, if you were to marry Buffy, and I were to marry Cecilia, than perhaps we could have one of those royal dippity-dos?"

Suddenly, that evil glare returned to the face of Weemus. The serious demeanor returned to his step. The deep, protruding voice also returned. "That's old school hair gel. I ate it one time, thinking it was grape Jell-o. I mean I had a friend who had his entire head shot off by a dippity doo. There you go... His whole entire head. So let's just keep that one a little quiet," Weemus stuck out his tush, put his hands on his hips and gave them a push.

"On the other hand, we will go ahead with the wedding, as long as I get to make the floral arrangements. And I know what I want my bridesmaids to wear." Weemus cast a hideous, somewhat bureaucratic smile.

"Father, who, may I ask, is my mum?" Winston was longing for something, as the momentous occasion of the super-duper wedding approached.

"No son, no chrysanthemums. They smell funny."

"I'm referring to my mum, father."

"Ah yes, that would have been telling," said Weemus, "But you've been a good little evil menace, for the most part."

"Wait, pardon?"

"Ooh, I forgot about that incident with the knife, though."

"Still, it is most delightful to hear you are proud of me."

"Wait, then there was the time you blew the game winning shot in that ancient basketball game," said Weemus. "I was mighty embarrassed to be your father that day."

"It is entirely unnecessary to dredge up old stories..."

"No, then there was the time you ate that entire plate of fudge I had specially delivered from Switzerland. Oh, but I suppose I was just really angry as opposed to regretting I ever allowed for your existence, so that doesn't really count. No, come to think of it, I was really looking forward to that fudge. So that's three times you've been a disappointment..."

"Father," said Winston, "Shouldn't we be planning this affair from the groom's point of view?"

"Wait, is that the man's side?"

"I believe it is..." Weemus Bobeemus and Winston stared at

199

the ground for a few hours, trying to figure out the theorem put forth.

"Yes, then I suppose we should let Buffy and Cecilia have all the fun with the dresses," said Weemus. "But I still get to make all of the flower arrangements..."

Buffy had no problem with this. "I have no problem with this."

"Excellent, then it's settled," said Weemus. Just then a security alarm tripped, with lights and flashy gizmos, um, lighting up the place. Ok, then you come up with another word for lights. Not as easy as it sounds, eh?

"What's this?" said Weemus, glancing at a series of security monitors along the wall. "Seems our enemies are nearing the swamps that surround the Great Hall. Winston, prepare to meet your arch-nemesis. Our final victory is near."

As Winston left and Weemus began sketching floral patterns, Buffy peered down at a poor little Styrofoam cup tied up next to her, also in a beautiful rose pink angora sweater. Otherwise people might get confused between the two, because the little Styrofoam Cup was also a cutie in disguise. Although I'm not sure what kind of disguises a Styrofoam Cup would wear. Oh well, it couldn't have been that important.

St. Elsewhere's Fire, Elmo, John Parr, Flabius and the Legion of Doom

Emperor Flabius Flaximus and his trusted sidekick, Biffus Palookus searched the countryside for a Cyclops. Their journey took them to Legion of Doom Swamp, so named for Hawk and Animal's early 1990s run in the WWF, back when WWF was awesome and not encumbered by that stupid E. Don't get me wrong, I like E's. Elvis was awesome, and who doesn't like Elvira, Mistress of the Dark?

But the WWF's pinnacle was the aforementioned 1992 Royal Rumble, won by the mighty Ric Flair, who connected on at least five nut punches on that fateful day at the Knickerbocker Arena in Albany, N.Y. Just ask Dave. Since then, WWF/WCW/ TNA/WWE, yeah, not so much.

Then Michael Rosenbaum, bearing a strange resemblance to Lex Luthor, walked by the mighty duo, followed in close order by Toyman, Sinestro, Captain Cold, The Riddler, Gorilla Grodd, Giganta, Bizarro, Solomon Grundy, Cheetah, Dr. Syn (aka the Scarecrow of Romney Marsh), and Wonder Woman. Lex Luger was not among them.

"Can anybody see Black Manta? Did he miss the bus again? Who was Black Manta's partner?" Rosenbaum walked at a brisk pace, occasionally looking over his shoulder to make sure that his cohorts were still following him.

"He said before we left that he wanted to be Brainiac's partner," said Toyman, in a high-pitched squeaky voice reminiscent of Ned Beatty in *Deliverance*.

"I told you guys before, no way am I sharing the screen again with Marsters," said Rosenbaum. "That guy hogs every scene he's in."

"Solomon Grundy want Cheetah for partner!" Solomon Grundy wanted Cheetah to be his partner.

"We already chose partners, Grundy. We're *trying* to find Black Manta," said Rosenbaum.

"I could be wrong, but are any of you King George or members of his naval press gangs?" said Dr. Syn. "I seem to have taken a wrong turn somewhere. I'm looking for Romney Marsh."

"Well, you've found Legion of Doom Swamp, Doctor," said Rosenbaum. "My advice to you is to find the nearest carriage for the coast and lay off the meds."

"Why is Wonder Woman here?" said Giganta.

Just then the Wonder Woman theme song started playing. Wonder Woman swung back and forth on a few tree limbs growing out of the swamp.

"I thought we went over this, Giganta. She's my girlfriend," said Rosenbaum. "It's not that I don't find you attractive anymore, but I don't find you attractive anymore. Or ever, actually... Now, can we please get back to finding Black Manta? He has the keys to the Hall with him. Wait, who are those guys?"

Rosenbaum and the rest of the Legion, including Dr. Syn (who wasn't really a member but didn't have anything better to do) turned their gaze toward Flabius and Biffus.

"Yes my good man... Emperor Flabius Flaximus, pleasure to make your acquaintance." Flabius offered a hand of friendship to the fiendish Rosenbaum, who accepted.

"Great. Just what I needed." Rosenbaum turned his attention toward the heroic pair. "Michael Rosenbaum, a.k.a. Lex Luthor, chairman and CEO of Luthorcorp, a multinational conglomerate secretly bent on world domination. Pleasure to meet you. Now can you tell me what *the hell* you are doing in my swamp?"

"Yes my bald-headed friend. We're looking for a Cyclops. Have you seen any?"

Rosenbaum wheeled around to his colleagues. "Well? Has anyone seen a Cyclops?" The Legion of Doom began conversing with one another.

"Solomon Grundy see Cyclops!" Solomon Grundy had seen a Cyclops.

"What kind? Was it a Cyclops wedge? Quick man, out with it!" Biffus Palookus was eager to leave the swamp and get back to the mission.

"Solomon Grundy see Cyclops wodge," said Solomon Grundy.

Biffus and Flabius looked at each other, puzzled. "Is that a real word?" asked the Emperor.

"A wodge, gentlemen, is a bulky mass or chunk – a lump or a wad," said Dr. Syn in his most excellent 18th century English dialect.

202

"Perhaps it would be more helpful if you explained to us why you need this Cyclops wedge?" asked Rosenbaum, clearly showing his exasperation.

"Well, we need to find the Purple Fortress..."

"Like the black one from *Krull?* And you need a Cyclops to wedge in the doorway before the fortress disappears?" asked Rosenbaum.

"Exactly," said the two travelers.

"Got it. Well, far be it for me to offer an opinion, but I would wager heavily that a Cyclops wodge would sufficiently stand in for a Cyclops wedge, especially if no Cyclops wedges avail themselves to you. Grundy, point them in the direction of the Cyclops wodge. Now, do you mind?" Rosenbaum then led his villainous gang deeper into the swamp. Wonder Woman swung after them, her theme song continuing to blare.

"Good day to you, gentleman, and good luck," offered Dr. Syn.

"Yes, and a find good day to you sir. For the record, we loved you in *The Prisoner*, although the last episode was kind of out there, which is really saying something considering the rest of the show. I also hated you in *Baby: Secret of the Lost Legend*, but I guess that was the idea in that one," said Biffus.

"Precisely," said the Scarecrow, as he retreated into the swamp after Rosenbaum and the others.

Biffus and Flabius looked around. At least they now had a heading to pursue, and with luck they would find a Cyclops wodge along the way. Just then, they ran into a Cyclops wodge.

Flabius, himself a man of brawny stature and immense height, looked up at the giant mythical being. "Very well, Cyclops, good day to you. We are here to request your help in fighting the evil wizard, Weemus Bobeemus."

The Cyclops peered down at him, his lone eye blinking blankly (or should it be blankly blinking? Take your pick), unsure what to make of this Emperor.

203

"I understand you can double as a wedge? Let me explain it thusly: somewhere out there is a purple-colored fortress, an evil place of people who are not particularly nice. It's called the Purple Fortress of People Who Were Not Particularly Nice."

"I've heard of it," said the Cyclops, continuing to blink.

"Well then if you've heard of it, my good wodge, you know that it disappears every morning at dawn. Unless we can reach it tonight, and get through the doorway before it vanishes, we have no hope of finding the Napkin of Doom, the last element needed to complete the vile Weather Dominator," continued the Emperor. "After we retrieve it, we can give it to the evil wizard Weemus Bobeemus, which will then allow us to officially stop him from subjugating the G.I. Joe team and the rest of the world."

"Two questions, why would you ever give the evil wizard the final device he needs to complete this weather dominator, and why exactly do you need me to accompany you?"

"Ah, excellent points, my good wodge, excellent observations," Flabius was quite impressed with the giant's keen insight. "On the first note, as you've already surmised, Weemus Bobeemus can't complete the weather dominator unless he gets the paper napkin, which is why we have to bring it to him. We can't prevent him from conquering the world unless he has the means to do so, which is why we plan to give him the napkin. That probably sounds worse than it actually is. Come to think of it that actually is worse than it sounds. Nonetheless it does offer me the opportunity to showcase my heroic skills, and thus elevates this chronicle from absurd to ludicrous. And on the second note, we plan on wedging you in the doorway so that we can safely make it past and go on to save the world per my previously discussed strategy."

"So, you're going to retrieve the last item the wizard needs to complete a device that could wreak havoc all over the world, and create the means by which he can enslave humanity, and once you have it you're just going to hand it over to him?"

"Yes, exactly. I'm glad you're getting this. Only, he could also use the completed set of destruction to conquer the known universe. You know, the universe is his oyster!"

"I still don't understand... why would you do that?"

"Well, for one, he's got my girl. And for two, how am I to *save* the universe from the clutches of the evil wizard Weemus Bobeemus if he doesn't possess the evil set of destruction by which he has the means to *control* said universe?"

"I guess that's logical," said the Cyclops Wodge, rubbing his chin. "On the second item, what happens to me after you wedge me in the doorway? What if I can only be wodged in the doorway?"

The ever-observant Biffus, who had been paying close attention, felt he had the knowledge to answer this question. "Ooh! I can take this one! We heard from this guy named the Scarecrow that we should be able to wedge you in the doorway, because wedge and wodge are pretty similar. Well, actually this other guy told us that we could probably do that, but he seemed a little preoccupied, so he might have been lying. Plus, I'm pretty sure you'll get crushed by the door after we make our way past you and into the Purple Fortress of People Who Were Not Particularly Nice."

"This other guy you spoke with, he wasn't a master criminal bent on world domination, by any chance, was he?" asked the Cyclops.

"Come to think of it, yes he was," said Biffus. "Although he might have just been an actor who plays a master criminal bent on world domination on TV. Why do you ask?"

"No reason. Ok, this plan sounds fine with me."

The trio then set off for the Purple Fortress of People Who Were Not Particularly Nice. Fortunately for them, the writer's hands were starting to get all achy and stuff so they arrived at the fortress almost immediately.

It was just before dawn. The trio climbed swiftly, being especially careful as they tried to avoid triggering any of the ancient laser guided security systems that had been installed all of those millennia ago.

Sure enough, as they started to scale the mountain, evil guards emerged, shooting lasers and throwing gazpacho and garbanzo beans at them.

Yet, the travelers would not be denied.

First, the Emperor threw a few beans back in the direction of the evil guards, causing their innards to explode outward. Then, carefully shielding themselves with the Cyclops wodge, Biffus and Flabius were able to ascend the rest of the way to the fortress door, at which point they wodged the Cyclops in the opening.

"Quick, enter the fortress before it's too late," said the Cyclops.

"Yeah, that's kind of what we were planning to do. Well, nice knowing you," said Biffus. Then the doors closed and crushed the Cyclops, just as the sun rose above the tree line.

"Ooh, you know what, I left my good cape with the mares. Do you think it's too late to go back for it?" Flabius was concerned about his good cape. He pried open the door, freeing the Cyclops and causing the fortress engines to stall.

"You came back for me!" exclaimed the grateful Cyclops.

"Actually I was just looking for my... I mean yes... Never leave a man behind, and all that," said the heroic Flabius. "Say, while you're free, would you mind going back to the mares and fetching my good cape? You're a good Cyclops Wodge."

Flabius patted the huge Cyclops on the head, kind of like you would with a soft-coated Wheaten Terrier, which we know from earlier that Flabius really wanted. He did this gently, of course, because not only would a hard pat shatter the Cyclops' head (after all it was Flabius doing the patting), but the Cyclops was now sort of mushy from having gotten stuck in the doorway of the Purple Fortress of People Who Were Not Particularly Nice. Otherwise he probably wouldn't have been able to reach the giant's head.

Speaking of the Purple Fortress of People Who Were Not Particularly Nice, another guy started speaking over the intercom system, clearly irritated with this new turn of events. "Okay people, who left the door open? Everybody knows we can't engage the disappear-reappear engine when the door is ajar. Now we have to call a mechanic, and it's not like we're getting a lot of professionals willing to come out to the citadel these days..." That was because the inhabitants of the fortress weren't particularly nice, and *not* because they had trouble finding ancient master mechanics who were well-versed on the intricate inner workings of the internal combustion engine.

As the Cyclops made his way down the fortress wall toward the mares, Flabius and Biffus explored the inside.

The castle was huge. But, the most impressive feature, beyond the large, evil paintings of evil people, past the enormous statues of the mean awful residents of long ago, through the giant arches built by guys who didn't know that the people they were working for were really not all that nice and so they eventually ended up getting eaten, was the little baby pool right in the middle of the place.

"Stay alert, my trusted light bulb, and don't touch anything. We need to go about this carefully. Hey look, a big glowing thing. I'm going to go touch it..." The object in question was actually a big DayGlo monster at the bottom of the evil pool, but Flabius enjoyed water, and he knew he must defeat any and all evil creatures that he encountered.

"No wait my liege," said Biffus. "It may be a big DayGlo monster at the bottom of that pool!"

But Flabius did not wait, and instead he plummeted towards the big 'glowing thing' at the bottom of the pool. The monster lashed out, defending its sacred prize.

207

Flabius and the creature battle back and forth, with the creature taking the advantage thanks to the watery battlefield. But Flabius held fast. He shouted to his assistant, "Quick my trusty little assistant who is going to save me, find my bucket of air, so that we might smite this evil creature!"

"Sire, just stand up. I have just come to the conclusion that the pool is only a foot deep!" Biffus was fairly certain that Flabius didn't need a bucket of air in order to smite the DayGlo creature, as he was taking meteorology classes online. "Besides, as soon as you're out of the water you are in the air, no matter where you go..."

"I understand my trusted scientist," said Flabius. "No, forget that. Let's stick to the original plan. Find me the bucket."

Biffus flipped over paintings, ransacked a couple of smart classrooms before coming across the fortress cafeteria. He quickly overturned the nearest trash can, at which point several guards said, "Hey, that wasn't particularly nice!"

Biffus had no time to argue, however, as his master was still locked in a death match with the DayGlo monster from the bottom of the kiddie pool. He scooped up the empty trash container, gathering some air along the way, before hurling it in the direction of Flabius.

The Emperor held the mighty monster out of the water as it was struck by the oncoming trashcan of air, not the actual trashcan, mind you, just the air that Biffus threw out of it.

In the aftermath, the dazed Emperor struggled to stay on his feet. The DayGlo monster had apparently vanished.

"My liege, I think we defeated the monster," said Biffus. "Look at your hand!"

Flabius looked at his hand.

"No Sire, your other hand... Yes, that... no you were right the first time."

Flabius looked back at his original hand again. There it was, the formerly gigantic evil super creature DayGlo monster laid vanquished in the wake of the mighty Flabius Flaximus. "We did it, my trusted guy who can't be trusted with buckets. The prize is ours, no thanks to you... Where was my bucket?"

"I... I... I just threw that trash can to you..."

"Biffus, my trusted Constructicon, a trash can is not the same as a bucket. So, what happened to the bucket we had brought with us at the start of this adventure but never mentioned until just now?"

"I ate it."

"Oh. That happens to me sometimes as well," said Flabius. "I am absolutely, positively, one hundred percent sure that this habit you have of eating important items will not come back to haunt us at some later juncture. Quick, lets get going."

"Hey Sire? Look at the bottom of the pool... It's the... the... the... line please!"

PAPER SUPER NAPKIN OF DESTRUCTION!!!!!

"Hey Sire? I bet that thing at the bottom of the pool is the Paper Super Napkin of Destruction," said Biffus.

"I bet you are right, my trusted forget-important-lines-at-critical-moments-and-eater-of-air-buckets chum!"

And there, at the bottom of the pool, was the last item on the list, the item to complete the set of silverware that Flabius and Biffus had been after for so long: THE PAPER SUPER NAPKIN OF DESTRUCTION!!!!!!!!!!

"I already said that," said Biffus Palookus.

Elsewhere or maybe Elsewhen? I'm not sure

The boat docked. The Duke and the Fairy made their way off of the Junk, in front of the donki. America. Freedom. And then, from out of nowhere, a super police force that didn't look like police at all, but the Impolitus Guard, surrounded the Duke and the beautiful Belle.

"Looks like we're surrounded."

Meanwhile, behind the guardsmen, millions rioted and

looted as the moon had just blown up. Things were sort of not looking very good.

"State the obvious next time, Duke," said Belle.

"Okay, looks like we're surrounded," said the Duke. "But I just said that. You should listen more carefully."

"You know, there isn't going to be a next time," said the Fairy. "We just got captured. Our story is over! This just isn't fair. I didn't even get the chance to fly or anything..."

The Duke looked around. Only the Impolitus Guard seemed disaffected by the fact that the moon had just exploded. The Duke addressed the guards. "You know, she has a point. Doesn't the apple look greener on the other side of the Fig bush? Isn't it always brightest before my hand forms a fist and makes contact with your face?"

The Impolitus guardsmen looked around themselves. They didn't have any cool things to do in the story, either.

The Duke knew it was time to react. In expert fashion, he punched his way out of the corner that he and Belle were in, even though it was more of a scalene triangle than a corner.

The guards were too busy consoling each other, however. When the Panzer division heard the tears, they too came to share in the misery of their comrades. And so the guards and the Nazis ran off toward the hills, playing footsies and singing "THE MOON WILL COME OUT... TOMORROW... TOMORROW!"

"Fat chance. It just blew up. Nazis. What do they know?" The Fairy had a way of stating the obvious.

But just as it looked like the Duke and the Fairy were going to make it, fate, in the form of Dr. Judy Darwinkly and hundreds of evil pansy-toting flower girls, intervened. "Hands up! You two wackos are coming with me!"

The Fairy turned around to see the good doctor, with a Howitzer mounted over her shoulder, standing behind them. "Well, lady? What do you want?"

210

"Don't you recognize me? I sat behind you in the 8th grade." said Dr. Darwinkly, dredging up a painful primary school memory. "You were always the most popular... The boys always went for you. What did I ever get? I didn't even have any wings. You never even spoke to me..."

"You realize, of course, that I grew up in Pixie Hollow. Actually I didn't even grow up, I just kind of sprouted." The Fairy wanted to clear the air before she was blown away.

"Come to think of it, I don't think I ever went to school either," said Dr. Darwinkly.

"Then how did you get to be a doctor?"

"That's a good question. Now that I've answered it, we're off."

"Where are you taking us?"

"To a little bar I used to frequent. We'll all be having a big party in a matter of minutes. Just because you can outsmart the guards and the Nazis doesn't mean you can outsmart the great Dr. Judy Darwinkly, Nobel Prize winner and snappy dresser."

"In those clothes? Those styles went out at least ten minutes ago..." The Fairy was downright disgusted, or possibly upright incredulous.

"I had other business. My car broke down. I needed a new toothbrush. I didn't have time to get to the store. Besides, you don't look so up-to-date yourself..."

"Not you, Duke. I'm talking to the doctor lady," said Belle.

The Duke was making a habit of talking out of turn.

"Well, what he said. Besides, what do you call your outfit?"

"I don't have any particular name for it. It's just a dress."

"Yes, exactly. At least I have names for my clothes." The doctor was starting to win the argument.

"Yes, but I'm a fairy. Besides, you don't even have any wings. You said so yourself." The Fairy won the argument.

"That doesn't matter. You're coming with me. A man by the name of Weemus Bobeemus has been feeding me information and supplies," said Dr. Judy, probably revealing

211

way too much. "I've been one step ahead of you two the whole time. I was ready when Dr. Blindofsky came a-calling. And then I iced him."

"He was shot, not iced. I was there." The Duke was there.

"I think they mean the same thing."

"Can we check a dictionary?"

"What's a dictionary?"

"Wait, who said that?"

"Anyway, I killed him," said Dr. Judy, I think. Maybe it was one of the flower girls. "Soon enough, I'll kill you too, Belle. We've got other plans for the Duke. An old friend of his will be visiting us soon. Now we must go to THE HALL OF PANZIES..."

DUNT DUNT DA!!!!!!

The three conversationalists looked around each other. Then, Dr. Judy continued to speak. "After we get there, we'll be visiting the Pub of Boogus MacDoogus. It's a bar you haven't been to for quite some time. And when we get there, your surprise will be revealed."

"Yes! I knew it. A surprise! Cool." The fairy was excited at the prospect of a surprise. She began jumping up and down. She didn't really have good ups, though, so nobody knew how excited she actually was. It was a mystery.

"Hey Belle, she said the surprise was for me. I get to open it. I'm not saying I won't share or anything, but it's still my surprise. Between you and me, I'm rooting for chocolate cupcakes." The Duke was also excited, but he didn't believe in ups.

And with that, the three were off, followed by the girls.

Elsewhere, but we have been with these two before

Dave and Cecilia wandered the swamps of South Central aimlessly. "Where is this hall, exactly? You know, I was looking for my grandmother out here, earlier, and I don't recall running into any super fortresses of destruction."

"Well, Dave, Winston said it was in some sort of multidimensional techno-babble Sub-Antarctic Egyptian fortress zone near the Jamaican Desert."

"That clears up everything, Claristinarta."

"It does?"

"Of course. Therefore, according to the laws of association, we should be in possession of the ability to transmorphigize our bodies into the reproductive cells of small rocks, at which point, we would fly off the planet until we landed in the Great Hall that Wabbinfath spoke of."

"Is there any other possibility, Dave?"

"It's just a long shot, but we might just end up at the Hall without any real explanation."

"Look Dave! What's that?" There, in front of them, was nothing. Cecilia and Dave, however, not to be disappointed, kept moving. Eventually, they found nothing more. And then, they showed up at the Great Hall. As Dave looked around, he could tell that it was in old California somewhere, just off the coast of Madagascar, among other places. Slowly Cecilia and Dave made their way toward the entrance. Before reaching the great and evil gate, Cecilia got an idea.

"Why don't we sneak in through the underground tunnel system?"

"Why, you're getting better by the minute, Cecilneena!"

"You too, Dave! That's the closest you've come to saying my name correctly in nearly 100 pages." And so the two spies entered the tunnels, through the codename 'manhole' sometimes known in strange literary circles as 'person-hole' and in still other places as 'thingy.' The caverns were dark and dreary beneath the evil hall. But it was safer than the direct approach. And then, something happened.

"Dave, something's happening," said Cecilia.

Yes indeed, Dave knew he made the right decision when he hooked up with this super intelligent spy-of-good. In the meantime, the walls were closing in, and the tunnel in front of them was blocked by a large piece of cheese, Gouda cheese.

"So we meet at last, Mr. Cheese. Let me just tell you, I won't be as easy to scare off as some of our country's senior citizens..."

The cheese held his ground though, and the walls continued to close in. The two started to battle, but the cheese was ultra-tough. Dave worked with everything he had, but was becoming exhausted. Cecilia, meanwhile, was shrieking up a storm when she noticed her dress had gotten soiled in the evil tunnels.

"Won't someone help us?"

Just then a cloud with some cheesy lightning special effects rumbled overhead. And from out of the mist an old-school phone booth plopped onto the Gouda.

Bill S. Preston, Esq., poked his head out of the booth. "Ted, I think you dialed the wrong number again, Dude."

"Excellent!" said Ted Theodore Logan.

"No Ted, we're running out of dimes, Dude. Wrong numbers are most heinous," said Bill.

"Sorry Bill, So-crates keeps pushing Abraham Lincoln into me," said Ted.

Socrates started speaking ancient Greek, gesticulating in the direction of Beethoven and Genghis Kahn, who were comparing musical instruments.

Just then the Gouda squeezed out from under the phone booth.

"Hey Ted, there's a piece of cheese over here if anyone's hungry," said Bill.

Just then the TARDIS came crashing through the roof of the tunnel, landing on the Gouda.

"Forget it, Ted. Some other phone booth dudes ran it over," said Bill, clearly disappointed.

The Fourth Doctor, wearing a long and colorful scarf, opened the door of the TARDIS. He addressed Bill and Ted in a most non-excellent manner. "You know gentlemen, we were doing this phone booth time machine thing before you two graduated out of your nappies."

Just then the Fourth Doctor was struck in the head by a frying pan and dragged back into the TARDIS. Peter Cushing, dressed as Grand Moff Tarkin, strode forth, as stormtroopers Mehmet G. Korkmaz and Chip Langston fanned out on either side of him.

"Dude, it's the evil dude from *Star Wars*," said Bill. "Ted, should we grab him?"

"I don't know Dude, we're supposed to be doing a history report," said Ted Theodore Logan.

"Yeah, but *Star Wars* is from a long time ago, isn't that in the past?" asked Bill.

Abraham Lincoln, not familiar with *Star Wars* but sufficiently versed in the project the boys were attempting to complete, tried to explain the difference between actual history and movie history.

"Gunnery Sergeant Korkmaz, have you located the Gouda?" asked Peter Cushing, who was beginning to sound more like the actual Grand Moff Tarkin.

"I think we landed on it, sir," said Korkmaz.

"Great, have Langston scoop it up. Emperor Palpatine plans on running it through some drills. This Gouda may become his new apprentice. The Emperor says that the cheese is reeking with the dark side of the force," said Cushing.

"It's reeking with something, all right," said Dave.

"Hey, isn't that the guy we tried to pull over back on Tatooine?" asked Langston.

"Cool it, Chip," barked Korkmaz.

"It's Kip, sir," said Langston.

"We've been over this already, Private," said Korkmaz.

Bill and Ted, having sufficiently understood Lincoln's history lesson, bid farewell. "Catch you later, evil *Star Wars* dudes!" They closed the door to the phone booth, and were off into another cheesy special effect lightning cloud.

"After them!" shouted Cushing, directing the stormtroopers back into the TARDIS to continue the chase.

The Fourth Doctor stumbled back through the doorway, almost knocking over Korkmaz, blood streaming from his head. "It's Dr. Who!" shouted the Fourth Doctor in the direction of Cushing, as the first, second, third and sixth through 11th doctors barreled out of the TARDIS.

"Hey, I've seen this guy before. He's not Doctor Who, he's Grand Moff Tarkin," said the Sixth Doctor.

"Of course he's Doctor Who, you dolt," said the Eighth Doctor, dressed like Lieutenant William Bush preparing to embark on the Renown. "Didn't you view the Dalek films?"

"Now, now, Eight. Be nice to the lad. We all know six is missing a few screws," said the Ninth Doctor.

"While we're here I'm heading out for a pint, you cheeky bastards," said the 10th Doctor. "Anyone else?"

The First, Second and Seventh Doctors quickly followed the 10th Doctor out the door. Eight and Nine looked at each other, shrugged, and followed suit.

"I'm only holding the TARDIS for 20 minutes," said Cushing to the other doctors, who headed for the pub of Boogus MacDoogus. "And someone better pick me up a Reuben, fries, and a few cases of extra stout. None of that non-carbonated pub draught, again."

The 11th doctor began inching toward the exit, before Cushing wheeled around. "Get back in there, eleven. You're *still* grounded!"

"I'd listen to him," said three. "If you think what he did to four was bad, it can get worse... much worse. Come on lad, I've got some smoking jackets we can try on." The third doctor put his arm around eleven and led him back into the TARDIS.

Cecilia, in the meantime began to run towards her brave

little warrior, who was attempting to catch his breath. "Come on Dave, we have to get out of here, before it's too late!"

The walls were starting to get closer. There were only a couple of inches left before Cecilia and Dave would be size negative zeroes, even though you can't have negative zeroes. You also shouldn't be able to have size zeroes unless your in the buff, because zero by definition is the absence of stuff. Which means Eva Longoria should just walk around without any clothes on because apparently she's a size zero. So therefore size zero equals no clothes and super bitchy desperate housewives. Cecilia, on the other hand, was not a size zero, but more likely a six or an eight. She struggled to get the weary Dave to his feet. She picked him up off the ground, and the two of them were able to scurry out just before they were crushed, or just use your imagination. If you prefer a size 20, then she's a size 20. She has to at least be a six otherwise she never would have been able to pick Dave up off the ground. So the size six-to-twenty Cecilia and Dave entered a new room, where they were met again by another villain, this one slightly larger than the cheese.

"So we meet again, Winston."

"Sorry chap, we haven't been in any scenes together."

"Right." Dave quickly wheeled around. Then he turned to face Winston, once more. "But now I can say we meet again."

"Well done, old bean. You're quite the barrister. Yes, quite the boffin of espionage, aren't we? Still, I shant be thrice defeated." Winston would not be thrice defeated. Spies have the most ultimate of ultimate conversations.

Dave was equal to the challenge. "So, now that we meet again, I will defeat you once and for all."

"Well said, old chap, but look, what's that on your face?"

Dave quickly attempted to look at his face, but he found that an impossible task while his eyes were still connected to it. As Dave tried to pry his eyes from his head so he could look at

217

his face, Winston grabbed Cecilia and took off further into the Great Hall.

"This is harder than it looks," said Dave. "I need that thingy that John Crichton had on *Farscape* when he ripped his eyes out of his head. Maybe that would work."

"No Dave, the evil Nebari used that eye thing to frell with all the good guys," said Cecilia, trying to keep Winston from gagging her. "There isn't anything on your fa..."

Dave looked up, and tried to figure out what Cecilia had meant, and why she was going. "Nothing on my fa? Wait. It must be code. I'll just get my trusty little book and... Drat, I left my book back in Cellameena's room."

Dave had to think and think quickly. Then, like a bolt of lightning traveling faster than a slow-moving bolt of lightning, Dave figured it all out. "Face! There's nothing on my Face! Of course! Fa is a long long way to run, and *Farscape* is on the B-side of Otis Reading's "Fa-Fa-Fa-Fa-Fa-Fa (Sad Song)," and everyone knows that a duet by Mary Poppins and Otis Reading would have been so fantastically awesome that it would have ripped a whole in the space-time continuum that would have had Doc Brown looking to buy a one-way ticket to Libya. And if Doc Brown were Fuzzy Wuzzy, then Mary Poppins really does have red hair, and she didn't have anything on her face when she was singing on that mountain. I'm off!" Dave was off, this time to finally settle the score with Winston.

All's well at the Pub of Boogus MacDoogus

Led at both gunpoint and pansy-point, the Duke and the Fairy swished through the doors of a very familiar looking establishment. It was exactly as Dr. Darwinkly had said it would be. The barroom was the same as the one from all those years ago, when the Duke was young and alive. Now, he was, um, I'm not really sure, ah, looking at the Fairy, who of course is a fictional character and also alive, except as a fictional

218

character. But Dr. Darwinkly had other plans for them.

"Do you remember now, Duke? Do you remember the humiliation you caused my love?"

"Hey lady, when was the Duke ever your love?" The Fairy had to speak. She had been angered when Dr. Darwinkly insinuated that the doctor and the Duke had been lovers.

"No, I meant that he caused someone that I call 'my love' humiliation."

"It wasn't enough that you had to drag us through that foul-smelling swamp? If I find out that the two of you were involved..." The Fairy was so angry she was incensed, except instead of smelling like incense she smelled more like fairy dust. Come to think of it, I'm not really sure if fairy dust smells like anything, so lets say Belle smelled like jasmine or roses. But not a person named Jasmine or Rose, unless they also smelled wicked, as in good wicked, like 'wicked sweet.'

"No! No, no, no, no, no! You just don't get it, do you? I said that I loved this guy, and... Forget it. It was Borpos, all right? You humiliated him, and I loved him. But he's back now, ready to settle the score."

Just then the 10th Doctor intentionally bumped into Dr. Judy, spilling Guinness Extra Stout all over her snappy threads. "We're quite the fit bird, aren't we? Come on love, where's the porpoise? Under your dress?"

Dr. Judy fought off the 10th Doctor, who was attempting to lift up her dress. "Young man!"

"Actually I'm a centuries old time lord, and I'm completely zonked," said the 10th Doctor, falling asleep on Dr. Judy.

The Duke and the Fairy looked at each other, and then back at Dr. Darwinkly.

"So, this porpoise is someone I've met before?" asked the Duke. "I don't recall befriending, or at least meeting, any aquatic mammals. I don't even recall eating any marine mammals. Can you eat marine mammals?"

"I have, mostly manatees. And some humpback whales in my youth." The fairy had a big appetite. "Hey, what about those orcas from earlier?"

"Those guys just owed me a solid. On the other hand, if I were to befriend any marine mammals, it would have to be either a polar bear or a walrus. Mostly because walruses are wicked sweet," said the Duke, now conversant in the latest lingo. "That means extra awesome."

"Ooh, I bet walruses taste really good," Belle was getting quite hungry. "Can we go out for surf and turf after this?"

"No, you cannot go out for surf and turf after this. I'm planning on smashing you into several small pieces, and plucking your wings, and doing lots of other mean things to you," said Dr. Judy, edging out from under the 10th Doctor.

"Jeez, Doc, that's pretty messed up," said the Duke.

"Well, she's the one that ate a manatee," responded Dr. Darwinkly. "Those are endangered."

"Speaking of manatees, there's this other species of the order Sirenia, called the dugong. Those are really chewy. I wouldn't recommend them," said Belle. "Cheese went to boarding school with one named Gary, and he was seriously strange. Seriously, are we going to go get something to eat or what? I'm starving."

"Ah, now I remember this Borpos guy."

"Doc, I don't think anyone cares if you remember," said the Duke, puzzled by Dr. Darwinkly's comment. Me too.

Nonetheless, Belle was correct: Dugongs are really weird looking. It's possible they're also chewy, but only a fairy knows for sure. Just then, Borpos walked through the door.

Elsewhere in the Hall of Panz... you know the rest

It was time for the big wedding. Winston, having retrieved Cecilia, wore a white tuxedo with tails. Weemus had borrowed Ron Weasley's dress robes. The Impolitus Guard joined the

220

Weasleys, a few Nazis, several evil flower girls and Black Manta in the chapel, as the Bishop from *Spaceballs* officiated.

"I hired this guy because he does really short readings," said Weemus.

"Good heavens! Why are the Weasleys in attendance?"

"You know, something borrowed, something blue. They're my something borrowed, the old guy bishop is my something old... I still don't have anything new," said Weemus.

"Or something blue," said Winston.

"Nope, got that covered. We've decided to replace you with *Hill Street Blues* actor Daniel J. Travanti."

As the two women made their entrance at the other end of the hall, escorted by the remainder of the Impolitus Guard, or rather forced up the aisle by the Impolitus Guard, a few Nazis zapped Winston with Scott Baio from *Zapped!* as Daniel J. Travanti quickly took his place by Weemus.

"Um, thanks, Dad," said Travanti.

The attendees rose as the wedding organist from *Sixteen Candles*, accompanied by the Trammps, started playing "Disco Inferno." Finally, the little white Styrofoam cup, wearing a little white dress, was dragged up the aisle by a few more members of the Impolitus Guard and some ultra-evil flower girls.

"Styrofoam... That reminds me, what happened with the knife and fork? I'll need those devices to finish off the Joes."

Travanti looked a bit lost. "Um, can it be any knife or fork?"

"You've failed me for the last time, Admiral," said Weemus, raising his hands as if to perform some act of evil wizardry.

"I played a police captain on TV..." said Travanti, before getting blasted into smithereens by Scott Baio from *Zapped!*

Dazed, Winston slowly got back onto his feet. "What happened?" he asked.

"You'll have to ask Scott Baio. Or Bob Loblaw."

Meanwhile, Buffy and Cecilia were getting acquainted as they were forced up the aisle by the Nazis.

"If we work together, we can escape," said Cecilia.

"I don't know, I think they got them at the Pottery Barn," said Buffy. "I wasn't really paying attention."

"Look, my ex-boyfriend kidnapped me, gave me this awful wedding dress... actually it's pretty nice... and forced me down the aisle... Look, I've got a friend on the outside. He can help us escape. We just need a diversion."

"Are you still talking? Fine. Yes, I still have the Angora sweater, and no you can't borrow it," said Buffy. "Wasn't it enough I loaned you my mascara?"

"No, you gave that to the cup. Why *is* the cup here?"

"Can I get a pizza delivered?" asked Buffy, talking on her new Virgin Mobile smart phone.

"What? A smart phone? And Winston with his pager," said Cecilia. "I should have known."

"No, that's some other girl," said Buffy, continuing to talk on her phone. "Yes, I know she's rude. Wait, she's looking at me. Pretend we're talking about something else. Yes, Mr. Flying Monkey, I do, I do, I do believe in spooks."

Cecilia wasn't sure if Buffy was talking about goblins or super spies. She grew leery that perhaps Buffy was onto her new status as a secret agent.

The three ladies slowly (very slowly) made their way further up the aisle.

Back at Boogus's

Borpos strode through the swooshy doors like a man on a mission. The swooshy doors made that swoosh sound, which, I'm assuming looks like Air Jordans. Borpos was ready. There, in front of him, stood the Duke, with the Fairy at his side, surrounded by Dr. Judy and the flower girls. He walked up to the Cowboy and cracked his neck from side to side.

"Do I know you?" asked the Duke.

Borpos cracked his knuckles and flexed his muscles. He

222

then motioned to Bob Loblaw to begin reading for him, as apparently Borpos had also lost his voice.

"So we meet again, cowboy, only this time I am the master," said Loblaw in a monotone, ah, tone.

"Yeah, we meet... when was it again? Thursday?"

"No, not Thursday," said Belle. "We were, um, staying at the Himalayan Ritz on Thursday..."

"Well then, it couldn't have been Thursday."

"Mr. Borpos, my time is up, now if you'll excuse me, I'm off to work on my law blog," said Loblaw, off to work on the Bob Loblaw Law Blog.

"Maybe Saturday?" asked Belle.

"That's today. Thursday was two days ago. That's not really all that long ago, even in fairy time," said the Duke.

"Why Duke, you remembered," said the Fairy. It was the little moments that counted the most. "Like when you baked me chocolate chip cookies, even though you knew I liked snickerdoodles."

"Pardon?"

"No I will not pardon your insolence!" exclaimed Borpos, having found his voice. "Also, if anyone has seen a pair of keys, with a little pink Minnie Mouse... I lost my keys."

The First Doctor strode up to Borpos, pointed up in the air, and acted as if he was going to say something important. Then he belched and sneezed on the evil planet killer, before returning to his Guinness.

"That's good, thanks for helping," said the Duke, watching the First Doctor go back to his seat, before wheeling around to face Borpos. "What's insolence?" asked the Duke.

"Oh, is that the new bubble bath you got me for our anniversary?" asked Belle.

"Sure, that sounds good. But wait, how did he get your insolence?" asked the Duke, returning his glower to Borpos. "You've crossed the wrong cowboy, hombre."

The Duke crossed over to the planet-killing super villain, ready to punch his lights out, and also probably him as well.

"Timeout!" said Borpos.

The Fairy lunged at Borpos.

"I said timeout!"

"That means it's go time, right?" asked the Fairy.

"No, that means timeout," said Borpos.

"Oh," said the Fairy. "So is it time in, yet?"

Just then, Dr. Darwinkly tackled the Fairy to the ground. The Duke made a move to help his sweetheart, but was blocked by the planet killer and a bunch of the flower girls.

"Are you ready, Duke? This time, it really is over," said Borpos. "And nobody forget about my keys, please. I'm double-parked and the swamp police hand out tickets like Tic Tacs at a garlic festival."

"You can say that again, Borpos," said the Duke.

"What, about my keys? Do you think those guys forgot? Oh, you meant about it being over. My bad," said Borpos.

"Do you mind? Can I continue?" asked the Duke. "I should have finished this a long time ago. Now you've given me the chance to fix that." The two men glared at each other.

"Wait, when you say a long time ago, are you referring to when we both hung out here in the 1920s, or are you referring to Thursday?" Borpos wanted to clear the air before the fight.

"Don't know. Let's ask this guy over here," said the Duke, motioning to R5-D4. The duo stared at the droid, waiting for an answer.

Over on the floor, Belle and Dr. Darwinkly fought it out. Dr. Darwinkly had taken the advantage, when Belle had tried to attack Borpos. She had Belle flat on her stomach, unable to reach behind to swing at the doctor.

Dr. Darwinkly was about to go in for the kill, when finally, after years of built up fears and unnecessary anxiety, Belle did it: with her left wing, she knocked the Howitzer off of

224

Darwinkly's shoulder. With her right wing, she forced the doctor off of her back. And with great effort, Belle was onto her feet, this time ready to face her enemy head on.

Meanwhile, R5-D4 continued to give the Duke and Borpos the silent treatment. Just then, Greg Marmalard, Danny Kaye, Ludovico Ariosto, Francois Mitterrand, Def Leppard, Donner the Reindeer, Mitch Albom and the entire Island of Molokai enter the room. The group began complex negotiations with the droid. The Duke and Borpos noticed their voices becoming increasingly agitated before Donner took control of the situation.

"Hey guys, you should probably just continue with your fight. I think this R5 unit has a faulty stimulus package," said Santa's head reindeer.

"Donner, tell them about *Tuesdays,*" said Albom.

"I believe he means a bad motivator," said Mitterrand. Greg Marmalard and Danny Kaye stared at the former president of France. "What? The film was translated into French. It was called *La Guerre des étoiles.*"

"That's not even a blinkin' beacon," said Donner.

"By the way, thanks for ditching me," said Marmalard. "Do you know how much a taxi costs from the Hoth system?"

"Don't answer that," said Danny Kaye to Mitterrand, who was preparing to speak, once again.

"What's all this about Tuesday?" asked Borpos.

Def Leppard started playing "Photograph." Borpos and the Duke decided to mutually restart the fight once Rick Allen started playing the cowbell.

Borpos harnessed his massive strength to crush the Duke.

"Go ahead. What are you waiting for? I ain't gonna flinch, pilgrim," said the Duke.

And so Borpos delivered the death blow (normally reserved for devouring small galaxies and space nuggets).

When the smoke cleared, only Belle, Dr. Darwinkly, R5-D4

and Donner the reindeer were left. Oh, and some other guy standing right in front of Borpos. Apparently everyone else was vaporized or went to the bathroom, except the 10th Doctor, who was still sleeping on the floor. Then Santa's lead reindeer kicked R5-D4 with his rear hooves, obliterating the little red droid. After that, he got a call on his cell phone.

"Hey dear. No, no, the scene's almost over... Yes, I have my credit card, why? Seriously? How many carrots can one reindeer eat? That's a load, dear, there's no way he needs beta-carotene to refuel his nose. That's absolutely nuts... No, as in 'absolutely absurd.' No, not peanuts... Well, if he needs it that badly, tell Rudolph I'll pick up some sweet potatoes and kale on the way home and that he better have his chores done... Because I'm sick of carrots all the time... Yes, kale is also high in beta-carotene. I just looked it up... No, while I was talking to you... No, I have been listening the whole time... I got one of those new smartphones. This wizard guy just got a whole bunch of them from Virgin Mobile... I imagine it's got pretty good coverage if you can call me while I'm in the middle of Legion of Doom Swamp... I'll be home when I'm home. I don't know... Well, if he's got a date tonight he'll just have to wait... I'm sure Clarisse won't mind waiting a couple of minutes... Well then her dad's an idiot. Are you sure we want grandkids with that guy's gene pool? I heard he doesn't even know how to fly... No, one of the guys told me... I don't know. It was either Comet or Blitzen. Probably Blitzen... Yeah, he might have had a couple of drinks. What are you insinuating? Look, *I* never ran over any grandmas... No I haven't had anything to drink... That's it I'm hanging up... No, I mean it. Seriously, I mean it... Fine, I'll also get some milk... Love you too." Donner then began to depart. "Ok, I'll see you guys later. I've got to go pick up some groceries."

Wait, somebody was still standing in front of Borpos?

"Nice try, Borpos. Now it's my turn," said the Duke, clearly not killed, vaporized, or sent to the bathroom by the death blow.

One uppercut, and it was over. Borpos was sent back to outer space, just as Danny Kaye, apparently hiding behind R5-D4 before Donner obliterated the astromech, found a set of pink Minnie Mouse keys.

"No!!!!!" shouted Borpos, as he was blown off the planet. "Please move my car, it's a 1993 green Honda Civic..." The force of the blow caused him to fly into the sky so fast, that he took all of the material that made up the moon along with him. As Borpos continued on his flight path, the strength of the punch forced the shards of the moon to reform in virtually the exact same configuration in which it had existed for the previous four and a half billion years. I say virtually the same because the eastern edge of the Mare Tranquillitatis was covered with dust from the Abul Wafa crater, but only lunar scientists would find that troublesome.

This was the second time in less than a month that the moon had blown up. People were beginning to ask questions. It all ended up being attributed to Rosencrantz and Guildenstern or somebody, so it was okay.

As Borpos made his way out of the solar system, faster than he had come, he looked back to see Neptune reforming. All of the space nuggets he had devoured somehow managed to retake their respective shapes.

It was a decent punch.

Dr. Darwinkly looked up as her champion left the galaxy. "Borpos, my love. Don't forget about me!"

Belle, not to be outdone by her beau, flicked Judy with her wings, sending the evil scientist on the same trajectory.

All over the world, people looked up, and felt a renewed sense of purpose. The Argentinians and the Brits stopped fighting over the Falkland Islands. Chile and Turkey stopped making jokes about each other. The Israelis and the Israelites became good friends. They invited the Arabs over for tea and crumpets. Dogs and cats *did* start living together, Dr. Venkman. The Enterprises NCC-1701 and NCC-1701-D completed a sign and trade agreement for James Tiberius Kirk, as he was the most awesome of all Enterprise captains, but only in the original William Shatner vintage. Even Fidel Castro shipped two billion tons of cigars to the United States.

Then, little Johnny Gacksford from Jeffersontown, Kentucky, called Bobbi Sue Blakely a big dugong. Confused but then later furious after discovering what a dugong looked like, Bobbi Sue responded that Johnny was nothing more than a weird little okapi. Then everybody else went back to his or her normal ways of killing and mass destruction.

Belle and the Duke breathed a sigh of relief that the nightmare of world peace would never come to pass. The Duke glanced down at his mistress.

"What? They always wanted to be together," said the Fairy.

"I will remember not to cross you when we get married."

"Who said anything about getting married?"

Yes, deep in his heart, the Duke knew that this was the girl for him.

At the White Wedding

"Smashing! Cecilia hasn't backed out on our nuptials," said Winston. With that out of his mind, Winston was back at the controls, flying the plane... free to pursue a life of...

"Wait, didn't I have a question for you?" asked Weemus.

"Are you going to ask me to be your best man?"

"That's right, I asked Travanti, not you," said Weemus Bobeemus.

"You asked Daniel J. Travanti to be your best man, not your one and only son?" asked Winston.

"Who said I had only one son? Black Manta over there is your brother. Why else do you think he got invited to the wedding?" said Weemus.

228

Just then, Michael Rosenbaum burst through the door, followed by his minions, Dr. Syn and Wonder Woman, and also probably some of Gru's minions. "Hate to interrupt, but we're looking for Black Manta. Hey, there he is. Black Manta, what are you doing here?"

"My dad and half-brother are getting married. I sent you a fax about it," said Black Manta. "I told Toyman, as well."

"Toyman!" Rosenbaum was furious. "Wait, a fax? We don't have a fax machine in the Hall of Doom. Speaking of which, where are the keys?"

Black Manta reached into his pants and grabbed some keys. "Some guy in a green Honda Civic blocked me in, though."

"All right, let's get out of here and let these nice folks get back to their wedding," said Rosenbaum, before turning to Weemus Bobeemus. "But I'm going to ask again, you zany Wizard, not to party past 10 p.m. I've got a meeting, bright and early, with Larry Ellison. We're trying to secure Legion of Doom Swamp for the next America's Cup."

"I told you before, Rosenbaum, you can't go out signing agreements until you first get the approval of the Legion of Doom Swamp neighborhood association," said Weemus.

"Is that really necessary, Mr. Wizard? It's the America's Cup for God's sake, only the greatest sporting event in the history of the universe. I think we all know the neighborhood association is going to side with me, just like they did when you tried to mandate uniform Christmas lights. Nobody likes *only* homogenized milk. Sometimes we like chocolate, or Yoo-hoo, or Strawberry Quik," said Rosenbaum. "Come on, Wonder Woman, I need a shoulder massage."

Rosenbaum and the Legion of Doom left.

Cecilia grabbed Wonder Woman aside just before she followed suit. "I just thought you should know that I love the outfit, and I'm hoping to get a lasso for our honeymoon."

"Dear, it might be best to leave the lasso at home for the

honeymoon. You wouldn't want anyone to get injured. Besides, he doesn't look like he'd last too long," said Wonder Woman, motioning to Winston, who was deep in conversation with Dr. Syn.

"No, not him. I'm going to marry Dave, my super spy hero. He invited me to go on this mission with him," said Cecilia. "Why Lex Luthor, anyway? Isn't he a bad guy?"

"As bad as he comes," said Wonder Woman. "And he is *Ah-mazing*, with a capital A."

"Really?" said Buffy. "Never would have guessed."

Wonder Woman then followed the Legion out the door, shouting back at Dr. Syn. "Come on, Scarecrow, time to go!"

"And then I was in *Ice Station Zebra*, where I played a British intelligence officer. Quite a good film. Had Ernest Borgnine in it," said Dr. Syn. "True what they said about him, as well."

"What was?" asked Winston.

"That he was faster than Jim Brown, of course. Now Brown was much better at lacrosse, but Borgnine probably would have been the superior NFL running back, had he chosen that path," said Dr. Syn. "Be seeing you."

"Jolly good! Don't forget you are all invited to the festivities at the Pub of Boogus MacDoogus following the nuptials."

Dr. Syn followed Wonder Woman out the door.

The Trammps, having finished "Disco Inferno," started playing a disco rendition of Milli Vanilli's "Baby Don't Forget my Number."

"You know, I swear I'm forgetting something," said Weemus. "I should really try that Lumosity crap."

"Psst..." said Fred Weasley, still very much alive. "Total fraud, that Lumosity. Waste of money. We should know. My brother and I run a joke shop."

Just then, Dave burst through the door, only to get stuck about half way through. Fortunately the Styrofoam cup had been leading Flabius and Biffus back to the hall, and he was

230

more than happy to knock Dave the rest of the way through.

Flabius and Biffus, only moments behind, followed Dave and the cup. The four warriors looked over at the guards, the Nazis, the flower girls, Winston and Weemus. And then, the guards and the Nazis ran off into a corner. The flower girls began pelting them with tribbles and pansies for their cowardice.

"Ah, the set of utensils! That's what it was," said Weemus.

Cecilia, spotting her true love, cheered for him to defeat the evil Winston Wallingford. "Come on, Dave!"

Dave was up to the challenge. "Well, Winston, I see now who your father is. I just want you to know that Cillidolina really shouldn't be wearing white."

"Wait, who shouldn't be wearing white?" Winston's follow-up question, however, was ignored, as Dave had come across the liner notes to his Bananarama vinyl collection.

Winston glanced over at his girlfriend. "Is this true Cecilia?" Winston was in a state of shock, of utter despair.

Cecilia was a little confused, but slowly came around to the super code that Dave was using. "White? Huh? Oh. I get it. Oh, I mean, no, I really shouldn't be wearing white."

"My apologies, darling, that hardly seems fair. What color would you like to wear? I would offer blue, but my father had Daniel J. Travanti vaporized," said Winston. "Also, I believe we still need something new. We've sufficiently addressed borrowed and old. Maybe tangerine? Would that be fair?"

Dave had no time to judge what was and wasn't fair, or serve as a magistrate on *X-Factor, America's Got Talent, Britain's Got Talent, Dancing with the Stars, Bailando por un Sueño, Pop Idol,* or *American Idol.* He hadn't practiced law in years. Instead, he made a quick decision.

"You know what's not fair?" asked Dave, before becoming utterly distracted by his liner notes. "Hey, where did these come from? I've been looking for these for weeks."

"I believe they belonged to R5-D4," said Winston. "That

reindeer fellow obliterated him, however, so I believe you can have them. Would that be fair? I saw the entire affair on this security monitor." Winston pointed to a wall-mounted plasma that carried security feeds from around the hall.

"Hey, does this thing get the DuMont Network?" asked Weemus Bobeemus.

"I'm pretty sure they used that joke in an episode of *Archer*," said Dave. "But thanks for the liner notes. That actually is kind of fair."

"Brilliant show, *Archer*," said Winston.

Dave and Winston looked at each other. Could they be long lost brothers? Could the two super spies, one like the white spy from *Mad* magazine, the other like the black spy, simply be two sides of the same coin? Could Winston be like Matt Damon in the *Good Shepherd*? Could Dave be like Lee Pace in *The Hobbit*? Could anyone ask another question that started with the word could?

"And you know what else?" asked Dave.

Winston looked around to see if there were any marsupials nearby, before responding, "I'm sorry, old chap, are you speaking to me?"

"I'm not going to pay a lot for this muffler!"

"Clearly. Who would?"

"I know that, now," said Dave. And with that, he began his long awaited battle with Winston. The two fought valiantly. I should rephrase that. Dave fought valiantly while Winston cheated and stuff, but to no avail. The fight waged across seven continents and 142 countries. DRD-1812 played the *1812 Overture* to make the fight seem even more dramatic. Eventually the two stumbled back through the doors of the Hall. This time however, it was with Dave dragging Winston by his nose, victorious.

"Make this failure number three, Winston. No, on second thought, make this number four. Yes, I think I have decided to count the fudge incident after all." Weemus Bobeemus was obviously upset, although possibly moreso because he couldn't catch any DuMont Network wrestling shows, featuring his favorite star, Gorgeous George.

"But father, I have a fudge allergy," said Winston, kind of in this nasally voice because of the way in which Dave had a hold of his shnoz.

"Well then, I'm counting it twice," said the evil wizard. But there was no time for that, with Flabius standing right in front of him. He quickly lunged for the Sacred Spoon of Chocococolate La and the Great Fork That Has Been Known to Wreak Havoc on Entire Countries, the two devices that still might save him.

"Even if I can't complete the Weather Dominator, this will still be enough to defeat the likes of Flabius Flaximus," said Weemus. "Of course I'll probably have to give Cobra Commander some of his money back, but, we can deal with that later."

Flabius was ready, also, as he engaged Weemus in a stare-down. "So we meet again, Flabius Flaximus!" Flabius then started counting to himself, before coming to the conclusion that he had spoken correctly.

Weemus, a little shocked and confused by the strange comment, made his shock and confusion known. "Yes, but weren't you supposed to say, 'So we meet again, Weemus Bobeemus?'"

"So I see the great wizard is a little confused, calling himself names. Just remember one thing, Weemus, I was recently a member of a barber shop quartet, and I should tell you, your son is a fantastic tenor. And, although I could be wrong, I'm pretty sure Frankenstein is the name of the guy, not the monster, who tends to be on the side of good in most modern retellings, such as that great film, *The Monster Squad*. Also, I'm going to defeat you now. Let me summarize by breaking into

233

song. It's a classic, and I'm sure you can all sing along...

"SOMEWHERE OVER THE RAINB-"

"Sire, please, let's get on with this. Besides, you are off key." Biffus was there to aid his master at all costs, including advising Flabius when he was singing a c-sharp instead of a d-flat.

"Thank you my trusted music teacher, I shall remember to use a metronome, next time. Anyway, now to you, Weemus Bobeemus. I'll still beat you, even with those super items. Because you are evil, and also confused, whereas, I am good."

"Confused? Not any more. But just out of curiosity, if I was trying to power a weather control device funded by Cobra, do you think I could use any set of utensils or does it have to be *the* sacred set of utensils?" Weemus Bobeemus held the vicious weapons of destruction in the general direction of Flabius.

Flabius, in retaliation, made a sort of grabbing motion toward his great ally, Biffus Palookus, as if he were waiting for Biffus to hand him something. "Quick, my trusted handler of sacred objects, hand me the knife and the super napkin!"

Biffus meanwhile, was just finishing a quick snack, of muffins and butter. He had been using the napkin to clean himself when Flabius made his call. Biffus glanced down at the soiled weapons. He gave Flabius that, 'Gee, sorry for using the ultimate weapons for a snack and thereby severely hampering your chances to defeat Weemus Bobeemus,' look. Flabius shook his head. He would have to make due with out any aid.

"Remind me to have a talk with you after this is all over, my trusted you-are-in-deep-trouble prairie home companion."

"Sorry, sire. I hadn't eaten in ages," said Biffus. Which may or may not have been true, depending on if he and Flabius had traveled forward in time or everyone else traveled back in time. *Gonna go back in time! Gonna go back in time!* Classic SNL skit. What fun. Can't find it online anymore. Totally bummed.

"I suppose you're right, my trusted fandango," said Flabius. "Hey, do you have any more muffins?"

234

"Blueberry or Corn?"

"Blueberry, definitely."

Weemus, meanwhile, had been circling around Flabius, waiting for the right moment to attack. "Hey, we're supposed to be having this great battle. Come on, let's go!"

Flabius looked up. "Oh, sorry. All right. So it's you and your spoon against me and the fork."

"No, I have both items. See?"

"Come on now, that's not very fair," said Flabius.

"No one said life was fair. I wanted to build a weather dominator, but somebody had to go and throw away the plastic butter knife of wonder and the paper super napkin of destruction. Okay, time to meet your fate, Flaximus," said Weemus Bobeemus.

"You know Weemus, I get the distinct impression I am forgetting something. What am I forgetting?" asked the great and powerful Flabius Flaximus.

"You know, I had that problem earlier. I thought about trying Lumosity but Ron Weasley's brother said it was a terrible idea," the evil wizard responded.

"What the heck is a lumosity?" asked Flabius.

"I'm not sure, something about video games but not video games. Hey, what about my other question? Do you think we could grab any old napkin and knife to finish off the Joes, or should we try to salvage the ones your buddy used up?"

"Great idea. Where can we find some?"

"So, you're saying we should try to salvage..."

"Heck no, Wizard. I hate recycling," said Flabius.

"Well, in that case, I think we might have some extra stuff in the Pub of Boogus MacDoogus. That's where we were going to hold the wedding reception," said Weemus. "Follow me."

Weemus and Flabius continued their battle through out the Hall, all the way to the pub of Boogus MacDoogus.

"Has this always been here?" asked Flabius. "Buffy and I

had our first dance together in this place."

"I believe so," said Weemus, carefully stepping over the sleeping 10th Doctor as he parried more strikes from Flabius.

"I could have sworn the kingdom of Boogus MacDoogus was now part of Rambo Brightus," said Flabius.

"It is. Actually, Gimpus Foo Foo is also part of Rambo Brightus," said Weemus. "Haven't you ever read your own map? That's the first thing I did when plotting your downfall."

"Wow, this place looks terrible," said Flabius, noticing a cowboy and a fairy diving under the cake table, both covered in frosting. "I wonder what happened here. Hey, maybe we could get some Guinness while we're engaged in this ultimate battle of devastation?"

"Excellent idea," said Weemus. "Barkeep?"

Lord Boogus MacDoogus poked his head up from behind the bar. "Yes, Wizard?"

"Hey, it's my future father-in-law," said Flabius.

"Actually he's my future father-in-law now," said Weemus.

"Right," said Flabius. "Um, do you have any Guinness on hand? Preferably extra stout?"

"Sorry, that roving band of time lords cleaned me out, sire," said Boogus. "I've got some decent house brews."

"You know, it's just not the same," said Flabius, deflecting several zaps from Weemus and the utensils, as well as Scott Baio. "You know what, this guy over here is starting to aggravate me. Do you mind?"

"Not at all," said Weemus.

Flabius flicked Scott Baio with his left pinky finger, dispersing his atoms into oblivion. He then peered over at the cake table, noticing a napkin and knife to replace the ones Biffus had wasted. "Hey look, maybe we can use these ones?"

"Let's give it a shot," said Weemus.

The pair headed back toward the chapel, stopping off on the roof where the weather device resided. Weemus loaded up

236

the spoon and the fork, generating untold amounts of power. "Okay, hand me the knife and napkin," said the Wizard.

Flabius tossed over the final two pieces of the puzzle, and sure enough, the device sprung to life. All around the world, countries that had just recovered from the blown up moon incident were thrown into atmospheric chaos. G.I. Joe was powerless to stop it. "Hey look it worked. Congratulations!"

"Excellent, now my plan can come to fruition. Time to surrender, Flabius Flaximus," said Weemus.

"Man, I think that Cyclops Wodge might have been right. This may have been a bad plan. Any ideas?" asked Flabius.

"Sorry, sell crazy someplace else, we're all stocked up here," said Weemus.

Just then, Buffy spoke up. "Flabius? Hey, Flabius? Remember me? Yes, dear, you are forgetting about your super roll technique. What is that called again?"

"Hee? Heeyah gaga? Heh, heh bemaga, great leap!"

Weemus Bobeemus knew what they were talking about, however. "No! Anything but that! Get away you... you... great leaper, you!"

"Perhaps a demonstration?" Flabius scurried along the ground. He looked right, faked left, did a 360 in the paint, a 900 off his skateboard, two salchows and a triple lutz wearing a blindfold, followed by a forward 4½ pike in tuck position from a nearby 10m platform and then went for it. It was too late for Weemus to react.

As Flabius soared through the air, making the correct calculations, Weemus was sent flying, along with his Impolitus Guard, the Nazis, and Winston, to the dimension where those ugly witches and the back-up dancers landed. It was enough to make the Styrofoam cup shed a tear.

"Flabius, you've returned to me, my love," said Buffy.

"Hega, fuffmie, it is I, the great and powerful Flabius of Oz."

"Flabius, you're last name is Flaximus," said Buffy.

"What did I say?"

"Yes, kidnapped. Can you believe it? And they forced me to wear this awful wedding dress. Come on, I'll go make you some fresh muffins. Wait, what's this?" Buffy glanced over the shoulder of the great supreme ruler of Rambo Brightus. Cecilia's former roommate could be seen running out from behind the door. Buffy's expression then changed to that of a wolf catching a glimpse of dinner. "Eek! A vampire! Excuse me a moment, dear."

Buffy leapt up, did a double back flip combination, causing her wedding dress to disintegrate. She then stabbed the ghastly blood sucker through her cold black heart with some leftover Tofurky from the wedding reception. After a quick roundhouse kick took off Becky's head, the threat was over.

"Okay, darling. We can go." Buffy brushed some vampire dust from her angora sweater lying nearby. She started to put it back on when Flabius stopped her, leaving her wearing only her sultry white undies, which were even nicer than Dave's.

"Nah. Nabama. Heeh, sweater, Buffy," said Flabius. "Oon sebaban. Some seeah, good bye to all of my friends."

By this time, the Duke and the Fairy had made their way from the Pub of Boogus MacDoogus, still partially covered in frosting. They had been partying with Blitzen, Mitch Albom, Greg Marmalard, Danny Kaye, Ludovico Ariosto, Francois Mitterrand, Def Leppard, and the entire Island of Molokai.

Well, Ludovico Ariosto more or less just stood around, but the rest of them were dancing on the ceiling. Only Bananarama could have guessed that Def Leppard's rendition of Lionel Richie's greatest hit would have exceeded Iron Butterfly's album version of "In-A-Gadda-Da-Vida," both in terms of length and pure rock awesomeness.

Unfortunately, Danny Kaye and Francois Mitterrand got into a fight over who better portrayed Walter Mitty. Then, someone decided to make Blitzen the designated driver, which turned out to be a terrible decision, mostly because the entire island of Molokai did not fit into Santa's backup sleigh. Not to mention, it's difficult to drive with hooves instead of hands.

"Don't ask me who gave him the keys, I have no idea how to drive a sleigh," said the Duke. "Where did Donner go?"

"I believe Mrs. Donner sent him to the supermarket on the way home. At least he is a responsible father. When will you start to show some responsibility?" asked Belle.

"So you *do* want to have children. I knew it! Let's get back to work on that," said the Duke.

Dave and Cecilia also held each other close. Even the Styrofoam cups could be seen embracing one another, although nobody could tell which was the boy and which was the girl, since they were both naked.

"My old friends! Thank you all for coming," said Flabius, grateful for the assistance of the dynamic team of champions. "Wait, who let in the reindeer? Come on, people, now we've got to clean up after him. And seriously, Merv Griffin? Don't you people have any respect for yourselves? He only replaced the greatest TV game show host of all time, Chuck Woolery, with Pat Sajak on *Wheel of Fortune*."

"You may be right about that, Emperor, but were it not for Chuck's departure, the world may never have had the opportunity to witness Vanna White flipping letters," said Danny Kaye.

"I hadn't thought of that. But you have to admit, Chuck Woolery and Vanna could have solved the secrets of the universe. Now, who's going to pick up after Blitzen?"

Blitzen, Mitch Albom, Greg Marmalard, Danny Kaye, Ludovico Ariosto, Francois Mitterrand, Def Leppard, and the entire Island of Molokai quickly scattered for the exits, exposing the Duke and the Fairy, who were in the midst of some heavy petting.

Flabius started making that coughing sound you make when

you're trying to get somebody's attention. After a good 20 or 30 seconds of awkward silence, the Duke and the Fairy finally looked up.

"Can we help you?" asked the Duke.

"It certainly has, my old friend. Why I remember it like it was yesterday," said the Emperor.

"Okay, we'll see you all later," said the Fairy.

The Duke strategically placed the Fairy between himself and the others, as they slowly made their way toward the door, shuffling backward, mostly disrobed. "Pilgrims!" said the Duke, saluting the others with a tip of his cowboy hat as he and Belle exited.

"Who were they?" asked Buffy.

"Heegaga not sure. Any gomumbu, I heeah you new friends," said Flabius, motioning toward the others.

Dave and Cecilia made their way toward Flabius and Buffy. Dave had much to say, so Cecilia spoke instead. "We're glad everything's okay now, sire."

It was now Buffy's turn to speak with her new friend. "Can I get my mascara back, now? Please?" Buffy and Cecilia had become close, almost best friends.

Dave turned to Cecilia, also longing for the return of his beauty products. "Sarsaparilla, the life of a super spy is never an easy one. There is death at every door, danger at every window, and doom around every corner. I can't promise you much, but I can promise you it will be ours together."

Cecilia's entire face lit up upon hearing those magic words. She was ready, now, to say what she had been waiting to say for so long. "Only if there is a lot more killing, and um, we make sure I won't need this white dress anymore."

"So when did you get to start wearing the bloomers in this relationship? That's it, I'm out of here." Dave opened a window and flung himself against a passing iceberg, knocking himself out instantaneously.

"Well I guess we'll be leaving now," said Cecilia, picking up Dave, fireman's carry style, and heading toward the exit.

"I'm serious! I want my makeup back. I only let you borrow it for the wedding," Buffy started to chase after the super spy and his girl, before Flabius reached out and restrained her.

"Buffy, mumfuffa, hejeya, wedding, ours!"

"Yes, I was planning on it, dear. I think we already covered that. Oh, I should tell you, though, I got engaged while you were away," said Buffy.

"Whobumba?" asked Flabius.

"This wizard guy," said Buffy. "He was kind of older, sort of ruggedly handsome, in a 'Dumbledore' sort of way."

"Like Richard Harris handsome or Michael Gambon handsome?" asked Biffus.

"Who was the first one? No, sorry, I meant Mr. Burns from *The Simpsons*, or maybe Sean Connery in *Zardoz*," said Buffy. "I should probably break it off with him before we proceed..."

"Hegagah, Muffmie, just sent Weemu Beemu to Phantom Zo... or some other nameless dimension that looks like a floating mirror in outer space," said Flabius.

"Well can't you call him or something?"

"Hegagah, Muffmie, don't know area code."

Flabius and Buffy continued their conversation, leaving the Hall behind them. Apparently the Styrofoam Cups got married and had lots of kids; at least that's what I was told.

The end (again).

Epilogue II: Biffus Palookus

"Why does the brilliant sidekick always get shafted? I protest. This is the worst ending in the history of letters," said Biffus Palookus, left stranded at the Hall of Panzies... DUNT DUNT DA!!!!! He was peeved at being left without a love of his own. "I'm going to find myself a supermodel to marry."

After searching for three weeks, the erstwhile sidekick of

241

Emperor Flabius finally found his way out of the Hall.

He ventured across the evil swamplands, through the magical forest, over the snow capped mountains of Tibet, to sunny Antarctica, where a famous magazine was having a swimsuit photo shoot. There she was, more beautiful than ever. Biffus could not stop himself from speaking to her.

"You, you light up my life. You give me the malarkey. You do that voodoo that you are capable of. You are the superstar that I have been waiting for. Say you will have me forever!"

Then Biffus realized that he was talking to his own armpit. The sun was coming down harder than earlier, and so Biffus called it quits.

Of course, the magazine security force found nothing odd about a medieval knight talking to the swimsuit model, but in the confusion, they fell asleep.

The model came running over, ready to throw herself into the arms of Biffus Palookus. Biffus, however, suddenly recalling some issue of high importance and elevated absurdity, turned in the opposite direction. This caused the swimsuit model to miss him completely, as she tripped over a walrus and got stuck, face down in the Antarctic soil.

"Did anybody shut off that weather doohickey?" asked Biffus. "I think those flower girls may have escaped, as well..."

P.S.

Peter Cushing stared intently at his watch, pacing back and forth as the Weasleys and Black Manta entered the TARDIS. Stormtroopers Korkmaz and Langston kept an eye out for a roving pack of time lords, hopefully carting crates of extra stout.

"We'll give them ten more minutes," said Cushing.

End number three.
Not counting footnotes.

Footnotes

Yes, have some.

Act I: The Saga of the Spoon

Chapter 1

1. *Tommy*: A classic rock-opera performed by *The Who* from 1969 to 1970 with some later performances when they got back together again.

2. *Dave*. a) Founder of Wendy's. b) A name for usually a guy. c) A plant cell.

3. *Moon*. It's this thing that is sort of like a satellite, but the same. I ate one a couple of days ago. They're kind of chewy. Also Keith Moon. AKA Mooney. Top five drummers all-time: Moon, Buddy Rich, Gene Krupa, Max Roach and Animal, as in the Muppet, not the wrestler. You could probably swap Krupa and Roach for Peart and Bonham, but I wouldn't.

4. *Don Juan*. A poem composed by Lord Byron in the early 19th century. Read it, you slouch.

5. *de Marco Polo*. nothing, unless you drop the *de*.

6. *Marco Polo*. If you don't know who Marco Polo is, you're pathetic. Okay, I admit, I am not particularly sure, but I think he may have been some sort of swimmer or something. He looked like Gary Cooper, though; I know that for a fact.

7. *Cecilia*. A really cool person who is a lot smarter than her roommate, and a lot better looking, and a lot nicer, and a lot more athletic, and not a slut.

8. *Moose*. Hey, ho, up the moose goes! Hey ho, watch that moose fly! Hey and ho and hey and ho, hey, Moose! Moose! Mooooooose!

9. *The Timpani Drummer*. The Timpani is a great musical instrument. It's these really big drums that you beat the hell out of. The drummer is the guy who plays these drums. In this case, the drummer is pretty crappy. Although his *Spaceballs* helmet is pretty cool.

10. *Monsoon*. I don't know. I don't particularly care for them,

myself.

11. *Mobile, Ala.* Socrates kept this most sacred of secrets with him when he drank from the cup of Hempstead that sent him to his oversoul.

Chapter 2

1. *Flaximus.* The family name for the greatest heroes in the history of heroes.

2. *Weemus.* The first name of people who tend to be Bobeemuses.

3. *Gimpus Foo Foo.* Ancient biblical place of the wandering Foo Foos. Usually accompanied by a Gimpus or two, who were not very popular during the time of Moses or Hammurabi.

4. *The Who Sell Out.* The best album *The Who* ever made. Get the remastered version. It's got even more cool stuff.

5. Did anyone see *The Walking Dead* season three? I loved the first 8 episodes of the show, but it's been a bit downhill since the third episode of season two. David Morrissey was pretty good as the Governor. Flabius would probably thrash him, though, along with Dr. Who.

6. *Chocococolate La.* The misspelling of chocolate that works when you are playing a video game version of *The Family Feud* and need to spell Chocolate correctly. Category found in: *Things you do with stuff.*

7. *Little evil ducks.* Self-explanatory.

8. *Crapshooter.* You are a crapshooter.

9. *Beautiful mares.* Refers to perhaps a large mammal known as a horse, of the female variety in that species. There is no factual information as to the validity of this definition, however.

10. *Johnny Lady.* It seems apparent that there is some sort of strange cross-dressing persona in each of the first few chapters, at least until the Duke comes along to set things back in their traditional order. Until he doesn't.

11. *Buffy.* Angora wearing goddess of looking good in Angora

245

in ancient Greek and Roman mythology. Refer to any Mythology dictionary for more information, like *Bulfinch's*.

12. *Chiasmus*. A friendly sort. Sometimes they are purple, if you are lucky. Stay away from the mushrooms, though. They give you highly flammable flatulence, followed by asparagus.

13. *Goldfish*. Scary.

14. *MiG-29*. Any chance we can get Flogging Molly to play Def Leppard in the movie version? That would be sweet.

15. *Nukes*. Because then you would have Flogging Molly playing Def Leppard playing Lionel Richie's "Dancing on the Ceiling." A banjo *and* a cowbell covering the former Commodore? That's why it would be sweet. Although we'd probably need Gene Frenkle if we wanted to hit ultimate sweetness. I think we can do it if we all work together, and page Bruce Dickinson.

Chapter 3

1. *CIA*. a) Central Ingonistical Alabamaboozledians. b) Cutting Incompetence Anastasia. c) Cap In (your-the) Ass d) Carpe Ungowa Diem. e) Frank From Ohio f) Candace Is Arboreal.

2. *Natasha*. Natasha makes me go yeeeeoooooowwwwwww.

3. *Daddy Warbucks*. You know, Daddy Warbucks! Daddy Warbucks, from *Annie*? You never saw *Annie*? You know, "the sun will come out," Everybody! "Tomorrow! Tomorrow!" Ah, you guys stink.

4. *Green Gables*. a) Betty Grable. b) Balthazar Getty. c) Clark Gable. d) Jim Carrey in *The Cable Guy*.

5. *More ducks*. The recurring motif of ducks in this story has this footnoter at a loss. There should be more of them, however. Ducks are cool. I can't be certain, but they are probably mallards, like Daffy Duck. Not white ducks like Donald Duck, who can kick Daffy's bottom any day of the week. Do ducks have bottoms?

6. *Outer space*. This space, which takes on an outer-like form, as opposed to an inner like form, which would not be outer, or

246

even middle.

7. *Chuck Woolery*. Was seriously the original host of *Wheel of Fortune*. He has the hair and YouTube clips to prove it.

8. *Sticky Fingers*. Something you get when you eat sticky foods, like maple syrup covered pancakes, and other stuff. Apparently the zipper on the Stones' album cover actually unzipped. I wonder how much one goes for on eBay? Apparently not that much.

9. *Golf*. Only if you think so.

10. *Putter*. And a happy new year. Now give us some figgy putting. Sorry. Now give us some figgy pudding. There, that's much better. Figgy pudding! Give!

11. *TV*. You can only see this on TV. Don't believe it, though.

12. *Bread Crust*. And the bread came back, the very next day!

13. *Bread Crumbs*. They never come back. They're unkind. I don't like them at all. You can, though.

14. *Croutons*. No thank you.

15. *The mysterious transforming space ship*. If you can tell me what a hunneringus is, I'll tell you what the significance is of *the mysterious transforming space ship*.

Chapter 4

1. *The Duke*. John Wayne. Come on, that was an easy one.

2. *The Fairy*. Tinker Bell. Okay, that might be a little harder, especially considering she is now full-sized (or is she?), but I tell you later on anyway. And if I spelled Tinkerbelle wrong, don't blame me; I've never even seen *Peter Pan*. Well, that's no longer true as of the twenty-third revision. Though I am still unwilling to accept any blame for any misspellings. It is always the computer's fault.

3. *Chevy Tahoe*. Good for everyday driving. Nice handling, 4-wheel drive is great when you live in the northeast. It snows a lot in places like New York, and no one likes to put chains on their tires, so Tahoes are popular their. Excuse me, I mean

'there' at the end of that last sentence. Sometimes I tend to type to fast. No wait, that's 'too' fast. Sorry again.

4. *1.23.22.7.Duck.13.* Okay, more ducks again. We'll have to recall the cultural impact that ducks have had on the last 150,000 years of human evolution. Ducks may indeed be the root of the entire civilized world, as we know it today.

5. *Value Meals.* Get a No. 1: The Big Mac. Just don't try that on Mark McGwire.

6. *G-Men.* FBI guys from the time of Hoover, J. Edgar. Does anybody know what the J stands for? I think it may be Jennifer, and you can quote me on that.

7. *Live at Leeds.* Is that a leading question? I bet Johnny Cochran would say so, or Jackie Chiles. And Sean Hannity, at least in the footnotes.

8. *Canada.* A country where Captain Kirk comes from. Although I also heard that he was born in Iowa from some guy that looks like T.J. Hooker. Because Captain Kirk will always be Shatner! And the second new *Star Trek* movie blew chunks. Unless you read this 15 years ago and thought I was talking about *First Contact*, which was actually halfway decent. As was the *Family Guy* episode with the entire cast of *The Next Generation*. Chunks of what, you might ask? No, I'm asking.

9. *Spock.* I don't know what country Spock comes from.

10. *Republicans.* Elephants should be embarrassed.

11. *Democrats.* Donkeys are embarrassed.

12. *Ross Perot.* We couldn't get in contact with any turkeys to ask them if they were embarrassed, because it was Thanksgiving. People actually knew who this guy was, once. Until Ralph Nader came onto the scene with John B. Anderson, John C. Frémont and James B. Weaver.

13. *Borpos.* Based on the 19th century god of filmmaking. All gods answer to the great god of the inky winky Borpi clan. No, I guess not. It was a nice try, though.

14. *Darwinkly.* I always wished I could have one when I was

little. You don't know what it is like. Then again, neither do I.

15. *Uranus*. Pluto, Saturn, Venus, Mercury, Zeus, Barton, Johnny Mathis and all of the Queen's men. That's the best explanation I can give.

16. *Space Nuggets*. Big things that are usually found in outer space, but not always. Sometimes they are found in other places. Sometimes not.

17. *Planet Killers*. Human Population, sign up here. Hey, I think, in order to be fair, the Hippos should also sign up. And the ducks. Let's not forget the ducks.

Act II: Of Forks & Mojo Cheetos
Ferdinand Franco

<u>Chapter 5</u>

1. *Cassius Clay*. Would have destroyed Mike Tyson if they ever fought. I'm not sure how he would have done against Mohammed Ali, though. Probably a toss-up.

2. *O.K. Corral*. Also would have kick Mike Tyson's butt, even if it's only a place, specifically a corral, as opposed to some form of life that can actually enter a boxing ring.

3. *Becky*. Terrible at athletics, mean, awful, tralk-like goddess of ancient Rome.

4. *Nerf*. Hardest substance known to mankind. Pardon me, humankind. I wouldn't want to not be politically correct at this point in the story when I have done so well up to this point — because clearly that's the point of all pointless writing. Or Tweeting. Or Twerking, is to do it in a politically unobnoxious manner.

5. *Wheel of Fortune*. Never buy a vowel, no matter how good Vanna White looks. Yes, she's beautiful, and really good at her job, but her asking price is way too expensive. She doesn't even bargain or do less for less money or nothing. That may not have been PC. Or an iMac.

6. *Sheila.* A pretty good song from the 60's, I think. No, I think I have changed my mind. *To Sir With Love* is a much better song, mostly because it was sung by Lulu who hates the name Sheila.

7. *Potatoes.* Once upon a time, potatoes ruled the Earth. Purples ones, from Peru. Eventually the Yukon Golds faced off against the Idaho Russets in a 'no holds barred' ladder match to set up a championship bout in Potatomania XX, but neither side scored a victory, likely due to a lack of appendages. This prevented either side from ascending the ladder and earning a slot in the heavyweight title match. Then the Russets started to grow appendages, or those weird root things that start growing out of potatoes if you leave them in the cupboard for too long. So that was pretty disgusting, and the rest of the world's population decided maybe it wasn't such a brilliant tactical decision to install tubers into governmental executive positions.

8. *Mash.* The movie was good, but the TV show stank. The potato version is by far the best, no contest here. Also spelled M*A*S*H.

9. *Buttocks.* I only used the word once, twice including this footnote. I hereby publicly apologize. It's a really bad word. Tush is even worse though. Now I have to publicly apologize for that. Okay, I apologize for using any really bad words. There, I said it. Read on. No, honestly, this footnote is over. No really, look away! I said stop looking! Come on, stop looking. Forget it, I just won't write anymore. I forgot I could do that.

10. *Winston.* Mostly a good name, but when coupled with Wallingford, it's pretty evil. Winston Churchill was a great man. The Winston Cup used to be the best sport to watch, in the world. Actually, you don't watch the cup. That would be sort of boring, but not completely boring. You watch people race to get the cup. I mean, they have a bunch of races where they

250

keep points and the one with... you get the idea. I once knew this guy who spelt boring as "boaring." I thought that was really neat, even if his name wasn't Winston. Winston Zedmore from *The Ghostbusters* was the coolest of all the Ghostbusters. Well, Ray Stanz was pretty cool. Igon Spengler just had a great name.

11. *Shrieking.* What Cecilias do when Daves jump out of windows. (voted by a panel of experts as the best footnote.)

12. *Quarter.* Fiscal years don't count that way. They used to, but then some dinkus broke the machines that run it. I think it was the Commies. They are really out to get the fiscal year. The two of them have always been enemies. To the death!

13. *Parameters.* As opposed to fartameters and the even lesser known gagameter, the parameters are as follows:

<u>Chapter 6</u>

1. *Gimpus Foo Foo.* Very big with the Romans as well as Hebrews. The Greeks never minded a Foo Foo or four, but they hated Gimpuses.

2. *Hall of Panzies.* DUNT DUNT DA!!!!!! It was actually built during the time of the Greeks, like everything else, but Zeus got pissed one day and blew it up. And by 'pissed' I mean drunk, not angry. I think that's a culture variant, depending on if you are in Gegharkunik Province, Armenia, or Pisco, Peru.

3. *Panzer.* Sounds like Panzies. They could have been pansies. We just don't know at this point.

4. *Puddle of Dread.* Sorry, no footnote, I just wanted to write a word that began with a 'P.'

5. *Impolitus.* You are very Impolitus. Could be sort of like you are very impolite to us. Okay, so it's a stretch. Who asked you, anyway?

6. *Palookus.* I just thought it was a cool name.

7. *Palookus.* A rare book of approximately 1,200 pages found all over the world and made from gymnastics mats. It tells the lost

story of the love affair between Ulysses and Lana Turner. It was presumed lost during the 15th century, but rumor has it that it was uncovered by a secret government organization bent on keeping information about aliens from the general public known as 'PBS.' It is said to have been written in the 1890's, when Thomas Jefferson first took office.

8. *Rosco Pico Train.* Sorry for not getting this footnote in earlier. Sorry.

9. *DDD.* Shhh. It's a secret. Shhh.

10. *Dudley Moore.* What ever happened to that guy, anyway? Didn't he used to have a partner that was a lot funnier than he was? What ever happened to that guy? I think he might have been in *The Princess Bride.* By the way, I feel that Andre the Giant was shafted by the Academy, that year. Nobody could ever rhyme "I mean it" with "anybody want a Peanut" until the Giant managed this intricate feat of articulation. But I would really like to know what happened to Dudley Moore's hombre. Actually I don't care all that much. Peter Cook! That was his name! I think. Well, maybe not. I can't remember. I haven't even seen *10* or *Arthur* or even *Arthur 2: On the Shizhouse when Snoop Lion Comes Over with some Homies.* That's really a pity.

11. *Frankensense.* That's how it should be spelt. Eye thinc ay speek fur everione aan fat won.

12. *Snow.* It's this stuff, you see, and it goes like this: Whoosh! Whoosh! Come on! Join in if the mood suits you! Whoosh! Whoosh!

13. *Big Bad John.* He was a lot nicer, once you got to know him. Especially if you invited him over for Jimmy Dean sausages.

Chapter 7

1. *Friends.* Not a reference to the TV show, but the lovely, you know, of Natasha, or any of the female *Friends* stars, I suppose, which would make it a reference to the *Friends* TV show. Sorry about lying, before.

252

2. *Mr. Roberts.* Was a movie character and a movie before a TV show and TV show star. See, so movies did come before TV! Tell that to the chicken and the egg!

3. *Las Vegas.* A great Elvis movie without the *Viva!* Part of the title. The lovely Ms. Ann-Margret never looked so good.

4. *Beer.* Unknown. Appears from the story to be some sort of liquid beverage. Further research required.

5. *Perfect.* Well, they were perfect.

6. *Bars.* Watch out, the juice is on to you. And if you think you can escape the wrath of the man with the golden neck, you are sadly mistaken. And you thought it was all a game...

7. *Nuns.* Even I am not that low.

8. *Old Lady.* Okay, I am that low. So here's the scoop: Two guys both named Frank, walk into a bar. Then they start a fight. Then they turn to each other and say: "Man, you shouldn't have hit that old lady, she's kicking your rear end, and she's not even a nun!" I try, just not very hard.

9. *Shooting Ducks.* I don't really think that there were any ducks in this chapter, but I just like to cover myself. You should do the same.

10. *Ducks.* Even worse.

Chapter 8

1. *Duke.* I already told you, John Wayne. For those of you who are really smart, I should use the name Marion Michael Morrison, or Marion Robert Morrison, or Marion Mitchell Morrison. No, John Wayne sounds better and is way easier. I wonder if he's related to Temuera Morrison?

2. *Fairy.* Yes, the Fairy is still supposed to be Tinker Bell.

3. *Mr. Moo Moo.* The moo moo is a large, dress-like super flower thing that people wear. You could also spell it mumu, I suppose. Or maybe mumoo or moomu. I wonder why Doc Blindofsky was wearing one? Maybe they are super comfy.

4. *Tibet.* All Tibetan hotels have airports. I know because I read

it from some guy who was telling a story he heard from this guy that looked like me but was.

5. *Breath-savers*. They're better than breakfast mints.

6. *Fairy-bath*. In biblical/mythological terminologistic societal parameter-minal-sociopathic collators, a Fairy bath is something a Fairy takes when she needs a bath.

7. *Giants*. The greatest team in the history of the NFL.

8. *Heat*. The cooling of the earth's surface as caused by the gamma radiation of the greenhouse solar wind storms of the ozone tornadoes.

9. *Casablanca*. Greatest film ever. Hands down. You that say "oh, but what about *Citizen Kane*," are just in denial. Those that say *Gone with the Wind* are gone with themselves, out to the candy store. I think I may join them. Personally, I think that *Citizen Kane* and *Gone With the Wind* are no better than 4th and 5th, respectively (and respectfully), behind No. 2 *All Quiet on the Western Front* (1930, the best war movie ever made) No. 3 *The Godfather*. The original. Please. Let's be serious. The second one was great, but the original is still the best. The epic format of 1 and 2 together is pretty cool. It gives it a truly "epic" feel, as it is, itself, described. This footnote is becoming epic.

10. *China*. I have never been there. Speaking of China, Bruce Lee was its biggest movie star, and he was also American. That's pretty sweet. *Enter the Dragon* was awesome. Here we are decades after the invention of the VHS and we still don't have *The Green Hornet* series on DVD, Blu-ray or for download or whatever other technology comes out after the publication of this book, which will likely not be on DVD or Blu-ray unless somebody tries to make a movie out of it, starring Bruce Lee and Daryl Hannah.

11. *Seven Seas*. Maybe even better than the South Seas. But, *Moby Dick* just wouldn't be the same if it was set on the Black Sea. Make sense of that.

The Inter-calorie Cheese Chapter
1. *Cheese*. Stuff.

ACT III: Where Butter Knives Dare

Chapter 9

1. *Clown*. An unusually diverse race of neoclassicists who draw upon the poetic genius of the great and powerful Pope as the greatest of the great poetic people that do stuff. The poet formally known as Alexander as opposed to that other pope guy. Wait, was there a clown in the story? I don't like clowns.

2. *Vermilion*. What about Ponytail Westerosi pants Qartheen gown dude? Or the Vegan in the congealed meat sauce?

3. *Large shoes*. The unequivocal existence that Emile Zola and Emmanuel Kant and Ernest Borgnine all sought... simply because their names began with the same letter. Borgnine has since denied the theory, but it was later confirmed by Hugh Jackman. Wouldn't it be funny if we all called him Huge Ackman, though? No? Why wouldn't that be funny? Because you said so? That's also not funny. So there.

4. *Othello*. Some guy who did some stuff but nobody liked him because they were all real jealous of Desdemona, who was probably really cute.

5. *Assorted vegetables*. Okay, I got this: Triscuits, a-tisket a-tasket, an alabaster basket, Konstantin Tsiolkovsky's space elevator, Rosie the Highland cow, Clan Macleod of The Lewes, rock candy, both red and green Boston lettuce, and probably some spicy bell peppers. Or Doug Ingle's organ. One of the three.

6. *'Scream like a scared little girly man.'* A spy device first incorporated by the NKVD in 1933 in their dealings with the Black Stallion. Next made famous by the famous Frank Frankenstein Frankincense of 127 Piccadilly Circus in 1883, during the eruption of Krakatoa, when he first laid eyes on... gasp... a piece of unfinished wood.

7. *Boston, Mass.* An adverb with similar meaning to the words 'frip' and 'frugillies.' You would say, " the man Boston, Mass.'d the refrigerator on all sides of the law, counting to five."

8. *Eliminated.* When someone fails on the Eliminator when competing on *American Gladiators.*

9. *Spaghetti Drainer.* Love child, don't you be pulling your spaghetti drainer in the most obsequious manner! Everything, in a very assertive and nonaggressive modus, otherwise I wouldn't be behaving particularly civilized, which is something I would never do.

10. *Space.* Nope, already had this one, too. At least, I think we did. Quick, somebody go back and check. Forget it, I'm too lazy. I can't ask you to do something I wouldn't do. That's just exactly what I will do, then. Go look. I know you want to. Look! Okay, I still haven't looked, either.

11. *Winston.* And you think Batman is a drinker? Yeah, come on! Winston must be like, the drunkest something or other ever! I don't know the origins of Wallingford, so I can't say what sort of drunk he is.

12. *Washington, D.C.* I am going to Washington, D.C. you all over this place. I will.

Chapter 10

1. *Havoc.* Something that could be fun if you were into that sort of thing.

2. *Fork.* Something that could never be fun no matter how much you were into it.

3. *Countries.* Something I heard about last week at the malt shop. I believe it will be a startlingly new concept that will be taught at school for generations to come.

4. *Private Dancer.* Let's not get into that, shall we?

5. *Musicals.* Personally, I think *Mary Poppins* is just great. She's really cute on top of being "practically perfect in every way." Then again, if that "every way" thing includes 'cuteness,' I

256

guess she would be practically perfect according to the story. I wouldn't go so far as to say perfect, but certainly within acceptable limits of interstellar travel, which is what "practically" refers to.

6. *Buffy*. Angora wearing goddess of looking good in Angora in ancient Greek and Roman mythology. Refer to any Mythology dictionary for more information. Or the Declaration of Independence.

7. *Rose Leslie*. Did anybody see *Game of Thrones* Season Three? Jon Snow is one lucky man. Of course then she shot him full of arrows, so that was pretty unlucky. Well, he at least broke even. Of course she is Scottish, so, I lean toward lucky.

8. *Styrofoam Cup*. The true hero of the entire narrative, but a fallen one at that. Many character parallels have been done discussing the ancient mythology behind this character and the similarities between him and Milton's Adam, and my friend Carter's pet Pewterschmidt named Frank. who is a very famous literary figurative alliterative character from "Song Sung Blue" by Neil Diamond. Not the Frank played by Henry Fonda in *Once Upon a Time in the West*. That guy was bad news.

9. *Towels*. Something we should all aspire to become.

10. *Litotes*. Um, this was on a test of mine. Let's see. Um. Just give me a second! I can get it.

12. *Catachresis*. I could have gotten that. Okay, this one is an intentional misuse of words. Come on, I am serious this time. Give me the credit. Wait a minute. Flashback. Woo. Scary. Sorry again.

13. *Assonance*. And you are not?

14. *Note cards are about as good as celery.*

Chapter 11

1. *Brunettes*. Brunettes are great.

2. *Blondes*. Blondes are great.

3. *Redheads*. Carrots do not have redheads, they have green

257

stuff at the top, you flaming-haired ginger. P.S. Rita Hayworth was one of the greatest redheads ever. Even if she started out as a brunette. Nobody is counting here. Also on the list: Lucille Ball, Maureen O'Hara, Rose Leslie, Ann-Margret... man, I'm getting tired of typing. I'm also thinking of redheads, so that probably doesn't help.

4. *Drunk.* There is an unusual amount of drinking in this particular chapter. The drinking seems to stem from the sociological inefficiencies of the main character and his inability to accept the world for that which it is: a big thing that we all live on.

5. *Beer.* I love it how Peter Cushing is the leader of the gang of Dr. Who doctors. He's also the only one who was ever called 'Dr. Who.' I don't know for sure if he liked Guinness Extra Stout but I will say it's far superior to the draught stuff. I need bubbles in my beer. Or beer in my bubbles.

6. *Jail.* Jail ain't so bad if you're not in it.

7. *Matters of Western Kentucky.* No, honestly, if you're not in jail, the bars don't seem to be quite so bad or restraining.

8. *Glork.* And if I were to be a cave man, I probably would have worn orange and pink, too. No, that's ugly. What about pink and green? Pink and anything? No? So much for my career as a fashion designer. I think I'll become a critic, instead. They don't need to know anything.

9. *Katrina.* I don't know what the fascination is with the Russian sounding names. It all started when I was four. I was not born on a leap year, however.

10. *Dr. Male-Pattern-Baldnificent.* Name one.

11. *Butch Wallpaper.* These are the guys that kill people and are underpaid.

12. *Frank.* I pity the fool who messes with Frank, especially because he's all ready dead. Come to think of it, if this chapter is set in the past, he could be not born or something. I don't know. Time does some pretty evil things in this novel. Boy, these

footnotes must piss off a lot of people. At least, I hope so.

Chapter 12

1. *Matter of Greece*. Hercules was half-god, but he still didn't know how to tie his shoelaces. I know, I asked him.

2. *Matter of France*. Charlemagne may have been an Emperor and all, but he knew how to tie his shoes. Although I don't think he actually had any shoelaces, so that's kind of cheating.

3. *Matter of Britain*. Arthur couldn't even dress without his mother's help. Of course, she was never really there for him as a child, so you can't really blame him, now can you?

4. *Jewels*. Jewel is a character from *To Kill a Mockingbird*. Jewelry was his full name, I believe. No, forget that, his name was Gem. Same difference, though, I mean both names are quadrat-gastrointestinal.

5. *Bunch*. Any group of people answering to the names of Greg, Marsha, Peter, Jan, Bobby, Cindy, Mr., Mrs., and Alice. Oh, and the dog Tiger, who later starred with Don Johnson in *Miami Vice*, or was it *A Boy and his Dog?* You know, that movie should have been called *A Dog and his Boy*. Thank you, Susanne Benton. Nice.

6. *Paladin*. I could never figure out what they were.

7. *Hippopotamuses*. I think that's the correct spelling. Honest.

8. *R2-D2*. The most powerful being in the Star Wars universe.

Act IV: The Final Napkin

Chapter 13

1. *Importance*. Forget it. It's just way too long to get into. Mostly because there isn't any.

Fin

259

ABOUT THE AUTHOR

Michael Parker is not a pen name for J.K. Rowling, Stephen King, Richard Bachman, Ernest Hemingway, Oscar Wilde, William Faulkner, F. Scott Fitzgerald, Ford Madox Ford, James Joyce, Bram Stoker, William Shakespeare, William Kennedy, Saul Bellow, John Milton, Miguel de Cervantes, Sidney Sheldon, Anne Rice, that *Twilight* lady, Derek Walcott, Eugene O'Neill, Geoffrey Chaucer, James Baldwin, Robert Burns, Herman Melville, Mark Twain, Percy Bysshe Shelley, William Carlos Williams, Mary Shelley, Edgar Allan Poe, T.S. Eliot, George Eliot, Langston Hughes, either Brontë sister, that other Michael Parker writer guy, or Arthur Miller. Just out of curiosity, does anybody know why Harper Lee only wrote one book? Speaking of books, *Catcher in the Rye* is a great book. If you haven't read it, go read it. Then try *Moby Dick*. It's long and you read way too much about blubber and hunting whales, but then whenever you're in a room with smart people or people pretending to be smart, you can say you've read *Moby Dick*. Don't tell them you've read *Finnegan's Wake*, however, because they'll know you're full of it, or they won't know what it is, so same difference. By the way, it's not the Finnegan whom Kirk beat up in an episode of *Star Trek*, nor is it the same as that Michael Finnegan song. Also, chin-ne-gan is not a word. As for poetry, *The Waste Land* is among the best. Try that instead, or *Paradise Lost*. Writer, pontificating bloviator and cantankerous carnivore, Parker lives with his wife and children in upstate New York.